POINT OF IMPACT

LAST CHANCE DOWNRANGE - BOOK 1

LISA PHILLIPS

TWO DOGS PUBLISHING, LLC

Copyright © 2022 by Lisa Phillips

All rights reserved.

No part of this book may be reproduced in any form or by any electronic or mechanical means, including information storage and retrieval systems, without written permission from the author, except for the use of brief quotations in a book review.

eBook ISBN: 979-8-88552-120-8

Trade Paperback ISBN: 979-8-88552-121-5

Larger Print ISBN: 979-8-88552-124-6

Published by: Two Dogs Publishing, LLC. Idaho, USA

Edited by: Christy Callahan, Professional Publishing Services

Cover Design by: Ryan Schwarz

1

Virginia

It wasn't Addie Franklin's choice to meet with a killer. The coffee shop had more than enough open seats. She chose the one beside the table occupied by a serial murderer because she'd been ordered to.

Before she even sat, the barista called out her dry cappuccino. She left her phone on the table and strode to retrieve it. As she did so, the voice of a coworker on the FBI task force sounded in her ear.

"You caught his attention."

Addie winced as though the cup holding the hot beverage were the cause. Sure, she was here tonight for precisely that purpose—to get noticed. She'd even worn a business-appropriate dress of all things.

But drawing attention to herself hadn't sat right since…

She could still feel the bugs crawl over her skin. A remnant of that day years ago, the night she'd been homecoming queen.

That had been another life.

The FBI profiler she was now, a Special Agent with the FBI, settled into her seat. She smoothed down the dress in the process and caught the eye of a rapist and murderer. Not exactly her idea of a fun Friday night, but considering her lack of social life, she couldn't say much about that.

Addie lifted the mug. The napkin it sat on came with it, then fluttered to the floor.

William Benning retrieved it out of the air before it could hit the tile and handed it back to her.

"Thank you." She opted for a polite expression. There was no way she would show interest. Though, with a guy like this, what might set him off was precisely the reason she was here.

The team needed him to admit enough of what he'd done that they had cause to bring him in and question him further. And they needed to know where he buried his victims.

Anything she learned would add to the profile already compiled on him.

"Can you believe how long it's been raining?" Addie held her smile and waited for his response.

The color in his eyes was so dark it bled into his pupils. His gaze seemed to track her like a laser targeting system as questions resonated in her.

What caused him to flip the switch and decide on destruction?

When he finished, where did he hide the bodies?

Lines ringed his mouth on both sides. Prominent cheekbones. The images they had of him didn't do justice to the impact of his presence. Life moved around him, the world that hummed with the energy of existence—those electrical impulses and the forces of physics that acted on every human being. This guy was a void. Existence ground to a halt when it encountered him.

Inside there seemed to be nothing. Stillness.

A black hole.

She'd seen it before, and yet every time Addie felt the impact as though it were the first time.

His expression shifted, a slight flex of his nose. "I like the rain. It washes away transgressions."

She lifted her brows and nodded as though considering that interesting statement. Internally she added "religious bent" to the profile she'd compiled of him and his proclivities so far.

Addie had grown up in church, going to summer Bible camps. How she felt about her faith the past fifteen years was… She pretty much tried not to think about God and how He felt about her—which was nothing good.

She took a few sips of the cappuccino and pretended to be engrossed in her phone.

Benning just sat there without even a newspaper or electronic device.

The task force had been hunting this guy for nearly two years. They'd finally managed to identify him, although it was pending confirmation.

They needed evidence that would remove any shadow of a doubt he was responsible for the disappearance of twelve women and the murder of at least seven of them. Five were still unaccounted for, but the task force had connected them to the case. To this man. When they were found, it would be twelve counts of first-degree murder.

This guy wouldn't see freedom.

Addie could use religion as an angle. Hyper-religiosity was something she'd studied as part of her psychology degree. It could be a way to connect with him. Possibly worth a try.

Her phone buzzed with a notification.

Addie frowned. Hadn't she turned off the app alerts for that TV channel? The notification was for a new show set to air in a few days titled *Where Are They Now?*

Her chest tightened until she had to take a long inhale and push it out slowly. That story began in high school when she'd fallen into the popularity track that led to being crowned prom queen and a TV special that aired around Halloween every year…and ended with this career as an FBI profiler.

"Everything okay?"

She glanced at Benning.

"Seems like maybe that wasn't good news."

Addie shook her head. "I don't like good news. It predisposes you to look for hope, and there isn't any. Better to face reality instead."

Her job held plenty of cold, ugly truth based on facts and what could be proven. Evidence. Convictions. People like William Benning were a puzzle she'd been trying to solve since homecoming, senior year. Three days later, she'd been taken to the hospital. She'd never gone back to school but instead finished with a private tutor her uncle had hired. As soon as she could, Addie left town. She'd barely been back since.

Just the idea of going there made her want to run out the door and not look back.

Benning said, "I find myself firmly rooted in reality also, though sometimes life can be sweet."

The way he said it made Addie's skin crawl.

"But the taste of anticipation…" He let that question hang.

"What is it like?"

"Lemons in summer. Sharpness and sweet in one touch of the tongue."

She was about to jump out of the chair. Only the mutter in her ear of the agent listening kept her grounded.

She was here to do her job. No way would she say the code phrase that would send the entire team swarming in the door. Even if going solo was the last thing she wanted.

They could decide to do it anyway, but she needed him to talk more before that happened.

"You know that taste. Don't you, Addie?"

Noise erupted in her ear, but all she heard was a buzzing as everything melted around her. All she could hear and see was William Benning. He knew who she was. That meant he knew *everything*.

"You know what fear smells like."

I know what your victims feel.

She'd been there. In that place where there was nothing but terror. Even though she hadn't been alone, it still enveloped her. Sank into her skin. The fear had become part of every inch of who she was. It had crawled into her soul and left a stain she'd never been able to get rid of.

"Yes." Addie fought the urge to shift in her seat. "I'll admit I do."

"It's probably why you do this job."

He knew who she was. Maybe he knew this entire encounter was an FBI attempt at tugging information from him. A long shot but deemed worth it. Now? Given the yelling in her earpiece, it seemed they'd decided to call it quits.

Addie wasn't going to get up and walk out. Not now that Benning seemed willing to reveal information.

"You've done your homework." *On the people chasing you.*

Benning probably wanted to know who he was up against. That had to mean he considered them formidable enemies. Or he needed the information so he could continue to work on the assumption he was so far superior to them there was no contest.

Then there was the regard he had for other killers like him. Did he consider himself unique in the world or part of a brotherhood of sorts?

His gaze remained steady on her. "I know all about you."

Everything in Addie wanted her to look away. Break their stare down. But she couldn't. He considered her of no more value than any of his victims—something she shared with them. They were nothing but an amusement to be used and then tossed aside when the fascination wore off. No one should ever feel like that. Which was the only reason she'd agreed to do this.

"You don't believe me." He paused. "But you'll see."

"You know my team?" She tried to brush it off. "I could say the same about you, for all you know."

"Not your team. You."

She lifted her coffee cup and took a sip, giving him a side view of her so he had a moment to seethe over her dismissal. Inside, she was the one seething. The FBI task force was a team. Why would he single her out? It made no sense.

The dance of this conversation had to be nothing but a curiosity to her. Though, she would never admit as much to her coworkers. They already thought she was a freak.

None of them knew why she didn't want to do this.

"You cannot comprehend what I am."

"No?" She glanced over her shoulder, but kept her body turned toward the counter.

If he wanted to make this about her, she would give him only what she wanted him to take.

Addie set her cup down. "You think I haven't seen exactly what you are? That I haven't *lived it* until I vomited up the taste of the foul *thing* that you are."

His jaw flexed. His Adam's apple bobbed as he swallowed.

"*That* is why I do this job. So people like you can be caged where you belong."

"All in reciprocity for the fact you were caged."

"In a cabin, with a friend of mine. A very long time ago." Words didn't have power of their own; they were just sounds. Syllables, vowels, and consonants. Speaking them aloud was a kind of exorcism—the release of not holding back anymore.

That lifetime ago event had altered the entire course of her life. She didn't even know who that girl was, the Adelyn Franklin she had one been, the girl who'd been so excited for the homecoming dance. The moment the clock struck midnight everything had changed.

He saw through it. "One day, you will not be so brave."

"Because you're going to hurt me like you hurt all the others?" She held the mug in both hands. Anything to warm her from the chill coming off him. "Bury me in some unmarked grave where no one will ever find me."

He stared.

"You don't want anyone to find me." Or the others.

After a moment of silence, he spoke. "Everything hidden will one day be revealed, and the lost will finally be found."

She leaned a fraction toward him, not feeling any of the bravado she tried to show. "We're going to bring them all home."

He shifted then. Her earpiece exploded, but she raised two fingers for them to hold. William Benning lifted a folded paper from the inside of his jacket. He reached over and laid it on her table.

Addie stared at the paper, then unfolded it and stared at the girl in the photo. Not one of his victims.

Her.

She'd been right. He knew exactly who she was.

She was vaguely aware of him moving closer to her until he whispered in her ear, "This one will come home to *me*."

Addie stood. The chair she'd been sitting on fell back. Coffee spilled across the table. She backed away from his smug smile, breathing hard.

The front door of the coffee shop burst open, and a swarm of agents rushed in. Guns raised. Her ears rang with the shouts.

Benning raised both hands and set them on the top of his head. An agent she knew well spun him, then slammed his torso against a tabletop. Benning was cuffed in time for her boss to see it when he walked in.

SAC Matt Zimmerman had been her boyfriend for three months before he'd quit attempting to get her to open up to him and take things to a "deeper" level. Whatever that meant.

They'd had bigger problems.

He strode right up to her while the others pretended they weren't listening to all of it. "What was that?"

Addie motioned to photo taken of her after being checked into the hospital. Fifteen years ago, but it may as well have been yesterday even if she wanted to forget all about it. One look, and she was right back there.

"Benning knew exactly what button to push." Zimmerman's jaw flexed.

Addie nodded. "Zimmerman—"

He cut her off with a shake of his head. "The next words

out of your mouth had better be that you need some time off."

"I told you I didn't want to do this."

"So you sabotaged the whole thing just to prove me right?"

She pressed her lips together. That was what he thought? There was no reason for him to be mad at her over this. What was going on?

"Take the weekend. Go home."

She shook her head. "I don't need—"

"We all need a break after this one." Zimmerman shot her a pointed look. "Once the details are wrapped up, everyone is taking a long weekend. But you're spinning out."

"The team has this handled." She wasn't going to let them fail.

"Good. They can handle it while you take a break."

Addie opened her mouth to argue.

His jaw hardened. "I don't wanna see you tomorrow."

Addie's eyes burned.

I don't need you right now, Ads. I have Greg, and you don't fit with that. Russ will take care of you.

Her mother's voice echoed in her head.

2

Washington State

Grandpa's truck rolled into the parking spot with all the grace of a coughing rhino. It was still Grandpa's truck even though Jacob Wilson had been the sole driver the past ten years since the older man passed away. Jacob owned a BMW SUV as well but rarely drove it downtown. Just over to the beach on the coast when he needed to get away from Benson.

Snow from the six inches that had fallen last week had been piled at the edges of the parking lot for Grassy Knoll Retirement Home. Situated beside a YMCA, the retirement home was brand-new and had been open for six months. Given the price tag, it seemed to be where the wealthy who lived in Seattle proper, an hour west, dumped their nearest and dearest. Close by, but not so near they'd have to visit much.

Jacob left the truck keys in the cup holder, grabbed his camera bag and backpack, and headed for the front doors. His boots crunched the salt on the asphalt.

He pushed inside and pulled off the beanie that kept his ears from going numb. His hair fell to the left. It was necessary to grow it out to cover the scar just behind the hairline on the left side of his forehead.

He ran his hand through it and headed for the receptionist.

He got a good look at the gray strands on the top of her head before he rapped his knuckles on the counter.

She flinched and looked up. "Oh, Jacob. Hey."

Naomi was older than him by a few years. He remembered her from youth group summer camps a couple of years in a row. The ones where he and Addie had snuck out during free time and hidden behind the tennis courts. When they got lost in the trees—and each other.

Probably not the most righteous thought to have.

The town had easily doubled since he was little and was almost a small city now. He could see the sky between the downtown office buildings from his apartment windows. Hopefully, Benson didn't get too big it obscured his view of Mt. Rainier.

Naomi was an RN now and on staff here. Though usually she didn't wear a nervous look on her face. She shoved the book she'd been reading under the lip of the counter where he was supposed to not be able to see it. *Too late.*

Jacob swallowed. "I'm here to see—"

"Mr. Harris, that's right." She handed him the clipboard so he could check in. "He's expecting you."

He signed his name on the entry log. Tried not to let on that this was the most conversation he'd had in four days. Talking to Mr. Harris was going to have him right back at his apartment with only the ambient noise of city traffic for company. His two cats were the only living creatures he spent time with until he was ready to venture downstairs.

He'd given up expecting people to understand why he was the way he was or how he managed it, especially when people insisted on reading that book.

Sure, it'd been a bestseller. The library next door to the elementary school a block from his building had sixteen copies, and most of them were usually checked out. He'd heard lately they were thinking about putting it on the high school English curriculum.

Someone had made a ton of money writing about the worst two days of his life. Whoever it was never got any information about what'd happened aside from compiling hearsay. Then again, he'd refused an interview and heard from his lawyer that everyone else involved did the same. None of them wanted to relive any of it.

People thought what they wanted to. Jacob just went home to his solitude.

He left Naomi to her bestseller and headed for Mr. Harris. He was eighty-seven next month and had some dementia but had agreed to talk. Jacob could take all the photos he needed.

When he reached the room and saw Mr. Harris in his high-backed chair looking out the window, the light caught Jacob's attention.

He dug out his camera and slipped the bags off his shoulder.

Jacob lifted the Nikon to his eye and looked at the man through the lens Grandpa had given him. A way for him to see the beauty in the world, the way Grandpa always did. The truth people tried to hide or walk away from—the good below the surface.

So he could experience it for himself, at least from a distance.

He'd needed it after all those hours at the whim of a man whose intention was to torture them until they broke. And that had only been the beginning of his plan.

Jacob had spent every day since—a span of more than fifteen years—purposely not thinking about it. Trying to find peace and see the good in what God had made. After all, he'd seen the bad. There was nothing worse left.

The click of the shutter reassured him. Like waking up to the relentless mew of hungry felines, waiting for him to dish out breakfast.

After getting a handful of good shots, he lowered the camera and took his things in. A pat on the shoulder jolted Mr. Harris out of his musing. The old guy roused as though he'd been sleeping, smacked his lips, and blinked.

Jacob pulled over a stool that might not bear his weight for long and sat opposite him. Mr. Harris wore brown slacks, wool slippers with tan rubber soles, and a threadbare blue shirt. Bumps ran up the older man's arms.

Jacob grabbed a blanket from the end of the twin bed. "Here." He waited for a second just in case the older man wanted to object, then settled it over his legs.

Mr. Harris clenched the edge of the blanket with knuckly hands. "Ah, yes. Our chat."

"If that's okay with you," Jacob said. "It doesn't have to be today."

Mr. Harris lifted his hand and waved away Jacob's comment. "I should tell someone."

The comment was plenty loaded, but Jacob wasn't about to ask questions on the man's situation. Mrs. Harris had passed away in the '90s—so coming up on thirty years ago now. Three children, seven grandchildren. They all lived in Seattle, and none had visited recently.

Whether that was due to them, or Mr. Harris, Jacob wasn't about to get into it. He was more interested in Mr. Harris's life as a young man. The stories were forgotten as the years passed, which he then compiled into a book. It was Jacob's way of giving a voice to too many who were overlooked. Silenced or simply neglected.

"Was there a specific time you wanted to tell me about?"

Jacob preferred to leave the interviewee to decide what to reveal. He wasn't worried about prejudice or corroborating stories to get to the truth. He wasn't a reporter. He simply wanted people to talk in their own words. He'd developed a radar for stories that were genuine and held back what he thought might be fabricated or embellished. Out of the thousands of hours of interviews he did for a book, only a fraction would be printed about the person.

And still, people insisted on reading the drivel published about him.

Jacob let Mr. Harris think about his question. He needed a subject for his new book and hadn't found the right person yet. The process had gone on so long it had set his schedule back.

God, is it Mr. Harris...or someone else?

A nurse came in. She spotted them talking and motioned that she would come back.

"There was a tree in the back yard. An oak, I think," Mr. Harris began. "We used to climb to the top before supper, and my sister would pull us down so she could be first."

Jacob recorded the conversation with a handheld voice recorder.

"She pushed my brother once. He fell and broke his arm. She told mother it was me, and I had to sleep the night in the shed." He swallowed. "I couldn't sit for a week."

Jacob wanted to smile, but that wasn't the kind of parenting he'd been raised with, and neither was it amusing or "just a fact of life." He didn't frame the stories he was told with his own experiences, just presented the words of the storyteller.

His upbringing hadn't exactly been full of peace and love. His parents had argued more than they got along—with him in the middle. Passed between them like a chess piece when they were "off" and ignored when they were "on again."

"That was the tree we buried Timmy under."

Jacob held the question on his tongue.

"The summers after the harvest failed. Pa took him to the shed. Two days later, the sickness took him to Jesus. Ma broke after that. Jennie took up with the preacher's son, and Pa kicked her out." He fell into a period of silence.

"What happened to your parents after that?" Jacob asked. Eventually he'd get to the old man's adult life, but that might take several conversations.

"Pa spent all day drinkin' at the creek." Mr. Harris blinked, the only movement aside from the rise and fall of shallow breaths. "Mama saw the preacher's wife at the house. I thought she had the same sickness as Timmy."

An orderly pushed another resident down the hall in a wheelchair. Only after the sounds of their conversation faded did Mr. Harris speak again.

"All day, muttering and carrying on. I was sick of it." His expression flexed like a tick in his cheek muscle. "She wasn't right. Yelling at me about peelin' potatoes. Holdin' that knife out, wavin' it in my face. That's why I grabbed the poker. Told Pa she fell over, hit her head. The blood had stained the floor, and she was cold by the time he got there. The water in the pot boiled until there was nothin' left. The gas ran out. He slapped me for letting the gas run out. Told me I was useless. That I couldn't even stop her from killing herself." Mr. Harris blinked. "He never even thought I could've done it."

Jacob held himself still. He'd learned not to show a reaction, or people generally shut down. When he could speak without inflection, he said quietly, "Did he ever find out the truth?"

"I told him," Mr. Harris said. "The night he had that heart attack. Told him he'd be going to hell, where I put her."

Harris blinked. It lasted two seconds. He said nothing and blinked again.

Jacob watched him succumb to a nap, thinking about what Mr. Harris had just said. Before he proceeded with the story, he'd investigate the man's background. See if he could find anything to provide insight into what Mr. Harris said. Jacob had met people who'd done bad things before, but there was something off about the unemotional way he'd told this story.

The sister he had mentioned might still be alive. Any of her children might've been told stories about the family.

Jacob looked at the framed wedding picture on the mantel. A bride and groom smiled, but it hardly told the whole story. He needed the words, which meant coming back and talking to Mr. Harris some more.

Not just to find out if he'd ever killed anyone else.

Jacob found himself in the hall with both his bags. He wondered how he got out there without realizing and looked back at the door for a second. No part of him wanted to associate with someone who could turn out to be at all like the man who'd captured him after homecoming, his senior year. A deranged madman who'd been given back-to-back life sentences for what he'd done to not just Jacob but others.

"Everything went okay?" Nurse Naomi stopped in front of him. "You look a little spooked."

She probably wanted him to talk about what she'd read.

"Everything's good." He could find out what he wanted to know on the internet before asking the administrator to reveal personal information for Mr. Harris's next of kin.

Jacob went to the lobby, where the administrator stood behind the desk with Naomi's relief. The administrator straightened her suit jacket. It didn't help the straining buttons. She shook her head. "I don't know what's wrong with that girl lately."

"Celia's been like this since she got a boyfriend." The receptionist pushed her glasses up her nose. "She said she'd be seeing him this weekend. Maybe they went out of town?"

Jacob frowned. Celia hadn't felt good about the boyfriend last week when she stopped him in the parking lot to talk. She'd said she wanted advice from someone older. It wasn't like he knew her well enough. They'd barely spoken before that, but she'd been upset. The whole thing seemed off to him, but he still tried to encourage her.

Until the boyfriend showed to pick her up. Jacob had just about managed to keep from getting a fat lip and a black eye, but it had been close.

Celia had simply hopped in the guy's car without a look back.

Jacob didn't think anything good had happened between them.

"Celia knew she had a shift." The administrator shrugged. "When she gets here, let me know. I want a word with her about her responsibilities." She glanced at Jacob, winced, and walked away.

The receptionist looked under the counter, then at him, then under the counter again. *Guess the book is still there.*

Jacob knew Celia enough to know the girl probably just forgot to call in sick. Or the receptionist was right, and she had spent the weekend with her boyfriend out of town.

He didn't need to get in the middle of a young woman's poor choices, though. It was none of his business, even if she was nice and that conversation hadn't had an ulterior motive.

He had work to do trying to figure out if he'd been interviewing a murderer today. Then he would dismiss Mr. Harris as a candidate and meet with someone else.

Jacob needed a story to tell.

3

Virginia

Addie leaned back in her chair. She tapped her pen on the desktop and compiled her thoughts. Except that there weren't any. Her brain didn't want to think of anything. It was blank.

Sure, Zimmerman had told her not to come in. Technically it wasn't tomorrow. She had a report to write and figured maybe he might've forgotten that order by the time she finished.

Meanwhile, the entire team sat around the office writing up their reports from the café operation. The suspect was being interviewed. She hadn't done anything since she sat down.

Now she had to wonder what was wrong with her.

Not that she'd let anyone else know there was a problem. Zimmerman may or may not let her in there to talk to Benning as part of the interview. It wouldn't have anything to do with whatever issues she did or didn't have. Addie still wasn't going to hold her breath that he'd ask her. Not after that conversation they'd had at the scene.

She tuned out the buzz of people moving. The general office chatter. Her profile for William Benning indicated it was unlikely she could persuade him to give up the location of the bodies he'd buried. Might not be impossible, though.

The seven they had discovered were in locations that held no connecting pattern. No way to predict where another would be.

The phone on her desk rang.

She picked up the handset. "Special Agent Franklin."

Dead air greeted her.

Someone had her extension and felt the need to call her whenever they wanted to disrupt her train of thought and interrupt her work. Always a blocked number. Even the tech guys couldn't figure out where the calls had originated. Someone spoofing the IP, calling over the internet.

She sighed. It hardly helped to dissipate the weight of exhaustion and frustration. She replaced the phone.

Addie had to contend with the frustration over unanswered questions with every case. Usually, she went for a run to bleed off the tension. Knowing there were possibly five young women out there who might never be found. Or, if they were, it was because of happenstance and no other reason.

Addie shoved her chair back and headed to get a drink. She should get water, but the truth was she would pour a cup of old coffee and she knew it. The profile she had on herself was the skinniest she'd ever done, but there were some key details on it. The rest she didn't want to know.

One of her colleagues, Bill from Albuquerque, left the kitchen with his own cup. He lifted it in salute.

"Hey." She passed him and headed inside. They'd

learned early on she had a hard time with small talk. Addie tended to answer only the question she was asked and didn't volunteer much else in terms of information. She wanted to do her job—solve the puzzle. She wasn't here to make lifelong friends. She wasn't wired that way.

Being relational meant attention. It meant people realized she wasn't worth sticking around for.

Sometimes attention led to…

She shook off the rush of memory laced with the tang of fear that not even coffee could get rid of when everyone knew coffee was magical.

Addie poured a mug anyway. She drank it black to have the most coffee in the mug possible. It burned going down but in a good way.

Considering she could muse about coffee for hours on end, she headed back to her desk. The murder board on the wall had been covered with victim photos, crime scene information, and an entire section on the suspect list they'd compiled.

It all pointed to one person: William Benning.

She should be satisfied he was in custody. Instead, Addie blew on her coffee and studied the other suspects. Benning could have a co-collaborator. A protégé, or mentor. She dismissed several possibilities as she'd done throughout this case. Each one still went on a list because occasionally, her assumptions were proven wrong.

"I need to show you something, Addie."

She spun around, careful not to spill her drink. Special Agent Mills, the newest member of the task force, had paled.

Addie frowned. "Everything okay?"

"Come on. I'll show you." Mills headed back to her desk and sat.

Addie looked over her shoulder.

"Carova Beach Fire and Rescue in North Carolina pulled a body out of the surf this morning. A young woman washed up just after five." Mills pulled up a photo.

The woman had been a blonde, but the body was marred and bloated. Given the markings, Addie motioned to it. "Same M.O?"

"Preliminary indications are that this is one of Benning's victims."

Addie wasn't sure that connection could be made at this juncture. She drew the line at giving killers fun nicknames that sold more newspapers or got more hits on social media. Publicity killed their ability to investigate when everyone had a bias over what they'd seen or heard or what a friend heard from another friend.

They'd succeeded in keeping this case out of the media. For the most part.

She struggled to formulate a question but managed it. "Has an ID been made?" Addie studied the photo.

Mills clicked to the open tab with the police report. "The ME has the body, and I requested the DNA be run to see if it's a match to any of our missing women. But this one has been dead only hours."

"So it could be someone we didn't yet know is missing. Someone Benning took in the last few days."

"Before we started to follow him."

Addie nodded. Had it been days?

Mills worked her mouth back and forth. She glanced up and frowned. "You okay?"

"Just tired," Addie said. "But no more than anyone else here."

"We've all been working pretty well around the clock the last few weeks."

Addie nodded. "He's in custody now. If we can get this case sewn up, we're all good to take that long weekend."

Zimmerman wanted everyone to have a few days off instead of ordering Addie to take a couple of weeks.

Like that would solve her problem.

"I'm looking forward to a break."

Addie didn't even know what that might feel like. Who cared about rest? "Send me what you have. I'd like to look at it."

Mills nodded. "Will do. You wanna drive down if it's one of his?"

She shrugged off the question—or tried to. Mills wanted to be, what? Friends? "I'll be here until Benning isn't, at least. I want to finish up with him." If Zimmerman let her.

Someone else could do the leg work if there was another victim. Tonight was the first time she'd gone out with the team on an operation in a couple of months. They compiled the evidence, and she formulated a picture of their UNSUB —an unknown subject, the label for an offender they hadn't identified yet.

If she needed to speak personally with a witness to get a better picture, she'd do it. But it wasn't often necessary when the people doing the interviews were highly trained FBI agents. They produced quality work. This team was the best.

She headed back to her desk, rolling her shoulders as she walked, shrugging off the idea that she wasn't the kind of FBI agent she wanted to be when she'd joined the FBI. The coffee hadn't done anything to perk her up, which was her fault since it would never be coffee's fault.

Zimmerman strode out the mouth of the hallway and spotted her. "You didn't go home yet?" He glanced at the clock on the wall.

Addie glanced around. "No one else did either."

He nearly said something else, caught himself, and motioned with a head tip to his office. "Sorry. That was unprofessional."

He only said it for everyone else's benefit. The entire office stared at the two of them like they didn't know what was going on under the surface. Like they didn't know she and Zimmerman had been a thing a few months ago.

"Thank you." Addie had to acknowledge his apology. "I'm sure everyone would like to know how your conversation with Benning went."

Zimmerman motioned again with his head. "Tomorrow."

Addie followed him to his office and shut the door behind her.

He took off his jacket and hung it on the hook. "I'd have thought you'd have gone home."

"No one else did." She didn't fold her arms. Everyone watching through the glass would see her get defensive in response to his words. "Why am I repeating myself?"

"Because you're burned out, and your mind can't think of a better response."

Addie frowned.

"I was serious about you taking time off."

He had something else on his mind. She could tell. "When the case is almost done?" Addie asked. "It can wait. This team pulls together."

"The team is no good if you're off your game."

Addie didn't know what to say to that.

Zimmerman sat behind his desk. "Besides, the case will never be over. Not when another will begin before it's wrapped. Then six years go by, and you realize you didn't take a single day off. I've seen it before. And I *won't* let it happen to you."

"I'm doing my job. Isn't that why the FBI pays me? Why they gave me this shiny badge?"

"You're a hair from losing it. You yelled at Stevens yesterday."

Addie winced. "They told him I'd sign that ridiculous book." The rookie had been pranked good, but he hadn't deserved her reaction. "I'll apologize."

"Yes, you will." Zimmerman sat back in the chair. "I thought I could help you, but I don't know now."

"Maybe you can." Addie braced herself. "My apartment building is being fumigated, starting tomorrow. I need somewhere to stay."

Zimmerman winced. "Ellie and I...we're trying again to see if we can make it work."

"I'll get a hotel room, then. It's fine."

"Everything on your desk is being handed to Clarenson upstairs."

She started to argue, but he interrupted before she even got started.

"This isn't coming from me."

As if that was all they were to each other. Or *had been*. Their thing was past tense. "You can't force me to go on vacation."

Zimmerman lifted one brow. "You'd rather I suspend you? Or get the doc to sign off on mandatory leave?"

Addie pressed her lips together.

"You need a vacation."

"What's going on?"

"He got under your skin." Zimmerman leaned forward. "You think any of us wanted to see that?"

She was the one supposed to be able to read the suspect. Put together the signs. Compile a profile that would lead to a conviction and the location of the missing women. If she dropped the ball and that didn't happen because she was too tired to see the connections in the pattern?

Addie sank into a chair. He was probably going to fire her anyway, kick her off the team and give her some trash assignment where it didn't matter that she wasn't a good agent and didn't have what it took.

"You've been going with this non-stop for months."

"So has everyone else."

"They don't know what you know." Zimmerman spoke quietly. "They don't feel what every victim feels. Not the way you do."

"I can do this job." She had to try, didn't she? She owed it to Russ to see if she could make him proud. After all, he was the only one who'd ever believed in her.

"Yes, you can. But the question remains if you *should*."

"And the answer is to shut me out? Leave me without the ability to give myself closure over this case?" She needed to know how bad this was.

He kept his mouth closed.

"What's going on?"

Finally, Zimmerman got down to it. "You're being reassigned."

He'd decided to make a go of it with his wife. She was being reassigned. "What did you do?"

"This isn't about us. Though we both have to admit the Office of Professional Responsibility would have a field day with the two of us." Zimmerman winced. "Are you planning to rat me out?"

"Why am I being reassigned?"

"It isn't a punishment."

She folded her arms.

"I promise. That's not the intention." Zimmerman sighed. "I told them not to do this." He shook his head.

"Someone upstairs has their eye on you, but they want a clean slate first. I didn't know how to tell you."

Addie didn't like the sound of that. "Where am I being sent?"

"The FBI recently opened a field office outside of Seattle."

The only place she knew of outside Seattle was…. "No. I won't—"

"There's nothing you can do. They need someone to run the branch, and yours was the name pushed to the top of the stack. You've got a new assignment in Benson, Washington."

She stood. "I'm being exiled."

"They want to see what you can do solo when you're given a chance."

Addie shook her head. "That's the worst idea I've ever heard." She was being set up so that everyone could see her fail.

Zimmerman frowned. "There's been a series of strange cases over the last few years. The office in Seattle is stretched thin, and the bureau wants someone in Benson full time." He lifted both hands. "It's not forever."

Home was the last place she ever wanted to be again. Facing the place that had destroyed the girl she'd been could fix what was broken in her. If it *could* be fixed. She didn't know if it was even possible, but she wanted to be brave enough to try.

And yet, what was the point when it would only go up in flames?

"Someone is setting me up so I can fail, so I'll be kicked out of the FBI." She grabbed handfuls of hair on the sides of her head. "I should never have become a fed."

Ivan Damen had taken everything from her. Addie had built the woman she was now out of that ash. But what good was it to try when she never succeeded? There was too much wrong with her.

"Addie—"

She gripped the door. "I'm being forced out and you know it."

4

The two women were seated at the table when Jacob walked in. The younger in a chair while the older lady had her wheelchair pushed up to the table. Even a cursory glance gave him the impression that these two were related to Mr. Harris, though neither shared his last name.

"Is that them?"

Jacob glanced over his shoulder and spotted the familiar face of his old friend, now police detective Hank Maxwell, in the doorway behind him. A fraction taller, which Hank had never let him forget. The guy had a scar on the underside of his jaw, was freshly shaven with his hair cut, wearing jeans and a button-down shirt—police badge on his belt. Brown Carhartt jacket. He was the only cop in Benson who dressed like he did construction instead of protect and serve.

Jacob looked back at the two women. "They seem like they'll be nice enough."

"Yeah, well. I'm planning on sticking around to find out either way."

"That's not why I told you this."

Jacob figured that was just Hank being Hank. Overprotective, and good at his job. Jacob had called last night to chew over everything. Apparently, Hank wanted to take the baton.

The two of them had been in high school together. Best friends at one point. Same classes. Same football team, though Jacob had been quarterback. Hank was what amounted to bestie for Jacob these days. That only meant he was one of the few people Jacob actually spoke to on a regular basis.

Not most people's idea of close. It worked for Jacob to connect with a friend and not have to face questions he had no intention of answering. Hank worked long and odd hours, so he'd answer when he could.

Jacob glanced back at Hank again. "Don't you have people to harass?"

Hank knew exactly what Jacob had been through because he'd been there that night. Even though Jacob purposely didn't think about any of that. Or the source of the scar on Hank's face. They could still be friends even if Jacob didn't want to think the word *victim* for the rest of his life.

That wasn't what he was. And his intention was that he never would be again.

Hank grinned. "Seems they frown upon that these days." He glanced at his watch. "I do have to go soon. There's some big shot fed set to show up in a couple of days, and the chief's freaking out."

"Huh." Jacob didn't exactly watch TV. He read the newspaper occasionally, but that was all local drama for the most part. So long as they didn't dredge up the past like the national news when things got slow.

"Just don't expect me to pay the bill for your breakfast." Jacob headed for the table where the two women sat drinking from full mugs of coffee. There was also orange juice and water on the table. "Good morning. I am—"

The younger woman looked up. Elaine Perkins. "I've lived in this town half my life. I know who you are."

Outside the diner window two fire trucks and an ambulance sped down the street with their lights and sirens going.

Elaine was slightly older than him, maybe by few years. She might have even been living here during the time it all went down. Where for three years in a row, each homecoming dance, a couple from the senior class were abducted at the end of the night.

Three years that a dangerous killer had gripped this town by its throat. Until finally he was caught, the night he had taken four teens instead of two. Maybe that mistake, that deviation, was why Jacob and his friends were recovered.

No one had told him how they'd been found.

Jacob turned to the older woman and held out his hand. "Thank you for coming, Mrs. Perkins. I appreciate you giving me your time."

Jennie Perkins put her crepey-skinned hand in his.

Before she could say anything, the younger woman butted in again. There was no other way to describe it. Especially given the almost belligerent expression on her face. Jacob wondered why she had even bothered to drive the older woman here.

"Not sure there's too much to say about Carl Harris." Elaine took a sip from her mug and said nothing else.

Jacob pulled out a chair and sat even though they hadn't invited him to. He was the one who had asked them to meet him here.

Hank had settled at the counter on a barstool, chatting up the new waitress. So new, she had no idea what she was getting into with the detective. Hank had left a trail of broken hearts across the whole county for the last fifteen years. Never settling down. Some of his conquests had even left town.

"You want to ask me about my brother?" Jennie Perkins had distant eyes and false teeth.

"I'd imagine I might not be the first person to do so."

"I'm surprised your friend with the badge didn't join you." She made no motion toward Hank. Elaine jerked around in her chair as though she hadn't even noticed the cop who'd come in with him.

Jacob gave the waitress his order and poured his coffee from the thermos pot on the table. "I'm putting together kind of a coffee table book. Photographs that I take myself, along with stories that delve into people's lives."

"And you got more than you bargained for with my brother?"

"Depends how much of what he shared with me was the truth." Some people enjoyed embellishing the past, though usually that involved posting online. Not telling a sordid tale that amounted to a confession of murder.

Elaine leaned forward. "Is your friend over there going to arrest an old man in a retirement home?"

"Even if it's true, how are the police going to find evidence?" Unless these women knew something he didn't.

The old lady watched him. Jennie Perkins had struck out on her own and married fairly early after she left her parents' house—before she even turned eighteen. She'd distanced herself from the family and maybe never completely reconnected. Though, she had remained local.

Jacob studied her. "Do you have any insight you can share into your brother?"

The waitress brought their food. Jacob waited through

those first few bites, unwilling to rush Jennie if she wanted time to think it over.

Eventually, she said, "Carl was always bad news. There was just something…wrong with him. I never could put my finger on it. Figured it wasn't worth sticking around, not after Timmy left us." She shook her head, the skin of her neck waving with the motion. "Things happened back then. My memory has become cloudy."

Jacob wasn't entirely sure that was true. She was more the kind of person who adjusted the truth to suit her needs. Meanwhile, her brother admitted to delivering a killing blow to his mother.

Carl had told Jacob that Jennie was the one who pushed Timmy out of the tree. It could be that whatever stained one had affected them all.

Either way, Jacob was going to drop Mr. Harris from the book. There was nothing in him that desired to uncover a decades-old mystery. To reveal possible murder—maybe more than one.

He wasn't going to tell a story and be revealed as a liar, whether he added the disclaimer that the words were not his but what he had been told. He wasn't a reporter. People could say whatever they wanted to about their own lives. Everyone embellished a little. Or they told outright fabrications.

The alternative was to withdraw entirely and never tell anyone anything.

He wondered what Addie told people about what happened to them. Or what Hank said about his experiences in the cabin where he'd been trapped with his girlfriend at the time. Hank's girlfriend had been killed, but that didn't stop the guy from trying to save other people. Something he respected about his friend.

Jacob chose to give a voice to those whose stories had never been told. Maybe so people would quit trying to hear his tale. The one he had no intention of telling.

No one wanted to be trapped by the past, but maybe it was unavoidable. Clearly whatever had happened to Jennie Perkins, she held onto some part of it even now.

Elaine Perkins glanced at her grandmother. "You get that we know you're lying, right? You've been sharp as a tack since my first memory of you, and that has not diminished even a fraction."

Jennie glanced aside at the younger woman.

Jacob waited, but she said nothing. He volunteered something that might serve to tug her from her malaise. "Was there a tree in your backyard? One that you played in as children?"

"Until Carl pushed Timmy off a branch. After that we weren't allowed to climb it." Jennie Perkins pushed a sausage around her plate. "Timmy was never the same after that. He just seemed to fade out, and dad had enough. The doctor couldn't find anything wrong with him. Dad made Timmy sleep in the shed so we didn't all have to hear him crying all night about the phantom pain."

Elaine winced.

He was inclined to agree with the sentiment behind that.

Jacob saw something in the older woman's expression. "He died out there, didn't he?"

"Because Carl helped him along." Jennie frowned, the wrinkles on her face scrunched. "I was looking out my window when I saw him go into the shed with a pillow. I thought maybe he felt bad about what he did so he was going to stay with Timmy."

"You think he smothered him with a pillow or something?" Elaine gaped. "That's insane! People don't do that."

Jacob shrugged one shoulder. "You'd be surprised what people do."

After all, he'd lived it for two days before the FBI busted in, and they were rescued. A dangerous killer was sent to prison for the rest of his life. The boot on the town's throat was lifted, and people began to live their lives again.

Jennie lifted her gaze and met his.

For a moment they were connected, siblings almost. If only in some existential way. Linked by a time when they had been birthed into a world neither of them expected. Instead of living in some place where things always ended well and people were good, they had stepped irrevocably into a place where terror was real, and evil things happened.

Yes, Jacob wanted nothing to do with this family. He didn't need shadows to add to the dark places already inside his head.

Elaine shifted, about to speak.

He shook his head. "Excuse me."

Jacob pushed his chair back and paid for all three meals at the counter while Hank sped up the rate at which he shoveled food into his mouth.

He strode outside to the cool February air and watched traffic stream past in both directions.

Hank called for him, but Jacob just marched to the parking lot and Grandpa's truck. It wasn't a deficiency in him that meant he wanted nothing to do with these people. There were plenty of stories to be told in the world. He didn't need to get tangled up in their back-and-forth, the accusations and blaming one another for terrible deeds.

It didn't mean there was anything wrong with him that he didn't want to spend more time with Mr. Harris. Jacob just knew what he could handle and what he couldn't. All the talking he'd done the last couple of days was enough to last him the rest of the month. He was ready to rush home and spend some quality time by himself. If he wanted to get online and chat with his counselor, or his pastor, that was no one else's business.

Jacob parked the truck in the basement garage and took the elevator to the top, using his key to access the floor where he lived.

He dumped his wallet in the dish on his entryway table and toed off his shoes. Strode through the living room, all the way to the wall of windows.

Jacob stared out at downtown while the rain fell in streams down the glass.

5

Washington State

Addie pulled up outside the house at the end of the street. Two days at the field office in Seattle getting briefed, and now she was here.

Okay, fine. So it had been more like a week of trying to convince someone—anyone—to take the assignment, so she didn't have to. But Zimmerman was right. The field office was overworked and understaffed, and no one was interested in Benson and a case that might not even be a case.

The only plus she could see was that the town didn't even look like the same place where she'd grown up.

She couldn't believe how far Benson sprawled these days. It seemed like the whole area was a mini-city, spread over what used to be forest. Now there were people and cars everywhere.

The front yard had been cleared of leaves, but the dead summer flowers still filled barrels on either side of the front steps. Maybe they were older than the last growing season. What did she know?

Addie hadn't been here in…it didn't matter.

She shut the engine off and looked back at the main street that led into the neighborhood, just in case she caught a glimpse of the white Toyota that had been following her. The last thing she needed was a tail that led right to the old rundown house where her uncle lived with her sister.

Addie didn't enjoy explaining the intricacies of her family situation to anyone. It was messed up whatever way she sliced it that days after she was released from the hospital, her mom and mom's boyfriend had packed up and officially moved to Arizona, leaving Addie with her uncle. A couple of years later they'd dropped off Addie's baby sister.

They hadn't been back since.

Addie had lost count over the years growing up, the number of times she'd been dropped at Russ's by her mom and whatever current boyfriend was the flavor of the season.

Preschool. Elementary school. Into middle school—until Russ told her to just leave Addie permanently with him.

After that her life settled, not uprooted by her mom whenever the wind blew that direction.

She climbed out of her car. There might not be much in the nuance between her mom's absence and hers, but she *was* better than them. She texted, at least. She called.

Mostly she worked. And what was wrong with that? There were people in the world who were alive because of Addie's commitment to her job.

Her calling.

Her *new* mission, and her way to do something for the greater good. Be part of a team. The Lord knew she was no good on her own. All she'd ever been was a pretty face, no substance. Being a cop meant something.

She'd stared evil in the face and lived to tell about it—as well as seek to understand. So she missed a couple of thanksgivings. That didn't mean she would one day be the kind of mother who abandoned her child just to live her life.

Addie grabbed her keys but none of her things.

The door was permanently unlocked, and today was no exception. Not many people here locked their cars or houses. She didn't even know where the key to this place was.

The entryway was empty, except for the shoes. Jackets and boots. Her uncle's keys hung on their ring, and his truck was down the side of the house. So he wasn't out. He was here.

On the wall beside the living room opening was a framed certificate—an award commemorating exceptional service to the US Government by Deputy Marshal Russell Franklin.

Addie inhaled. Her uncle had quit smoking cigars years ago, but the house still held that oaky tang. "Russ, you here?"

There was a two second pause of complete silence, and then, "Addie?"

She yelled back, "Yeah!"

"Office!"

Buster's leash still hung by the door. He should've thrown that out with the cigars.

Addie wandered through the house to the office where he'd worked for as long as she could remember—taking cases freelance after he retired from the marshals. Skip tracing. Who knew what else. She'd learned it was best not to ask because he certainly wasn't going to offer up the information.

He stood at the doorway, a frown on his face as she approached. Addie was trying to figure out how to play this off when he said, "You need a nap."

She'd never been able to pull anything over on a man trained to spot the inconsistency in any story. "That's only part of why I'm here."

Sure, she needed rest—according to Matt. According to

him, she also needed to get to work, so she figured Zimmerman's opinion didn't matter. She was here now, under the Seattle office assistant director.

Matt Zimmerman's view didn't have any sway.

He motioned over his shoulder. "I'm in the middle of something. Then we can talk about this new assignment of yours."

"You know about that?"

He just smiled that grin of his.

"Coffee?"

"Sleep," Russ ordered. "You've been driving, and you haven't stopped working since you landed, right? I'll make the coffee, and when you wake up from a nap, we can have a conversation."

Uh-oh. Addie winced. Seemed like he kept close tabs on her. "Sounds great."

She wasn't going to admit she liked the idea, even if it was snooping.

He peered toward the front door. "Moving truck?"

"I didn't get that far before I left." She'd figured she was either not staying in Benson that long, or she would pay someone to pack her things and move them here.

While he finished up whatever he was in the middle of, she would get back in her car and find a bed and breakfast… the next state over.

She peeked over his shoulder and saw two men on the monitor of his computer. One had dark hair that fell over his forehead. The other filled the screen, a blond guy with a muscle shirt on—and one arm missing just below his shoulder.

She frowned.

Russ cleared his throat.

"Okay, fine. I'll disappear again even though I just got

here." She walked away down the hall.

"I know how to find you."

She waved, though a pang moved through her. She wanted to be the kind of person who was found—especially by a good man like Russ. But did it always have to be her uncle? Couldn't she be seen by a hot guy who just *got her* without either of them having to explain?

At least she had this relationship with Russ—because her mom sure hadn't given her anything except abandonment issues. Addie had stayed away from Benson too long, but the fact she and Russ cared about each other wasn't something likely to change anytime soon.

Too bad she couldn't be good at her job *and* the kind of niece and sister who visited regularly. The two were not mutually exclusive. It didn't work like that—kind of like life. It wasn't possible to have everything. If it was, she would know someone who did.

Addie hauled her suitcase and purse in from the car and dumped both inside the door of her old bedroom. It looked the same, except he'd hung a photo from her FBI graduation on the wall. The two of them stood together, Russ smiling in a way she'd never seen.

Mona had been at an elementary school science camp that week.

Addie looked at the screen of her watch. Her sister would be home from school soon unless she was working her job at the chicken sandwich chain in town. Maybe she and Russ could go there for dinner.

She pulled her cell from her purse and laid on top of the comforter. Four missed calls, all from an unknown number. No voicemails.

Addie tapped and scrolled through her apps, then the social media accounts she kept but rarely posted on. She wasn't connected to anyone she knew—mostly, they were used for work when she needed to look up a victim or suspect. She played a couple of rounds of a word game and realized her eyes were getting heavy.

When she woke up, the lamp beside the bed was on, and she had a blanket over her.

Instead of it being dark outside, light streamed between the curtains. Muted by the cloudy sky and the rain that pattered against the glass.

A shadow outside shifted.

Addie blinked.

A figure stood out the window, hood up. Face in shadow.

She gasped and sat up. Her stomach muscles clenched. She reached for a gun she usually set on the side table. It was still in her suitcase, in the lockbox.

She looked once at the door, then back. The figure was gone.

Addie shoved back the covers and moved to the window. She stood beside the frame, out of sight, and shifted the curtain to peer out.

No one.

The house was cold enough she had to fight a shiver. Addie pulled the blanket from the bed and wrapped it around her.

Probably just a figment of her imagination. The remnant of some forgotten dream.

She still wore her suit from yesterday. After a quick shower, she changed into layers of every warm item she had, wrapped the blanket around her again, and headed for the kitchen.

A young woman in jeans and purple Converse sneakers stood at the counter with a T-shirt and jean jacket on her top half. Her hair had been straightened to within an inch of its life and was the same color as Addie's.

The print on the wall was different. Before an old reproduction of a Thomas Kinkaid hung there. Now it was a striking black and white photo of Mount Hood that seemed familiar.

"Hey, kiddo."

Mona turned toast in one hand. She took a huge bite. "Hey."

She'd gotten better with makeup since last time. Addie had handed down her old car when she upgraded two years ago—the summer Mona passed her driving test.

"School today?"

"Yep. Math first, and my teacher is a pain, so I've gotta go." She left her plate on the counter, along with the jam—the lid beside it—and breezed to the door with the remains of the toast in one hand.

Addie sighed to the empty kitchen and brushed back her wet hair. She kept the blanket around her while she poured herself a cup of coffee and trailed down the hall. Russ sat at his desk with the door open. Since there was a couch there, she took a seat while he pecked at the keyboard.

"You should take a typing class."

"You should keep your opinions to yourself." He looked over and gave her a toothy grin.

Addie took a long mouthful of coffee and then leaned her head back. "I slept a while."

"You slept nineteen hours."

Addie blinked.

"How long have you been pushing yourself?"

"Big case," Addie said. "All hands on deck, and a complex profile to construct. It took a few months." The two days in Seattle had been no less busy.

"You caught the guy?"

She closed her eyes. The report was going to say that he'd gotten under her skin, and she hadn't wanted to follow orders even before that. Benning had played her because he knew more about Addie than she knew about him. That she hadn't been able to handle the stress of being that close to the suspect.

Her jaw clenched. Now she'd been reassigned.

The writing on the wall.

"You didn't catch him?"

She held herself still under his scrutiny. "Benning is in custody. I was told to come here."

"A new assignment?" Just like that, he was back in "police" mode. Addie had to fight the squirm of being under the spotlight gaze of a seasoned investigator.

She took a sip of coffee. "Seems like you might know more about it than me."

"I make a point to be informed. Planning on staying here?" Gathering intel. Forming a conclusion. What would he find her guilty of?

"I can get a hotel room."

"So you can tell yourself it's temporary. You're only here for a trip, so you've got an out when it gets too hard, and you can't handle it anymore."

Seriously? "If it does, it'll be *your* fault."

"Now you sound like Mona."

Addie frowned. "What's wrong with Mona?"

"Other than the fact she's a teenage girl?" He patted that barrel chest and the denim shirt that covered it. The guy was built like an ox. Or an old oak nothing could fell. "I'm what's wrong with her."

"I'll talk to her." Addie sipped her coffee.

"She gets straight As. She shows up to work and she

doesn't spend all her money as soon as she gets paid. I don't much like what I've heard about that new boyfriend of hers, but she always gets home before curfew. What's there to talk about?"

Addie took a sip of her coffee. She needed fortitude in the form of Russ's pancakes if she was going to venture into this minefield. He'd basically raised her. She shouldn't be concerned now he was raising Mona as well.

They needed a change in subject. "We could talk about who it was at the FBI that assigned me here."

He snorted. "That boyfriend of yours gave the order, right?"

"We aren't dating anymore." Because he was reconciling with his wife. "And I'm going to find out who sent me here." Then she'd know if this was worth fighting.

"Hmm."

Addie wasn't going to ask what that meant. "You know why I can't be here." She sighed. "I need breakfast. Want anything?"

"There's a sausage breakfast casserole in the fridge. One of the ladies from church saw your car yesterday and dropped it off. Cinnamon rolls, too."

"Seriously?"

"You're home." He shrugged. "It's a big deal." He turned away.

Addie gathered the blanket and now-empty mug and moved to the back of his chair. She leaned down and kissed his prickly face. "I missed you."

He said, "Hmm," again, but nothing else.

"What was that video call about yesterday?"

Russ reached to a white envelope on the desk beside his mouse and slid it under a manila file. "Nothing. Just some business."

Addie rolled her eyes and went in search of sustenance. It was either nothing, or it was business. It was unlikely both of those things.

She laid the blanket on a chair and stared at the kitchen. What on earth was she going to do? Probably it was the season that left her feeling like this. The way she'd felt when her mom left her on the porch.

Russ hadn't even been home. Back then he'd locked his doors. Until she sat there for three hours after her mom left her. Forty-five degrees. *Eight years old, Viv. How could you do that to her?* She'd walked out of the room before he finished his phone conversation.

Nothing good ever happened in February.

Still, at least it wasn't fall. Homecoming…

She shuddered. She should start by not thinking about that. Then get to work.

Being back wasn't about closure. Neither was it about that case file with her name listed as the victim.

Just the hundreds since then with her listed as one of the investigating agents. The lead profiler, part of a team that saved lives.

Clean slate.

Hardly. Someone was trying to get her kicked out of the FBI, and she was going to find out exactly what Benson had on its hands.

Take down a killer.

Figure out who sent her here.

There was no reason she couldn't do both, even if the odds of her success were nil. Like the odds of her convincing her mom to stick around.

Just stay here. Russ will take care of you.

It didn't matter what mom had said to her.

Addie was going to take care of herself.

6

Jacob always parked in the same spot at the grocery store. It took a whole blink before he realized someone had parked a white compact in the spot. *His* spot. He hit the brakes and swerved, missing the Hyundai by an inch. He yanked hard on the wheel and rattled into the neighboring space.

He stared hard at the car beside his, trying to decide if it was okay to be mad or if he should learn how to deviate from his routine sometimes.

He could do something different if he wanted to.

If he wanted.

Jacob pocketed his wallet and headed into the store. The carts were all wet after spending hours in the rain before they were collected by some high school kid earning a few extra bucks for gas money so he could take his girl to the lookout point and try his luck.

Not that Jacob had ever done that.

Except that thought brought up memories with Addie. The *before* of their relationship.

He pushed the cart down the first aisle and allowed

himself the indulgence of remembering a few evenings with Adelyn Franklin where they'd gone a little further than they should have. Sure, he'd been raised Christian—they both had. He just thought he knew better, which pretty much all teens did. They'd thought they could do whatever with no consequences.

Except in their case it led to the two of them being abducted by a crazed killer.

Not great for keeping his head on straight about what God did to punish those who didn't follow his law. Instead of being hyper-religious, Jacob's counselor had steered him toward not absorbing warped ideas about following the rules or feeling responsible for what happened.

God had grace. He gave it to Jacob.

It was up to Jacob to show it to himself when needed.

He might not have done anything to deserve what happened, but processing all that had taken some time. He'd rather forget about what happened and focus on now. Think about the good. Didn't mean that was the right thing to do exactly, but it kept him sane all these years.

He liked his ordered life. His routine.

Jacob wasn't going to lose it just because someone parked in his preferred space.

The store was nearly empty this time of night—the way he liked it. Still, two employees who were barely adults whispered to each other over the broccoli. One glanced at Jacob.

He shoved the cart toward the onions.

"…probably killed her."

Jacob twisted around to where both stared at him. Long enough Jacob spotted a shift right before they glanced at each other.

"Is there something you want to say to me?"

Those pimply faces were about to dissolve in fear. He saw one lip quiver.

Jacob rolled his eyes and went back to his shopping. Soon as he got home, he would call Hank and ask if there was a reason for that whole thing. Maybe the town was talking about him. Or someone had seen what happened with Celia's boyfriend.

He didn't even know that guy's name, but maybe he should visit the sheriff's office and tell them what he knew about Celia. Which, admittedly, wasn't much. Still, her boyfriend could have hurt her.

If it weren't for the police chief and the captain, he would have. Lachlan was probably the person who told all those true crime authors how that killer tormented the town. Maybe he thought there was something Jacob never told. As for Captain McCauley? Jacob didn't know what was in that guy's head.

It was like they'd already decided he was—

Jacob stopped. *Surely not.*

He dragged the cart back three feet and glanced down the dry goods aisle.

Blinked.

Adelyn Franklin.

Addie looked up from the box of brownie mix in her hand as if she could feel his attention on her. She blinked just like he had.

All of it rushed back in an instant. The cabin. The terror. Those insects crawling over every inch of everything. Music pounded so loud they couldn't hear each other, not even shouting as loud as possible.

Hours.

It had lasted for hours.

Pitch-black. Then bright white. Silence, then more hours

of deafening music. Until he wanted to scratch his ears off. Until the weapon the killer left on the dresser started to look like a viable option.

Jacob sucked in a breath through his nose. *That's not who you are.*

He bent forward over the basket of his cart and took a long inhale, followed by a slow exhale. In his mind he pictured the experience. As he blew out, he forced the image to move farther away. As though he could control it, push it away, get it as far from him as possible.

A light touch registered. Her hand on his arm. "Are you okay?"

Jacob opened his eyes and stared at her hand. Her clean fingers. Tidy nails. Some kind of pale polish.

He took a couple more breaths to gather his composure and lifted his gaze to her.

"You okay, Jake?"

Jake. He'd always been Jake with her. He said nothing.

"I can't believe it's you." She shook her head. The darkness he lived with was there in her eyes. She wasn't immune to it.

Their connection. He could feel it in her hand on his arm and in her attention. The warmth of her gaze did something that'd never happened with anyone else. Not before her. Not since. This woman understood him in a way no one else would.

She gave him a nervous smile. "Of all the people to run into at the—"

He spun around, slid his arms around her waist, and tugged her to him.

At the last second her eyes widened. He realized kissing her right now was a bad idea. Instead of acting and not thinking it through, he pulled her into a hug that felt so familiar his knees nearly gave out. Their cheeks touched.

There was still the option to kiss her for a moment, like a question left unanswered. Rather than push his luck, he slid his head alongside hers and held her close.

He found his eyes had shut.

Felt her sigh in his arms. Heard her breathy, "Well."

He wasn't sure what that meant, but she didn't push him away. Yell at him. Slap him. All of which she probably would have if he'd laid his lips on hers. Fifteen years, and he realized he'd grabbed her. Said nothing.

"Adelyn." Her name was a groan from his lips.

Neither of them made a move to exit the hug.

"Jake."

Fifteen years ago she'd hated to be called the shortened version of her name, while he'd loved being "Jake." But neither had realized how quickly things could go bad.

She shifted. Jacob let go of her, his cheeks flamed. "Sorry. I shouldn't have ambush-hugged you."

"It's different when it's you." She glanced aside, a slight smile on her face, and he heard a muttered, "Always was."

Jacob shifted. He didn't know what to say to that. He settled on, "How are you?"

They'd gone their separate ways, seeing each other only once after he was released from the hospital. She'd stayed under observation for longer. The last time they'd seen each other had been a disaster, what with her mom being there and all. Not knowing what to say to each other.

For so much of their relationship, they'd settled on a physical release rather than talking. He could argue they were just teens who didn't know better. Or that proved how futile it was that they hadn't had a foundation to stand on when things got real.

It also wasn't something they could change now. He'd had to process it as part of his moving on from their shared trauma, but no one could erase the choices they made.

Fifteen years later, they'd never even spoken once since the hospital. Both of them laid low. Then she left town, and they'd lived separate lives.

Addie winced. "I'm…okay."

"Yeah?"

She nodded. "I'll be in town for a while." She rolled her eyes, looking a lot like the teen he'd known and been smitten with. "A work thing." She shrugged, but he didn't believe it was at all casual.

"It's good to see you."

"You, too. Seriously." She reached out again and laid a hand on his arm. "I didn't mean to cause you distress. It is really nice to see a familiar face."

Jacob nodded. "Nice to see an ally." At least, it seemed like that might be the case still. Truth was, he had no idea if she'd be on his side or not.

She frowned at that but didn't ask him to explain.

"It was unexpected, seeing you." His voice remained soft. "But that doesn't mean bad."

She nodded. "I agree."

A handful of questions sat on the tip of his tongue, but none emerged.

"I have to get a couple of things." She motioned down the aisle. "Walk with me?"

Jacob turned his cart even though he only bought smoked paprika and olive oil in this aisle. He got plenty of exercise at home but didn't need to do extra to account for additional calories. And what reason did he have to celebrate anything? There was never cause for cake. Not even on his birthday.

He had enough issues. Indulgence wasn't one of them, at least not with food. Indulging in more than a hug with Addie? The desire for that had caught him unaware. Now he couldn't get his equilibrium.

It had him off guard to such an extent he didn't know what to do now. Or what to say.

"You still live in town?" She picked up the box of brownie mix and set it in her cart. When she looked at him, he nodded.

She'd matured since high school. *Duh.* Good thing he'd kept that thought to himself. He didn't need to say idiotic things out loud.

"What do you do for work?"

Jacob eyed her. "How do you know I do anything? Maybe I'm a bum."

Her mouth twitched, but it seemed like she didn't know if she should laugh. She looked down at his shoes and back up. "I'm not thinking 'bum.'"

"I'm a photographer."

"Really?"

He shrugged. It was mostly true, and he couldn't help thinking about his new book. He needed a subject that captivated him.

Who captivated him the way Addie did? No one, if he was honest.

Not one single subject had ever moved him like her. But then, maybe that wasn't the nature of how things should be in his work. He might be chasing an idea.

A dream.

Nothing more.

"Your mom had a camera, didn't she?"

"She gave me my first one in middle school. I didn't use it much." Not when his parents used it as a point of contention. "She got it out of the closet again, right after..." He didn't finish. "It helped."

"Good."

"They moved to Florida a few years ago." He'd never been, and they'd given up calling. Jacob had no desire to be dragged into their battle. "And you're FBI now? I thought Russ mentioned that."

"You know my uncle?"

Jacob shrugged. "We have mutual friends. We talk sometimes."

He knew enough to know she hadn't been in town in the last couple of years. He didn't blame her since he lived in a penthouse apartment and only came out when he *had* to. Their lives weren't so different in that respect. Except that she had left and built a career for herself.

They chatted and walked the aisles. He didn't know half of what he threw in there but hoped it made sense. He should pull the list from his pocket. Only then he'd have to go back through the store and get what he'd missed. That meant Addie would go through the checkout, and he'd lose her.

They headed for the door together. Pushed carts across the lot to where they'd parked. She headed for his space, at the far end of the middle row under the light that had broken months ago—maybe longer.

"So you're the one."

She glanced over. "What does that mean?"

"Nothing." She would think he was crazy, going on about "his" parking space.

Addie turned to him. "Is this it?"

Jacob frowned. "Do you want it to be?"

After everything, he'd feel weird asking her out to coffee. Or dinner. Would she come to his apartment?

Addie beeped the locks on her car. The trunk opened on its own. They both loaded their groceries—his on the passenger seat and footwell, bags of he didn't know what. Random things he'd tossed in the car while they talked about nothing in particular. Winding through aisles.

He didn't even care.

A car stopped on the street, idling in a random spot. It didn't pull into the parking lot. Jacob turned back to her. "Addie?"

He probably would've told her it was good to see her.

She crossed to him and lifted on her toes, though there was about a half-inch difference in their heights. "Want to give me your cell number?"

Jacob hesitated. Maybe it was better not to get tangled up with each other again. What if they got to know each other again and she didn't like what she discovered?

Something crossed her expression, disappointment or hurt. He couldn't pin down what it meant. He figured she was building a profile on him in her head. Maybe she didn't do that with everyone, just dangerous killers. "Never mind. Maybe that's a bad idea."

"I'm sure we'll see each other around." Jacob headed for his driver's door.

If something was going to develop, it was better to let that happen naturally. Right?

Addie pushed her cart across to the return corral. One that was farther away than the one he'd used. Like she needed all that space from him.

Jacob gripped the steering wheel and watched her, as entranced as he'd always been by her. Sure, she was different now. He was as well. They weren't anything like the kids they'd been. And yet there would always be something about her.

The car at the curb pulled in. Addie turned and headed back for her car.

An engine revved.

Addie froze. It picked up speed. Jacob laid a hand on his horn and kept it there. The car drove directly at her.

Jacob shoved out his door too late.

7

Addie's knees locked. It was all too close. Too near. Too familiar.

White—the brightest of lights right in her face—blinded her to everything but the pound of her heart and the taste of fear on her tongue.

Her life, her present, swallowed in that night years ago.

Jake. Jacob.

The roar of a car engine broke through her awareness. Addie blinked against the brightness. *Car.* At the last second, she dove out of the way of the oncoming car. Wind whipped her hair. She slammed on the pavement of the parking lot, jarred her hip, and cried out.

The car roared past.

She reached to her hip for a gun that would've been there if she wasn't due to start her new position tomorrow. Back in her hometown. With Jake.

She blinked at the sky.

Benson, Washington. Otherwise known as the worst place ever.

"Adelyn!" His voice carried over the receding engine.

Addie glanced at the fleeing car, then watched him race to her. She held out a hand both to ward off her past, and in case he might hold it. *There's something wrong with you.* Probably too much sleep lately, because nothing else in her life pointed to this kind of sudden whimsy. He was terrible for her. That was all there was to it.

Something she already knew.

"Are you okay? Hurt anywhere?"

"Just bruises." She gritted her teeth. For a moment she'd entertained the tragically bad idea of going on a date with this guy. Her first boyfriend. First love. First…everything.

As though one impulsive hug on his part meant a summer fling—in February—would ever be a good idea.

She thumbed 9-1-1 on her phone. Resisted the tendency to report an officer down and declined an ambulance. Having her name associated with a hit-and-run wasn't the best way to start her new job.

The dispatcher said, "A patrol car is on the way."

"Great, thanks." Addie hung up and told Jake, "They're sending a black and white." It was probably just to take her statement, except that meant they'd have her name on record. Her first case—and not because she'd reported for duty.

"Good."

His tone jerked her from bemoaning the state of her life, and Addie surveyed his pinched expression. "Why don't I believe that?"

"What?" He glanced once at that rust bucket he owned. Didn't photography pay well? She didn't want to be judgmental, considering she was currently living in her childhood bedroom, but whatever it was didn't seem to bring that much income.

It wasn't any of her business. Not just because she was deflecting so she didn't have to think about her own issues.

"You have a beef with the local police?"

She didn't even know who the chief was these days. Plenty of people had a low opinion of cops these days. She tried to do the best job she could—which had led her right to burnout. And reassignment.

"Who is the chief these days?"

His jaw flexed. "Alan Lachlan."

"Wasn't he the lieutenant when we…?"

"Yep." Jake frowned. "He still thinks I had something to do with it." Before she could ask him what on earth would cause Lachlan to think that, he shifted. "Want to get off the ground?"

Jake held her elbow so she could stand. She hobbled over and leaned her bruised pride against the hood of her car. He'd want to know why someone tried to run her over when it wouldn't ever be his business. Not just because she had no idea.

"Was the car white?" It could've been the exact vehicle that followed her on the highway from Seattle. The same person making those harassing calls to her cell and work number. The figure outside her window this morning.

"It was." He stood in front of her, irritated but not at her she didn't think. "A white compact. Sure you don't need an ambulance?"

Physically she was fine. The rest was up for debate, except that at least now she knew she didn't need a psychiatrist.

In this light who knew what he saw in the shadows on her face.

"I'm not her. Not anymore." The words were out before she could recall them.

Some part of her needed him to know she wasn't anything like the girl he had known. She *couldn't* be that girl. Not anymore.

Tomorrow she was starting at the FBI office adjacent to the police department. She had to be the profiler and field agent who'd made a name for herself. Not someone struggling or damaged. That wasn't the way to garner respect in an exploding small town with an entrenched police department. Probably a bunch of good ole boys set in their ways who didn't want a woman in their business.

"I'm not who I was either." He settled on the hood beside her with a sigh. "So maybe we should get to know each other. The people we are now."

He glanced over, but she didn't meet his gaze. Across the lot, the cop car pulled in. Lights flashing. Addie lifted a hand to wave them over to her.

"I should go." Jake practically jumped off the car, then hesitated like he didn't know what to say. "I'll come find you?"

It sounded more ominous than he probably intended, but she nodded anyway. Then watched him jog to his driver's door and peel out in reverse.

The officer pulled the car right in front of her and climbed out, saying over the car roof, "Something I need to know about that?" He motioned toward the truck now halfway down the block.

Addie frowned. "Why would someone undertaking a hit-and-run then park and stick around to chat?"

"Oh, I assumed—" The cop had a tight haircut and no ring. He was young, maybe midtwenties. Blue eyes. She could make some assumptions but judging someone's outward appearance wasn't usually a quality assessment.

"I wouldn't if I were you." Addie winced. Just the frustration and bruises talking.

She turned her phone over on the leg of her jeans. It would be easy enough to get the mayor on the phone and figure out if this was par for the course in Benson. Then again, she didn't start until tomorrow. Maybe he had no clue who she was.

One could hope.

She wanted to get this done and get home. "Does the grocery store have cameras?"

He glanced at the closest light pole. Hesitated. Frowned.

Addie stood. "I'll go ask inside." All the frozen stuff in her trunk would be toast, even if it was freezing out here. But maybe they'd replace it. She couldn't leave right now.

Addie didn't get up from the trunk. That thought about leaving stumped her.

She *could* go home now. This wasn't her case, or her jurisdiction—yet. She didn't need to get her hands dirty on her last day off. Working a hit-and-run that was *probably* random but might not be.

"Does stuff like this happen in this part of town, or often?" Frustration or not, did she want to get in the middle of the police doing their job?

The young officer pulled out a logbook. "How about you just tell me what happened?"

Lights.

She'd frozen there as the past resurged like a dragon woken from sleep. "White car. I didn't see a license plate on the back as it sped away. There might've been one on the front. Maybe the security picked it up—we can check."

He looked up from his notepad and blinked those eyes. "Because there's a reason you're authorized to do that?"

Addie decided then that his looks disarmed criminals and witnesses alike. He was either irritated by that or used it to his advantage regularly. She showed him both of her hands, palms out, then reached her back pocket. She turned slightly and showed him the fabric of her pants. She used two fingers to pull out her wallet.

"You're a cop."

"FBI Special Agent Addie Franklin."

"The new agent that starts tomorrow." He nodded slowly.

Addie studied him, looking for some indication of how the local police viewed her impending arrival. She wasn't some unfamiliar face—whether that proved to be good or bad. "I grew up in Benson. My family lives here."

He nodded. "Everyone knows Russ Franklin."

Addie looked at his name badge and stuck out her hand. "It's nice to meet you, Officer Hummet."

"You too, Special Agent Franklin."

"Addie is fine if we're not both on the job."

"Sounds good."

Either he didn't know about her history or was professional enough not to mention it. Addie could appreciate both, whichever it was.

She set off. "Let's go check with the store about cameras."

Hummet used his radio to call in that he was headed inside the store. "Had a call here a few weeks ago. They have a system. It's glitchy, so I guess we'll find out if they dumped the money to fix it or upgrade."

"Guess we will." Addie hobbled over the entry mat. Tried not to let on that her hip hurt quite as much as it did.

"Want some ibuprofen while we're in here?"

Addie glanced over her shoulder and pouted just for show. "Fine."

Hummet grinned. "Broke my arm last summer. Took me two weeks to admit it was bad. I tried to take down a huge guy running a gambling ring. Nearly cried like a baby."

Addie smiled back.

"Thankfully it didn't need surgery because it'd started to heal wrong by the time the sergeant ordered me to the doctor."

"That's good."

Addie found the manager and explained what they needed while the guy glanced between her and Hummet. As if the cop needed to provide authorization for her request. Sure, this wasn't her investigation. She was the victim. But did he think that would hinder her from finding out who did this?

"Just show us where the office is," she said. "I'm sure we can find our way around your computer ourselves."

He squinted at her.

Guess not. But it got him to snap to and take them there himself.

The manager settled in a rolling office chair. They got a great view of the bald spot on the top of his head. "Let's see…" He clicked the mouse and scrolled the wheel, moving the feed on the monitor like rewinding an old VHS tape.

Addie stared at the car. "Too far away to make out the plate."

She wasn't even sure there was one on the front bumper. Glare meant she hadn't seen it—momentarily blinded by the headlights and her trauma.

Hummet hissed out a breath.

Addie didn't look at herself falling. She waited for a second and watched the part where Jake raced to her.

"Friend of yours?"

"Old acquaintance."

One she wasn't sure she wanted to see again. Being in Benson was about work, not reviving a relationship murdered by Ivan Damen—and Addie's mom. Whatever they'd had, it was gone. Had been for a long time.

She couldn't believe she was thinking about pursuing it. After fifteen years, the likelihood of something happening between them was as probable as a resurrection. Addie certainly didn't have that kind of power.

The manager turned, interest on his face.

Addie wondered why he thought she might tell a juicy story. "I should head out." She turned to Hummet. "I've got an early start tomorrow."

"I'll walk you to your car."

As soon as they cleared the store—after Hummet detoured her for pain killers—he glanced over. "Any reason that driver made a beeline for you that you can think of?"

Addie worked her mouth back and forth. "Write it up as an accident. There's no reason to believe it's connected to something else."

His jaw flexed as they walked.

"You want me to read you in if it is?" Some cops wanted to stick through the aftermath of a callout. "I just figure you have enough to do without wading in."

"And if I'm interested in federal work experience?" Hummet adjusted his belt. "A way to see what life is like… across the hall."

Addie reached her car. She turned and folded her arms. Assessed the officer. It was tempting to think of him as a kid, but he was a professional. A colleague. "Give me your card."

He pulled one out and handed it over.

"Now I know one cop in Benson." Addie lifted the card. "I need someone, guess whose name I'll mention when I'm talking to your chief?"

Hummet's smile broadened. "I appreciate that."

Addie nodded. "Have a good night."

8

Jacob was early, and he knew why. He just wasn't prepared to think on it too much. He entered the code for the warehouse door and disarmed the alarm.

Inside was an open space, his photo studio. The shooting area at the end had a light bar hung above, various spotlights and strobes hung from it. White on the floor, white on the walls. Four lights on tripods with umbrella reflectors.

A refreshments bar stretched the length of the left wall between his office and the changing rooms—bathroom at the end.

His assistant wasn't coming in until later because she had a still life class this morning, but she'd left a note. The clothes had been set out, and since the photos were meant to be historical, they'd use some makeup but not the full makeup they might if this was a fashion shoot or even senior photos.

He did those all the time. But this wasn't work for hire. It was to get more stock photos for his portfolio, now that he knew he wasn't using Carl Harris for the new book he was putting together. Or it would be when the two young models he'd hired for the spread showed up.

Right now, Jacob knew what he was looking for, and it wasn't the cameras he kept in the locked cabinet in his office.

He glanced back at the door. It wasn't in the camera bag he'd left beside the door.

Jacob headed for the storage room. At the back, on the top shelf, were a series of boxes. He pulled out the middle one and flipped the lid. Carried the album he'd put together to his office and sat in his chair.

Stared at the cover.

Are you going to let this have power over you?

Jacob dumped the album on the desktop, and his pen rolled away. He flipped the cover and stared at the first image. He'd taken the picture himself a long time ago—some of the first good photos he'd taken.

Almost as soon as he'd known how to take good images, he'd gone back to that place and clicked the shutter a hundred times. The files were buried on his cloud storage. Some he'd printed. He could see the level of skill he'd had back then. Clearly some talent there, but a few of the technical aspects he'd do differently now. The lighting wasn't great in spots.

As if he'd have dragged studio lights out to that cabin where his life had all but ended.

He was just grateful the cops left it intact. At least long enough he could go back through. He'd needed desperately to look at the details through his lens, like that kept him separate from the scene even if he stood right there in that place to take them. The spot where he'd listened to Adelyn cry. He'd cried as well. They'd both lost their voices from the hours of crying and screaming. Calling for help. Clinging to each other.

The instructions.

The torture. Mental and psychological. Tied to chairs.

Breathing in some kind of gas.

Waking up on the floor with no bindings but new bruises.

They'd barely had scratches and a few abrasions on them when the cops picked them up. The most damage had been below the surface.

Sometimes he wished he'd lost a limb, though that might seem strange. It felt like he'd had something taken from him. Torn off or amputated.

Jacob blew out a long breath.

Seeing Addie again would dig up everything he'd been trying to bury for fifteen years. He really couldn't run the risk of allowing it to be exhumed. He wasn't sure he would survive it again.

The buzzer for the front door sounded.

Jacob shoved the album in the top drawer of his desk and strode to the studio area. Two college age kids came in, the door closing out the day's sunlight as they moved toward him. The young woman practically bounced on her feet. The guy was playing it cool. Both of them were excited.

"Thanks for coming." He shook both their hands.

Sammie and Dylan were relatively new to modeling but came recommended by the college art professor.

Dylan said, "We just need to get changed?"

He nodded. "Everything is laid out in the changing room, outfit number one first. We'll work through all three and see what we come up with. Sound good?"

Jacob was paying them for a full day, and by the end of it all three of them would be exhausted.

Six hours later he called for a break, unsurprised when Dylan sat on the floor to stretch out and lay flat.

"Watch the outfit, yeah?"

Dylan nodded, breathing hard.

Jacob had run them ragged, but the shots of the two dancing as war era young couple in love would be worth it.

Dylan about to go off to war. Or maybe newly returned and unscathed—at least on the outside. They'd taken a range of pictures from happy couple in love to arguing spouses. The two of them had held each other. Jacob had coached them through an argument, giving them dialogue and motivations.

Sammie popped the top off another diet soda—she'd had about half a dozen while he and Dylan polished off two pots of coffee.

Dylan shut his eyes. Sammie sidled up beside Jacob and laid her hand on his arm, peering over at the camera display. "Can I look at some?"

"I do some editing work on the computer first, before I do anything with them." Jacob smiled. "But you guys did a really good job. If you need references, I'm happy to write up something."

"Thanks." She squeezed his arm.

Dylan didn't open his eyes. "Thanks, Jake. 'Preciate it."

Sammie hesitated. Jacob tapped through menus on his camera. Eventually she took a sip then said, "Can I ask...it's okay if you don't want to talk about it."

Jacob looked up. Saw her expression. He *didn't* want to talk about that. Too bad everyone asked—eventually. Except Hank or Russ. Even his mother insisted on bringing it up, especially on the anniversary of Becca's death.

Hank hardly ever talked about the girl he'd lost that night, abducted with him like Addie was with Jacob. Becca's death had sent Hank into a tailspin, and Jacob wasn't sure he'd ever crawled out of it. Not completely. Even after channeling his frustrations into police work, the guy had never bounced back to the kid Jacob had known.

Maybe none of them had, or ever would.

Sammie said, "You are…that guy, right?"

"You want to know if I'm the same Jake Wilson who was abducted?"

She bit her lip. Tenacious, but still unsure what his reaction was going to be. She shifted a fraction too close with her hand back on his arm. She glanced once at Dylan, then slid her arm around to his back and down. She traced her hand on the back of his belt, over the T-shirt on his waist.

"I can't imagine going through something like that."

Jacob's synapses fired, locked between the images he'd looked at hours ago now in that photo album. The ones that never left his mind. Then there was her presence beside him. It wasn't like he felt anything, let alone attraction. She was far too young, and he wasn't interested.

He stepped away. "Give me a sec. I need to plug in this camera before it dies."

As he strode to his office, Dylan rolled over on the floor. "We're done, right?"

"Yep."

The two of them could get changed and leave as far as he was concerned. They'd tell stories about the temperamental photographer, but that wouldn't ding his reputation at all. In fact, it would likely serve to enhance it more than anything.

He did need to plug in the camera.

Movement at the door caught his attention. He looked at the same time he set the camera on the desk. "Hey."

Sammie shut the door behind her. "Sorry if I upset you. I really can't imagine going through something like that."

"But you're interested in the morbid details?"

She shrugged one slender shoulder while she crossed to him. "I've seen almost every horror movie ever made. I love being scared. It's—" She inhaled an excited gasp. "Exhilarating. You know?"

"Do I?" He didn't remember fear being the same thing as excitement. Far from it, in fact.

"You were with your girlfriend." She did the hand on his arm thing again. "I couldn't imagine being alone. It's much better to be with someone you care about. Someone you can share with."

"Mostly I don't think about what happened. Ivan Damen is in prison, and he'll never get out. It's over."

"Have you ever"—hand squeeze—"visited him?"

"Why would I do that?" Jacob shook his head. "Damen means nothing to me."

He'd tortured them, tried to birth something ugly and evil in Jacob. It hadn't worked. They'd been rescued, and the rest was an exciting blurb for a TV show because the network needed something sensational to play when not much else was going on in the world. True crime podcasts and shows loved to re-hash all of it. Every few years, some new study was written—a spin.

His favorite was the one that said Jacob had killed Becca in a pact with Hank so they could both be in a relationship with Addie. He only knew the gist of the book because his agent had told him she read it on a cruise and thought the whole thing was hilarious. Then again, she knew Jacob wasn't some kind of amorist.

His last relationship was…

He didn't even know.

It must've been a while, considering he still felt Addie's hug. It was the closest he'd been to anyone in years.

Until this.

Jacob crossed to the door and held it open even though it

didn't need assistance doing its job. Sammie looked like she wanted to give whatever this was another try.

"Go get changed."

She breezed out in the shirtwaist dress his assistant had found. Muttering something that sounded like, "Your loss."

Jacob gave himself a minute. He wanted to know if Addie got questions like that or if no one ever mentioned it to her.

People in this town were always trying to drag him back into the limelight. It sounded like the worst idea ever, and he'd managed to keep his success pretty unnoticeable so far. Not many people knew he was the guy behind the Life in Story books—the writer and photographer.

It probably said something that he wanted to tell stories for others and had no interest in his own.

He grabbed checks for the two of them from his safe and met them at the door. "Thanks, guys."

Dylan gave him a salute using the check. Sammie grabbed hers and ducked out the door.

Jacob stared at the sunset that washed the sky in pink, then went to get his ringing phone. He still had to clean up and close the studio, and he was wiped. Who was calling?

The number wasn't one saved in his contacts.

"Jacob Wilson."

Silence greeted him. Then a choke, as if the person on the other end couldn't contain their distress.

"Hello?"

"I'm...Celia. I'm her mother, Carinne."

Celia had never mentioned her mother's name, just that she lived with exacting parents who hadn't liked her boyfriend. "Carinne?"

"Do you know where my daughter is?" The female voice was accented. Interesting enough he wanted to hear a story.

"I only met Celia a few times at the retirement home." And fought with her boyfriend. "I don't think there's anything I can provide the police to help them find her."

"Unless you're the one who took her."

"Ma'am—"

She cut him off. "Your history and all, and you said you know her. She's gone. No one knows where she is."

"I'm a suspect as far as you're concerned?" He worked to rein in his frustration. "I had nothing to do with her disappearance."

"So you say." She sniffed. "The FBI is getting involved now. That's what the police said. Some profiler who catches dangerous criminals and finds people. She'll sniff out the truth. You won't get away with this."

9

When Russ found out she'd taken his hammer, he'd be mad. Though, it wasn't like Addie would use it to commit a murder. If she did, he'd have something to be mad about.

The sound of the hammer echoed in the empty room. Empty bookcases. Desks, also empty. She had a laptop and her cell phone.

The city of Benson wasn't going to provide the federal government with anything, so she was surprised even the furniture was here. She'd tried the chair someone wheeled in and immediately gone online and ordered a new one she paid for out of her own pocket. Forget requisitioning.

How much time would she even spend in the office? Maybe she'd be out in the field. On undercover operations. Who knew what this position would bring up? She was the only one out here, miles from the closest field office. An outpost.

Exiled.

Given where they'd sent her, she couldn't help assuming

this was a demotion. There weren't many dangerous deviants to profile out here. Maybe that was a good thing. After what happened with William Benning, she needed a break from that field of study. Get back to her roots. Catch some bad guys.

Maybe she would buy a leather jacket.

Except that she was here to solve a case—to solve multiple from the sound of it.

Her phone vibrated across the top of the desk. *Unknown number.*

She dismissed the call on her watch and didn't even cross to her phone. That stuff wasn't going to creep into her life here. Whoever it was, they could go away as far as she was concerned.

The next call came almost immediately.

She nearly dismissed it before looking, assuming it was the same guy. Instead, the name *Zimmerman* flashed on her watch face. She went to the phone but didn't pick it up. On the screen flashed a picture of the two of them she'd never taken off.

Worst move you can make, baby girl, taking up with a superior.

As if Russ knew anything about it. He'd hated every guy she'd ever dated. Except Jake.

Addie went back to her task with a sigh. She hung the photo from her bedroom on the office wall. Her, getting her badge. Russ beside her. Both of them smiling.

She would have to get her own place if this assignment stretched into months. The longer she stayed at his house, the more entrenched she'd get into life there. Forty years from now, she'd realize she'd become Russ and never left.

Addie loved the scratchy old guy, but that wasn't the future she envisioned for herself. The dream didn't include being alone at a satellite office. Local LEOs her only backup, right where she had faced her worst fears.

Still, she was a big girl. She could make the most of it.

"Looks good."

Addie spun around and nearly dropped the hammer. "Hank?" She spied the badge on his belt. "You're a *detective*?"

He laughed. "Don't sound so surprised." He opened his arms, and she went in for a shorter hug that was a lot more perfunctory than Jake's.

Hank had been a good friend, mostly during their shallow high school days when they thought the world revolved around how they looked. Now? He was a handsome man but with an edge of something else. Not that classic bad boy. Something dangerous, though. Undefined. The kind of guy who might intrigue the profiler in her if she hadn't sworn off relationships for a while. She didn't need a repeat of the Zimmerman thing.

She needed to change the image that came up when he called.

"It's good to see you, Ads."

She stepped back from the hug. "You, too."

"Now you're a hotshot FBI agent." He grinned. "So it's not just me with a shield."

"Mine is a badge."

"Yeah, yeah." He shoved her shoulder playfully.

"Any idea what cases the PD is handing over?" She waved at her empty desk. "I don't think I've worked a day in my life as an agent without having a stack of case files. The first day on my first assignment, they handed me cases before I even sat down."

"I've got fourteen opens on my desk."

She winced. "I'll swing by if you want a second set of eyes."

Something flickered in his expression, and she realized she'd stepped out of bounds. He didn't want help.

"Then again," she said, "I'm probably about to get handed a box of files any second now and realize this free time is just an illusion."

He smiled, the effect much dimmer than before. "I don't know much about what you're doing here, but I do know there are several open cases that seem to be connected."

"I don't get the feeling you guys are just stumped and can't figure it out."

His face lost a fraction of its tightness. Hank hadn't been this expressive before. He needed to figure out how not to give away his thoughts so much if it was real. She'd crafted a blank expression a long time ago. For when people insisted on asking her questions she never in a million years wanted to answer.

It had served her well when she worked cases that involved individuals who performed reprehensible acts until she was burned out and unable to filter her reactions.

That thought made her think this was for sure a punishment. Had someone read the report so quickly they'd seen what happened to her—and why—and sent her here to deal with putting the past to rest finally?

"That doesn't look good." Hank settled on the edge of the desk. "But enough about work. You wanna tell me about that over dinner with me?"

Was he asking her out?

Before Addie could think if that was a good idea or not, he continued, "Have you seen Jake yet?"

Word hadn't gotten around about Jake and the hit-and-run yesterday.

Addie pushed the hair back from her face. She needed to find her hair tie and make a ponytail, or she'd look like she'd been dragged backward through a hedge before lunch.

"You have."

She rolled her eyes. "It wasn't a big deal."

Just the best hug she'd had in years. Addie let out a long sigh.

"Girl, you been back in town like five minutes. There's already a Jake thing?"

Addie rolled her eyes. There would *always* be a Jake thing, no matter if it had been five minutes or five thousand years. "If I've got cases coming, then I should do a daily Bible reading on the app now, or I'm not going to survive being back here."

She might not have gone to church much the last fifteen years, but she knew where the help came from.

He tipped his head back and laughed.

Addie shoved his shoulder. "It's not funny. You don't know faith is serious business?" She made a face and shoved him off his seat. "That desk is my space. Don't get your jeans all over it."

Hank didn't quit laughing.

She shoved him to the door and opened it for him. Tried to figure out how to hit him in the butt with it and not break the glass.

A man stood on the other side. Hank jumped back and to the side. "Mr. Mayor."

Hank nodded and as soon as the suited man entered, he slipped out. One glance back and he mouthed, *Good luck.*

Addie frowned and closed the door. The mayor wasn't someone she recognized, but she hadn't cared who sat in what chair in town as a teen. Just that she wore that homecoming crown. These days she'd rather garner zero notice.

The mayor crossed the room. His leather shoes clipped

against the tile floor. Hands in his pockets. Silk tie that probably cost as much as her rent.

He pulled out one hand, and they shook. "Simeon Olivette."

"Addie Franklin, sir." *Ugh.* She was going to have to break her lease. Live with a Benson address again. Her life sucked. And why that was finally hitting her now, she had no idea.

"Russ has a lot of good things to say about you." He wore a mustache over thin lips. Gray temples made her think of the men's hair dye that left some gray, so it didn't look like you were overcompensating.

"I'll have to thank him."

"We have a problem, Special Agent Franklin."

Somehow, she didn't think it was exactly *her* problem. Just that she was here so he could make it her problem.

"Lately we've had a rash of unexplained deaths. Some with the odd distressing characteristics." He sighed. "The police have done what they can, but you come highly recommended. I'm hoping you can shed some light on what's happening here before it goes public and people start to panic. I'm sure you of all people can sympathize with the epidemic of fear. It affects all of us."

"Of course." For once someone wasn't digging for information on her experience. Instead, he lumped her in with everyone so that she was no different than the residents who hadn't come face-to-face with a killer.

Trusting that the man the police had in custody was the culprit. Hoping nothing happened at homecoming. They'd been safe at home watching news reports and praying they weren't next.

SHE HAD BEEN NEXT. And she had the scars to prove it.

Zimmerman had told her she was uniquely qualified for this. She understood things about dangerous crime that the average cop only reported on. They, hopefully, would never live it.

Addie squared her shoulders. "None of us wants the public to panic unnecessarily. I'm here to do everything I can to figure this out."

He nodded. "With your expertise and background, I've been assured you're the right person for this job." He clipped to her and held out his hand again. "If you need anything, go ahead and let my assistant know."

"Yes, sir."

"I'll let the chief know he can have those files sent over."

"Thank you, sir."

She watched him leave and tried not to jump up and down with glee. Once again, she couldn't help thinking that nineteen-hour nap must have loosened something in her. Whatever it was had been wound tight for years. It was that or being back in town that brought out a little of who she'd been before life beat her down. The idea of diving into work was a familiar salve on that wound.

Addie couldn't be the teen she'd been, not if she was an FBI agent here. She'd be the professional she was.

Being in Benson wasn't going to turn back time. She'd been an adult for years, but no one here saw that. They only knew the teen she was back then. Which meant she needed to prove who she was now—so they'd all see that when they looked at her.

Minutes later a train of uniformed agents headed for her door. Addie held it open and watched them file across the hall with cardboard boxes. Coming from the police department across the hall into her tiny office. They had nearly seventy-five staff. Those with shields and those who worked for the department as civilians. She was supposed to hire an assistant, but only if she needed one.

If she needed backup immediately, she had to call PD. If she required personnel, the Seattle office would send agents to her. But the assistant director there had made it plain they had no one to spare unless it was an emergency, or she was compromised somehow.

"Special Agent Franklin." One of the officers strode past.

"Hey, Officer Hummet. How are you today?"

A couple of the others looked over, like the two of them were a curiosity. Addie shook his hand. "Dumping all your work off on me. Is it cause I'm a girl?"

Hummet barked a laugh and lifted both hands. "I'm not touching that one"—he saluted—"ma'am." He hurried to the door. "There are plenty more boxes to bring."

Addie grinned. "Coward."

Someone snorted. Addie figured the road to getting them on her side would be rocky but might be best served by bringing donuts. No, they'd think she was making fun because they were cops. Scones? Cupcakes? Something good. She'd have to find out if the bakery in town delivered.

Maybe a giant "Welcome to the FBI" cake, so it looked like she thought they worked for her now. Addie nearly laughed out loud at that thought. She'd have to find out if they could take a joke first.

A tall African American man rapped his knuckles on the doorframe. "Make it fast, people. We just got a call from the high school on Pinter. There was a scuffle in the lunchroom, and we've got multiple students injured and even more involved."

"Yes, Captain." A stocky man in slacks and a shirt dumped a box on top of another and spun around. "Let's move out, people."

He gave her a nod and headed for the door.

Addie grinned to herself alone in the office, now full of boxes. She'd done something detrimental coming home and taking that nap.

She was looking forward to this.

10

Jacob put the towel over his shoulders and headed out. The building had a gym, and his preference had him using it before dawn when few others showed up to work out.

The routine didn't settle his mind. Even with his earbuds in, running seven miles should've calmed him, but he still heard the words of that distraught mother in his head.

He wanted to think about Addie.

Instead, he found his thoughts drifting to Carl Harris and the conversation he'd had with Jennie and her granddaughter. About signs he should've seen but hadn't. People who buried terrible secrets.

Who hurt others simply because they believed they had power.

His counselor had told him many times that some things just weren't his to carry. It was true—he knew it. But getting his heart to believe it was a different story. Doing that almost felt like growing cold to other people's pain.

Jacob wasn't sure he wanted to be that guy. It sounded an awful lot like Ivan Damen. Whether he'd wanted to be caught or not didn't matter. He'd taken life. The problem was that Jacob still hadn't figured out what guy he wanted to be.

Sixteen floors up he let himself back into the apartment, where a set of keys that didn't belong to him sat in the dish on the entryway table. "Hank?"

"Kitchen!"

Jacob toed off his running shoes. "There better be coffee."

"Why do you think I'm here? This fancy Colombian stuff you order is gonna wake me up." Hank stood at the stove stirring what looked like more cheese than eggs, and the oven was on.

"Bacon?"

One of Jacob's cats wound its way around Hank's boots, which meant his friend had fed the animal several treats already. How long had he been here?

"You know it." Hank attacked the eggs like they were an uncooperative suspect. He wore jeans and a button-down shirt. It was Saturday, but that wasn't precisely the uniform Benson PD required. Hank had always pushed against authority in ways that might not make sense. As far as Jacob could tell, he just needed to be who he was. Considering Jacob's path, he could honestly say he understood his friend.

Both of them had been altered. Hank's girl had been killed by a dangerous man who'd nearly destroyed the rest of them.

"Why do you need my coffee so bad?" Jacob got water from the fridge. "Long night?"

"Yeah, but I wasn't working a case. At least not as a cop." Hank lifted his brows.

"Dude, you need Jesus."

Hank laughed like Jacob wasn't completely serious.

Jacob said, "How long on breakfast?"

"You don't want to hear about her?"

"Hard pass."

Hank didn't turn. "Six minutes?"

By the time Jacob got out of the shower, Hank had pulled the tray of bacon from the oven. He'd have leftovers for three days.

Jacob sat at the breakfast bar with a mug of coffee. His friend ate standing up with his hips against the counter.

Two bites in, Hank paused. "You saw her already?"

Jacob frowned, the fork almost to his mouth. Of course Hank would ask about Addie. "Did she put that in the hit-and-run report?"

It was his friend's turn to frown. "What hit-and-run?"

Jacob laid his fork down and told Hank about seeing Addie in the grocery store aisle and what happened after.

"I didn't see her name in a report, but I'll follow up with the responding officer. Make sure we're good."

Jacob nodded.

"I wouldn't worry about her, though."

"Because she's a trained FBI agent?" Jacob still thought the car had come at her on purpose. That meant whoever was driving knew who she was.

Who would do that just for the sake of it, injuring a random person they didn't know or hadn't ever met? More likely it was targeted. She'd been here only days from what she'd told him and hadn't done much but catch up with her uncle and sister.

"She's got so many files to go through she'll be stuck in the office for a month." Hank seemed to think that was a good thing. "Can't hit-and-run someone at their desk."

Jacob wasn't so sure he—or Addie—would agree that desk work was a good thing. Then again, Jacob had never held down a real job in his life. He hated filing and he rarely had to do it since he paid all his bills online and e-signed everything.

Addie probably hadn't become an agent to sit in an office. Then again, what did he know? Her coming home had thrown them all off. His routine was out of whack. Things had to get back to normal eventually, though.

He still wondered what kind of agent she was. Then he got sidetracked with mental images of the young woman he'd known, now carrying a gun and looking all tough. And gorgeous.

He already knew he'd never feel about anyone the way he felt about her. But did she have to occupy this much headspace?

Jacob shook his head. "What is she working on? Does Benson have that many federal cases?"

Hank set his plate in the sink. "Just between you and me?"

Jacob nodded.

"There's been a rash of murders the last few years. Adds up to a handful, but we've been trying to track down the UNSUB."

"What's that?"

"Unknown Subject. For when we haven't identified the person we're looking for. All we have is a profile, and it's not much to go on. We've pulled out every case we think might be the same guy. They're spread across two counties and several years." A muscle in Hank's jaw flexed.

Jacob didn't blame him for being mad. "This has been going on for *years*?"

"The mayor wanted it kept under wraps. His brother is a senator, so he called in a favor and posted a fed here. They picked Addie. She's got a background in profiling so she's a natural fit. She knows the area. People here." Hank shrugged.

Jacob wasn't sure she was happy about being here but didn't know for sure. He wanted to ask her. See how she felt about being reassigned. "It's gonna be a one-woman office?"

"She'll get support staff when she chooses them. The field office in Seattle will visit, and she's got regular conference calls with her SAC to keep him updated. She's not on her own."

Jacob wasn't so sure about that, but still. "You guys are right across the hall, yeah?"

Hank nodded.

Jacob figured that on top of all that she had support. Between the two of them, he and her uncle would give her a safety net. His gun might be dusty, but he had one. If they were hanging out and she got into trouble, he could help.

Except that was ridiculous. As if she wanted his aid to do her job. Hank would never accept it, and she was probably cut from the same cloth. They were both cops, so he figured he knew how it would go down. Jacob nearly shook his head, but then Hank would ask what it was about. No way did she want a photographer as backup when she could call other cops, or feds, to help her.

Jacob pushed his plate away and leaned back on his stool. She would call anyone else before she called him.

Same thing had happened when he was picked as the quarterback in high school. Junior year, he and Hank had been vying for the same spot. Soon as it was announced, his friend ghosted him. Hank never forgave him for getting it. They managed to stay friends, but things weren't the same after that.

Jacob's backpack was on a chair at the dining table. On

top was the photo album from the studio he'd put in there. Open on the table.

"You kept those?"

Jacob didn't take his attention from the book. He also didn't go over and look at it. Maybe later. "It helps. When I build it up too much in my head, I look at it. I remember it was just drywall and vents. A sound system. One man."

Just the shape of him. Jacob never saw his face. "Lights powered by electricity. The time on the clock on the wall, ticking closer to our rescue. The furniture. Just a place with no idea it was being used for evil intent. Objects that have no hold over me."

"Like he had."

Jacob didn't want that. "Not anymore. It was hours, sure, but then it was done. We got out." He winced and glanced at his friend. "Sorry."

Hank looked away. "Becca wouldn't have wanted us to be victims like she was, still walking around but dead inside. Killed by the same thing that killed her." His voice didn't sound anything like what Jacob was used to.

"How do cops deal with seeing stuff like that?"

"Talk it out." Hank shrugged. "Process it. The way you're doing with that album. Remember that what happened is in the past, and it doesn't hold you now. You never forget, though."

"You never forget." Jacob blew out a breath. "Doesn't mean I don't wake up in the middle of the night in a cold sweat wishing I could. Wanting to be done with it. Forget all of it. Be who I was before he took us. Live that life and see where it might've gone."

He'd dreamed that so many times. What life would've been like if they'd graduated, and he and Addie were still together. If they got married. Made a family. What he'd have done for work. If he tried to be who his dad thought he should be—when his parents bothered to remember he was there. Burying the artist he hid inside. Being the football star instead of the kid who was the reason his parents had split.

After what happened he'd given up the pretense of trying to be both things just to keep them happy. He'd managed to persuade his mom that he wanted to be a photographer like her. But only so he could capture what'd happened and deal with it in his own way?

Jacob couldn't help thinking he was probably as much of a disappointment to everyone now as he'd always been. He'd taken the steps he thought were right. So had Hank.

He didn't even know anymore.

"What?"

Jacob shrugged. "The two of you became cops."

"And you think you should've as well?"

He hesitated. "What do you think?"

"Would you be happy as a cop?" Hank assessed him like Jacob might've asked an insulting question. "Reporting for duty, following instructions. Brushing off the frustrations of the justice system. Seeing innocent people get their lives destroyed."

"No, I wouldn't be happy." Still, hiding hadn't given him peace either. It was quiet, but that wasn't the same thing.

The only thing that ever gave him peace was…

He glanced at the blinds. If he opened them now, would he see the dawn the way Grandpa had shown him?

Maybe Hank and Addie were more alike than he wanted to admit. That was the crux of it. They were both the kind of people who worked tirelessly to bring the evil in the world to justice. He'd tried to live his life the way he needed to, just like they had.

What had that gained him?

Hank rounded the counter and got in his face. "Aren't you exactly where you wanted to be?" He paused half a second. "Penthouse isn't all it's cracked up to be?" Hank laughed and slapped him on the back.

Jacob shoved his friend away. "I offered you a place to live."

"I like my yard."

Jacob rolled his eyes. The expression on Hank's face said it might have more to do with this being his building rather than an apartment having no yard. It wasn't like he rubbed his success in his friend's face, but who knew what Hank thought about it?

His friend shot him a look. "When the renovations are done on the fourth floor, you should move down there. See how the other half lives for a while. Get some perspective."

"I can do the same on a cruise."

Hank laughed and looked at his watch. "I should get going. Wanna go to the Gopher game later?"

Jacob made a face. "The quarterback needs some help."

"Maybe since you're the one who set the state record you should show up. Give him some pointers."

"Yeah, the coach will love us butting in." The two of them might have been football stars, but after what happened they'd been famous for entirely different reasons.

Maybe one day Jacob would realize it had been weeks and no one mentioned it. Nothing happened to remind him. But he wasn't holding his breath that would happen anytime soon.

Hank's phone rang. "Detective Maxwell." He listened for a second. "Text me the address. I'll be there in ten." He hung up.

"What happened?"

Hank hesitated. "Fine. A hiker in Prospero Park found a body. Preliminary ID is Celia Jessop."

Jacob blew out a long breath. "When you have time of death, call me. I'll come by the station, and we can get it on record that I was nowhere near her. Because I *didn't do it.*"

Hank tossed his plate in the sink with a terrifying clatter. "I've got to go, and you're gonna lay that on me?"

"It's not a big deal. I just want it confirmed it wasn't me. Officially."

Hank reached up and squeezed the back of his neck. "You're unbelievable. But just so long as you're clear, right? You've got issues, my friend."

They both knew that wasn't what was happening here. "Just call me when you know."

Hank headed for the door without a look back. The cat meowed after him, but Hank shut the door in her face.

11

Early morning wind whipped through the canyon just outside of town. Addie braced against it, closed her car door, and buttoned her wool coat. Her badge hung from a chain around her neck. She should've brought a beanie. Or gloves.

Addie shoved her hands in her pockets and discovered a wrapped piece of gum. She popped it in and discarded the wrapper in a trash can beside the row of marked police cars. The ME's van was here. She'd had to park three rows from the trailhead just to find a space.

The guy she now knew as Captain McCauley stood beside the trailhead map waiting for her. "Thanks for coming out."

She stuck out her hand, and he shook it with his gloved one. "I appreciate being looped in even though it's only my second day."

"How's it going? Being back?"

She wasn't sure if she was supposed to remember who he was from high school. He seemed like the kind of guy who aged but managed to look the same. Just more refined.

Addie shrugged. "The town has changed a lot. It's probably double the size it was."

"Small town people think this is the big city. Big city folks come here for the slower pace of life, but they can still get those conveniences that aren't in a small town."

"That's for sure." Some places people drove all over for work and groceries. There was no need to drive an hour unless necessary in a town like this. Everything was fifteen minutes away, give or take. Seemed like that anyway.

"Want the rundown?"

"That would be good, thanks." Addie preferred to know what she was walking into.

That, and the fact she'd been called here in the first place, meant the police department had reason to believe the body that'd been found was connected to the cases she'd been brought here to solve.

Considering Addie didn't have a crime lab, or fellow agents on hand, the cops were the ones who would work this case. If it proved to be the same suspect as the ones she'd been handed, having federal weight behind the arrest might make a difference.

McCauley kept a steady pace. "Celia Jessop went missing three days ago. Twenty-three, steady boyfriend. He's a loser, but we checked him out, and he had the flu. Claims they broke up a while back. He was bedridden the last week, so he hasn't seen her for fifty-two hours at least."

"Her car?"

"Still looking for it." McCauley motioned back at the parking lot while the path ascended around the hill. "Wasn't parked here. No one has found it abandoned around town. There's a BOLO still out on it."

"You think this is connected to my cases?"

"You'll see, but yeah." McCauley scratched at his chin.

"At this point, it's more of a gut feeling than anything else. None of them have the same MO. No correlations in the victims. No other way to link them or predict who he will strike at next."

She'd been sure about Zimmerman—namely that she could trust him—and look how that turned out? One dumb mistake. Now he was getting back with his wife, and she got exiled. To advance her career. Supposedly.

The common denominator was the fact she couldn't trust herself because she was putting her trust where there was no foundation.

She should probably call the Seattle field office and ask for help. Get a team here, so it wouldn't be so obvious when she faltered.

They rounded the corner, and the scene came into view, taped off. Guarded by an officer and several others. The ME and his assistant. Crime lab, collecting evidence.

Addie laid a hand on his elbow. "I'd love to talk to you more about this. Dig into that gut feeling. It'll help me work up a profile."

McCauley nodded. "I'll pencil you in."

They approached the tape, and she realized the cop was a familiar face. "Officer Hummet."

"Special Agent Franklin." Hummet nodded, all business. "Captain." He noted their names in his logbook before lifting the tape so she could step under.

"Thank you." Addie nodded and headed for the victim.

Hank stood over the body, talking with the ME. "Hey, Ad."

She lifted a hand but wanted to get a look at the body and not have to wait through an entire conversation before she got her questions answered.

"Our resident FBI agent?" The woman who looked up

had red hair. She wore a silk blouse and black slacks under a heavy winter coat. Expecting to see heels, Addie found winter boots on her feet covered with booties to protect the scene from her tread prints.

Addie stepped back so the ME knew she wasn't about to touch anything and contaminate the evidence any more than she did simply by being here.

She held a hand out. "Adelyn Franklin."

"Sarah Carlton." She removed a glove and shook Addie's hand.

"ME. PhD. More than one, isn't it?" Hank stuck a thumb in his belt.

The ME looked over at him. "And yet you turned me down."

Hank said nothing.

The captain jumped into the conversation. "Now the introduction is out of the way, do you have a cause of death?"

The ME shifted in her crouch and worked her mouth back and forth as she considered the question. "There are no signs of drug abuse. There are indications she may have had a cardiac event or been strangled. I'm afraid I can't pin this one down without a thorough examination."

"Anything you can tell us about what she went through before she died?" Addie figured if the captain was correct and this guy had her for a couple of days, she might have been held somewhere.

The ME hadn't even said the word *murder* yet.

Dr. Carlton tipped her head from one side to the other. "Signs on her wrists and ankles that she was bound. Looks to me like chains, but I'll confirm that and the state of her treatment." She glanced at Addie, who read her gaze.

Both wanted to know if the girl had been raped.

Addie nodded.

"What about the time of death?" Hank's jaw had remained hard since that exchange with the doctor a moment ago.

Addie didn't know if she even wanted to ask either of them what that had been about. She thought Sarah might be someone she could be friends with as well as colleagues. After all, they'd only just met and seemed to be on the same wavelength.

"This Rizzoli and Isles thing you guys have going on is cute and all." Hank folded his arms. "But we need to find who did this."

Dr. Carlton stood. Before she could say anything, McCauley motioned to the trees. "You need to take a walk, Maxwell?"

"No, sir." Hank seemed to force out the words. "If we could have time of death, Doc?"

Carlton nodded. "Given the liver temp and the ambient, I'd say six to eight hours ago." She looked at her watch. "So, somewhere between one-thirty and three-thirty this morning. But I should be able to narrow that down."

"Thanks." Hank strode away.

Addie wanted to talk more with the ME, but the information she needed would likely come after the autopsy. She excused herself and followed Hank.

Addie caught up just beyond the tape. "Hey," she called out to him. "What's going on?"

Hank slowed. He seemed to need a few extra steps to walk off whatever ran through him, giving him this edgy vibe.

"You just don't like murder?" She shrugged one shoulder. "Cause not many cops do." Or this was more personal.

Maybe he needed to feel as normal as she did. Knowing

what they went through and the fact he'd lost the person he'd been closest to back then. Now another woman was dead, possibly held for a few days first.

It didn't serve to draw those lines of distinction and separate them from everyone who hadn't had their innocence stolen like that.

They were like patient zero of a disease—the three of them—and the infection spread from there. Or the point of impact of a gunshot. The effect rippled out as the energy dissipated.

Sometimes Addie didn't want to feel different. She wanted to feel like she was the same as everyone else.

Not that she ever had been. After all, most people's parents stuck around and cared for them. They didn't drop their child with a relative and take off to live the high life with nothing to chain them down. Then when they came home, they threw their drama around and caused havoc.

Probably it was just her.

"I'm fine." Hank lifted both hands then dropped them to his sides. "And I don't need a buddy. Not when you're going to go back to your cushy federal life as soon as possible."

"Mmm. I do like my cushy life." She folded her arms.

"Fine, I know nothing about you." He lifted a brow. "Whose fault is that?"

"You haven't changed, have you?" She shook her head.

Hank took a step closer to her.

Addie resisted the urge to retreat. "You switch moods the way most people change their mind about what food they feel like." She kept her arms tight across her chest. "Always have. Though you seem to have it buttoned up for the most part. So what do you do when it gets too much?"

"You don't want to know."

"Okay. Fair enough." Addie studied him. "What got to you?"

"Looking to build a profile on me?"

"Yes, clearly I think you had something to do with this. Or I can't be 'friends' with anyone. I have to see them as a project. So since you're right, and we don't know each other all that well, here's a pro tip, Hank. I'm on your side."

"Yeah? What if my side and Jake's side are opposite?"

Addie frowned. "Explain."

He wouldn't have said it if there wasn't something to it. Whatever had gotten in his head, he was ramping up to spin out. The fallout wasn't going to be pretty. She'd seen Hank on a rampage, like after his dog died. He'd punched out two of the defensive line at practice, yelled at the coach, and thrown his helmet so hard it cracked.

"I was at Jake's when the call came in."

Addie nearly asked where Jake lived, but what business was it of hers? He'd said he would find her. He hadn't done it yet. Maybe because he'd changed his mind? She was trying not to care.

"He asked me to tell him when we found out the time of death." Hank ran a hand down his face. "So he can figure out his alibi."

Addie frowned. "He wants inside information from the police to eliminate himself as a suspect?"

Hank lifted his hands and exhaled a long breath that expanded his chest. His build made him formidable. He was bigger than he'd been in high school. The guy could pack a punch if he wanted to. Jake, on the other hand, was leaner and fast. She tried to believe that neither of them would hurt her. They should have solidarity after what they'd been through together. But she was only certain that Jake would never have hurt her.

Despite the fact he'd torn out her heart at the worst possible moment.

"Jake probably thinks everyone has him on their suspect list for everything. Maybe he's paranoid, living in that huge apartment all by himself." He shrugged. "Who knows? I mean, we all have a dark side. Right? You of all people know we all hide the truth behind a façade."

She shook her head, unsure what that meant.

"Because you get into people's heads."

"You think I want to get in yours?"

He grinned, and she knew the storm had passed. "Might not be a good idea."

"You're right about that." She glanced back at the scene. "I should head to the office. Look at the files and see if this one fits. Any ideas where to start?"

Something flashed on his face. A matured expression she couldn't decipher. "Thea Ackerman. I'd love to get the guy who did that." He practically spat the words.

"Thanks. I'll keep you in the loop. And you do the same?"

He nodded.

Addie spoke with the captain, got the ME's card, then walked alone—down the trail, across the parking lot, to her car.

The whole time, she couldn't get rid of the crawling sensation on the back of her neck.

Someone was out there.

Watching.

12

The knock on Jacob's door came just after he'd finished leftovers of last night's dinner. The pot pie his housekeeper made was big enough for four people, so he stretched it out when he didn't have the brainpower to choose what to have for dinner and sometimes froze a serving or two for later.

He tugged the door open wearing shorts and a T-shirt, his feet bare. Hair a mess. On his doorstep were a uniformed police captain and Addie, in her official capacity, since she immediately flashed her badge at him. "We'd like a word."

Jacob stepped back.

The man entered first. "I'm Captain McCauley, and I believe you know Special Agent Franklin."

"Not exactly in that capacity. But yes, I know her." He closed the door behind them and ushered them to the living area. "Care to sit? Coffee?"

The captain glanced at Addie. She shook her head and turned to survey the apartment. Four thousand square feet. His agent had recommended an interior decorator. Jacob hadn't thought about what she did with it. All he cared about was that the couch wasn't uncomfortable, and he could see the TV without straining his neck.

The view from the windows was what sold him on the place.

He motioned to them with a tip of his head. The skin around Addie's eyes flexed, and she headed over to look. "Wow."

"It's even better when the sky is clear. And at night, when you can see the city lights." He could see why people loved big cities like New York and Chicago. Downtown bustled with life. The fact he was up here alone most of the time didn't matter when he felt like part of something. One in the crowd of a community.

Grandpa had taken him to the top of Golden Hills Bluff early in the morning, many times, so they could see the sunrise. There Grandpa had told him that anytime he saw the dawn, he would know there was always hope.

He hadn't been able to look at it since. But he still liked the sky.

"Mr. Wilson?" The captain tucked his hands in his pockets. "The police department received a call last night from a young woman recently in your employ."

He'd only done one shoot recently.

"Sammie...something." Jacob shook his head. "I paid them in cash, but I've got their information written down somewhere."

"Why her? When I mentioned a woman, why do you assume it's her?" The captain had a staid expression that made him extremely hard to read.

"How about you tell me why she called the police department?" Then he'd know whether he needed his lawyer.

"The statement she gave is that you harassed her. She's not pressing charges but wanted it on record just in case you, in her words, 'tried it on some other unsuspecting girl.'"

Addie turned from the windows. What did she think of the view?

Instead of asking that, he said, "Is this something the FBI usually investigates?"

The corner of her mouth curled up. "Harassment against women?" She shrugged one shoulder. "Maybe it should be."

He turned to McCauley. "She made it clear she was interested. Touched my arm a couple of times when Dylan was either not paying attention or out of the room. Asked too many questions."

"And that made you angry?"

"Excuse me?"

McCauley shrugged. "I'm just trying to gauge your state of mind."

"Of course." Jacob held it together on the outside even though his head spun. "Is she pressing charges?"

"No. Like I said, it was only a report."

"Is there anything else?" He'd figured this was about the body Hank had run off to look at. Assumed it was about the missing girl who worked at the retirement home. Maybe she wasn't dead.

"Yeah, there is." McCauley glanced at Addie.

Addie put her hands in her coat pocket. "Can you confirm for us your whereabouts between midnight and five this morning?"

So this was about Celia. She'd been found dead, and right now he was the prime suspect. Instead of answering the question, he said, "Why would I need to do that?"

Hopefully Sammie hadn't disappeared as well since she called the cops to report her own actions. He didn't get people sometimes. Why sabotage his reputation and business, all because he'd shut down her advances? It didn't make sense to him.

Then again, people rarely made sense to him.

"Celia Jessop's body was found this morning," McCauley announced.

Jacob walked to the couch and sat. He knew, of course, since Hank had told him. Still, he couldn't help that it hit him.

He ran his hands down his face and thought about that woman on the phone, Celia's mother. She'd accused him of being the one who took her daughter. But the grief in her voice? The pain she felt had caused her to lash out, looking for an explanation where there may not be one.

Or she heard about that fight he'd had with the boyfriend and drew her own conclusions.

"I'm sorry to hear that." He hated that a life had been snuffed out. "She was a sweet girl. That's a…it's a shame." Her family would know what it was like to lose a loved one too soon.

"As I said," McCauley started, "where were you last night?"

"Midnight to five?" Jacob glanced at Addie, and she nodded. "Here. In my apartment—alone—until three-thirty." Both of them stiffened, just a fraction of a shift. Jacob's life was about visual nuances. There was something significant to that time. "Then I was downstairs at the gym. When I got back up, Detective Maxwell was here making breakfast."

"Does Hank do that a lot?" Addie asked.

"He has a key."

"Do you do that a lot?"

He didn't exactly know what she was asking. "He's the

only person who has a key. If for nothing else than he can get in if no one's seen me for a few days because I slipped getting out of the shower."

"Like one of those medical alert things?"

The captain cleared his throat. When they both looked at him, McCauley lifted his chin. "Can security for the building confirm you never left?"

"My key logs entry and exit. It'll show when I went to the gym. And that I never left the building. It might suffice." Jacob shrugged. "Until you discover I own the whole building, and the salaries for all security and housing staff are paid out of my accounts."

Addie shifted, a movement he spotted out of the corner of his eye. "You own the *building*?"

She glanced around, and he realized he'd surprised her. He'd figured she would do her due diligence. Run his credit and see if he had a rap sheet. Unless she'd had no intention of seeing him again—until it became necessary to question him about a murder.

He might've hugged her, but clearly he meant nothing to her aside from ancient history. How long until the cops heard about the incident with Celia and her boyfriend?

"The fact you have the means to craft yourself an alibi doesn't bode well for you." McCauley assessed him with a long stare.

"My cell phone will confirm I was here all night."

"You could've left it here," McCauley pointed out.

"So prove I was somewhere else. The onus is on you, I believe. But I can save you the trouble. I didn't kill Celia. What reason would I have to end her life?" He included Addie in that question. After all, she was the one who figured out what people were thinking.

"But just so you're not surprised when you learn about

it." Jacob paused. "Celia and I had a conversation in the retirement center parking lot. We happened to be leaving at the same time, and she asked for advice. What she should do about her boyfriend."

McCauley snorted.

"Continue," Addie said.

Jacob didn't mention the fact it hadn't felt genuine. But what reason would Celia have had to play him like that?

"She asked what I thought, and I asked her a few questions in response. To try and get her to think it through and decide on her own. The boyfriend showed to pick her up, saw us talking, and lost it. He ran up and tried to shove me around. He hit me. I hit him. It was over pretty quickly, and no one was hurt badly. I didn't let it escalate, but Celia was freaked over his reaction. She left with him."

"And you didn't call the police?" McCauley seemed to think that was suspicious.

Jacob stood. "That's all of it. So if you have any further questions about anything, you're welcome to direct them to my lawyer."

Addie had turned away to study the photo he'd hung above the fireplace. The sunrise above the bluff, a picture taken by his grandfather years ago. The only part of the decoration he'd had input into, and that was only to tell the lady which of his framed photos he wanted to be hung there.

She moved on to study the books on his shelf. Jacob twisted around and winced, thankfully where McCauley couldn't see. That stupid scrapbook Hank had pulled from his backpack and left on the table. He still hadn't put it away.

If she saw it…

Part of him wanted to know what she would think.

Did she do the same, processing what had happened to them and the hold it still had—while at the same time trying to convince herself that it was done? It was nothing. The past was over.

Jacob didn't want McCauley realizing what he had in his possession, and neither did he want to explain it. The captain wouldn't understand. Not the way Addie might.

He strode to it and put the scrapbook in his backpack. Addie shot him a questioning glance. Since she had no intention of seeing him again, what was the point of letting her into what his life was like now? It wasn't like she cared.

"One moment." He headed for the study and pulled a business card from the desk drawer. Back in the living room he handed it to the captain. "Here's my lawyer's information."

McCauley took it, but the guy didn't seem happy Jacob shut them down.

"Some place you've got here."

Jacob shrugged.

"Is this all down to that book you did? My wife has a copy in the guest room."

"Life in Story?"

"That's the one." The captain lifted his chin. "Her dad is part Cherokee, so she liked reading all the firsthand accounts of your grandfather's life."

"I'm working on another one." Jacob figured he could at least use it to solidify his case. "That's why I was at the retirement home. I'm interviewing some of the residents, trying to find a story to tell."

He didn't tell them he thought one might be a murderer, since cops tended to react to stuff like that. What was the point of dragging an older man with dementia into a court case when he might not even live to serve out a sentence? Hank knew about it, and he hadn't seen reason to drag the past back up. They also hadn't talked about it since the diner.

But Jacob knew he needed Hank's advice on the whole thing.

"That's how I knew Celia." He wanted to ask them to pass on condolences but figured the family wouldn't be receptive. Jacob didn't want to cause them more grief. "She was a nice girl who didn't deserve to be killed."

He was only assuming this was a murder. After all, they wouldn't come around like this if it were natural causes or an accident.

The captain turned. "Special Agent Franklin?"

"I have no questions, but I'd like a minute. I'll meet you at the elevator."

"Very well."

Jacob figured he'd be on the other side of the door, which McCauley would leave open just in case he had to rush back in and save Addie.

She walked to him but stopped several feet away. The couch between them might as well have been as wide as the Atlantic.

"I didn't kill that girl."

She nodded. "I'm glad to hear you say that."

"But you're still wary of me because I might be a murderer. So you'll stay over there just in case I did kill that girl."

"I'm not exactly supposed to get close to a suspect or person of interest."

"But you want to?"

Addie shook her head, the ghost of a smile on her face.

That was all the answer he needed.

"You've made a nice life for yourself." She glanced around, her cheeks pink.

He shrugged.

"I've seen that book. It's amazing. I didn't realize it was you."

"Thank you."

"I should go."

He nodded.

"You're very talented." Addie crossed to him, hesitating a fraction. As though she might kiss his cheek or offer her hand to shake. Instead, she did neither. Just headed to the door and slipped out. He heard the murmur of conversation, and the door clicked shut.

Now he knew how it felt.

After the hospital. The reporters. The recovery. That conversation they'd had in the hospital, where her mother had screamed and wailed in the hall and Jacob had snuck into her room during the drama. They'd been talking when her mom interrupted, and their breakup had been inevitable after that. Neither had wanted to admit they were in pain. They just took it out on each other in the moment—with her mom adding her opinion.

When it had all died down, somewhere between Christmas and the new year, he'd shown up at her house. Half drunk, the only way he'd gathered the courage to talk to her. Tell her he couldn't see her anymore. They were over. After being all either of them had during that time, he just hadn't been able to do it again. Be alone with her. Find comfort after all the pain.

He'd walked out of Russ's house and never looked back. Before the door shut, he'd heard her start crying.

"Goodbye, Addie."

He wasn't sure how long he stood there before his feet numbed on the tile floor, and he remembered how much work there was to do. Jacob winced as he walked sensation back into the soles of his feet.

He found his phone and sent a text to Hank asking why he never got that heads-up.

Hank didn't reply.

13

"I'm done."

Addie gripped the phone. "That was fast."

"Yeah, well," Dr. Carlton said. "Maybe I'm trying to impress the new fed in town. What can I say? I work long hours, and I don't have time for Bunko group even if I wanted to play games."

Addie felt the amusement bubble up. "What about a book club?"

"When do I have time to read? My commute is six minutes. Do you know how many workdays it would take me to listen to a twenty-two-hour epic that's supposed to be tragic, and I'll be destroyed by it?" Sarah sighed. "I see that every day, and they don't want to hear about my tragic story."

Addie turned and sat on the edge of the desk, the phone sandwiched between her shoulder and ear. That thought only made her hungry for an actual sandwich. How long had she been at this? "I don't suppose there's a twenty-four-hour diner in the vicinity of Fourth and Trenton that serves cheeseburgers and milkshakes."

"Be still my heart. I think I just found my new best friend."

Addie chuckled. "You know if we do this, that Rizzoli and Isles thing is *never* gonna die."

"You think those two would care about that? No. They just keep wearing uncomfortable heels that look fabulous and do their jobs." Sarah paused. "Not that I want to be there to catch the bad guys."

"Noted." Addie remembered Sarah's reason for calling. "So, Doctor Carlton, how did Celia Jessop die?"

"Petechiae on the face and bruising to the trachea suggest she was strangled."

Addie blew out a breath, and her throat tightened reflexively.

"It was done from behind, and I estimate that her assailant was taller than her."

"She was what, five six?"

"Seven and a half."

Addie pulled over a notepad and wrote that with the stub of a pencil she'd found in one of the drawers. "Thanks. Anything else?"

"No signs of sexual assault, though she was active recently."

"DNA?"

"None."

"Doesn't mean it wasn't about power."

"True." Sarah paused. "Were you serious about that milkshake?"

"One question before we switch topics." Addie tried to fight the shudder. "Were there signs she was bitten? Like a spider or some other kind of bug." She realized she'd started thumbing the inside of her thigh just up from her knee.

"Actually, yes."

Addie stretched out her fingers. "I'll need a copy of your report when it's finished. And seriously, would *you* ever joke about a milkshake?"

Sarah was quiet for a second. "No way. Especially if it's chocolate."

Addie smiled. "Call me when you're done for the day. I'll meet you there."

"And if it's two in the morning? I mean, you mentioned twenty-four hours, and I know just the place."

Addie looked at the clock on the wall. It was just after eight in the evening. "Doesn't matter what time."

"Okay." Relief rang in Sarah's voice. "Gotta go."

Addie hung up the phone and stayed where she was. Her legs ached from standing for so long. Since that interview with Jake earlier, she'd spent hours pulling files from boxes. Noting case details. Trying to establish a pattern.

A white board standing on wheels the police had brought in was to her left. After she filled that she'd asked for at least four more and they'd delivered.

One board held three-by-five cards that detailed a case number for reference, and basic details like the victim's race, manner of death, the date, and anything else she'd deemed relevant.

One board was about cause of death. Another was mapped locations of crime scenes where the bodies had been discovered. Even if she wasn't sure the perpetrator was the same for each crime, Addie wasn't ruling anything out by assumption. Not until she knew for sure.

The next board had witness sketches from three of the cases and everything compiled about the person who did this—the beginning of a profile. Anything and everything that might prove relevant to her solving this case.

Hank had been right that this appeared—at least at first

glance—to be the work of one person. Or a small group of people. If she aligned the kills in the order they were done, it did look like someone who was gaining skill.

She'd looked at the victim he'd mentioned, Thea Ackerman. Even if she didn't see significance she planned to start there.

"Knock, knock."

Addie flinched around to the doorway.

"Sorry." Russ held up both hands.

She shook her head. "Don't worry about it, I was deep in thought."

He nodded and scanned her office. The boards had been arranged in a semi-circle. Tables in the center held all the boxes in a semblance of order, but she was going to have to fix that fast or she'd lose all sense of where anything was and what it related to.

"You've been busy."

She pushed off the desk and strode to the board that listed the manner of death for each victim. "Take a look at this for me. Tell me what you think it looks like."

He met her at the board and tugged his glasses from the pocket in his shirt. Russ slipped the readers on his nose and still squinted.

He smelled so familiar, like an old ache for a lost dog. For a moment it caught her off guard.

"What am I looking at?" he asked.

She ignored his question. "It keeps hitting me how fast this all happened. Seems like one minute I'm working with a task force in DC, and the next I'm back here, and nothing's changed. Or everything has changed. I can't figure out which."

She'd been part of a team. Now it seemed like everything was riding on her being successful solo.

He studied the photos and reports on the board. "Bad thing?"

"Just different."

"Work is a safety net. It's familiar. It doesn't matter where you do your job, right?"

"Yeah, that's right." She didn't tell him how she might've made a friend. She'd never had many of those, even as the captain of the cheerleaders. At least not friends of any quality. Jake had been the best thing in her life until everything went wrong.

"What's this?" He motioned at the crime scene and autopsy photos.

"First one was summer six years ago. She was cut up and left to bleed out. Looks like slowly, judging by what was reported from the investigating detectives." She slid her finger to the right. "I made a timeline. Next, a couple years later, there are two more. Now we've gone from a blade to blunt force trauma." It correlated with another element. "He's got a new method to try and subdue them. Makes it messy. One he finished off with a gun. But a couple of these, I'm not even sure they're the same guy."

"But that one." Russ pointed at the collection at the end. "Two years ago?"

"I think he's trying out different methods. Experimenting. The captures are cleaner, and the manner of death is... cold." Addie's brain tried to connect the dots figure out some kind of pattern. "And now I think he's started up again."

"Okay, back up from that fact for a second." Russ shook his head. "Why did all these get flagged?"

"I was given a lot of cases by PD. I asked for these as well, and several others. I still need to nail down what's the same guy, and what just relates in some way but I can rule them out."

"Okay."

"In each autopsy, with a couple of exceptions where the death was caught up in my search for other reasons, it was noted the victim had received a bug bite prior to their death."

"A bug bite?"

She shivered again even though she tried to stop it.

Russ turned.

"I know what you're gonna say."

"Do you?" He pulled off his readers. "You know me so well you know exactly what I'll say? Seems to me like you haven't been around much. Your sister is practically a stranger to you. I'm not much more than that."

"Is that the reason you came here?"

Russ sighed.

"Don't worry about it. You can go. I've got plenty to do."

"Sure. Keep pushing away what's perfectly obvious to everyone else."

"Russ."

"What?"

"It's not him." She bit the words out. "Ivan Damen is in prison where he belongs. He didn't do this." She waved at the boards.

"And your job is to find who did. No matter that it eats at you from the inside." He folded his arms.

Addie closed her eyes. "You're determined to make this as hard as possible, aren't you?"

"You do that to yourself," he said quietly. "Pushing away what's real so you can pretend things are okay. You did it with your mom because it was easier to deal with her when she was gone. You're doing it now."

"Maybe I want to understand." She stared at one of the

victim photos. "Maybe I want to see the truth." *Of why Mom left.*

"What if there's nothing to understand. Just pure evil. That doesn't mean it was your fault." Russ tapped a finger on a young woman's picture, terror in her dead eyes. "You think this was her fault?"

"Of course I'm not—" She exhaled. "I know what you're doing."

Addie was fully aware she had become an FBI agent to understand what she'd been through. To give a voice to the victims no one had been able to save, the way she was rescued. Addie could bring the empathy of knowing exactly what they'd felt and experienced. To help walk a victim or witness through that first step toward healing.

"It's not a bad thing." Russ lifted a hand. "It's what life gave you. What the Good Lord chose for you to carry. Until you're willing to give it to Him."

Addie didn't even know how to do that. Maybe she *wanted* to carry it. After all, it was hers and it didn't belong to anyone else. What she'd been through made her who she was. Without it, she wasn't sure who was left over.

"Just don't forget that the rest of us are still here. We'll *be* here."

Addie loved that earnest, pained look on his face. She always had, even if it meant she'd disappointed him. He cared about her. As much as she tried to make herself believe she didn't need anyone.

"You got a whole lot of work done in just a few hours," he said. "But if you need help, I'm happy to come in."

She lifted one brow.

"I won't give you a hard time." He patted the buttons on his shirt. "I think I got it out of my system."

Addie lifted her chin. "I'll talk to Mona. Hang out with her."

"She needs you. And I think maybe you need her, too."

Addie didn't want to admit that was true, at least not out loud. "This assignment is supposed to fix something in me."

"Maybe it will. Is that a bad thing?"

"Someone at the Bureau thinks I could be more than I am, but they think Benson is holding me back."

"Is it?"

Ugh. His questions were infuriating. "Like everyone doesn't have hang-ups? Does every agent have to go back to where their trauma happened and get over it so they can get promoted, or assigned somewhere good or whatever?" This made no sense—and she needed to figure out what the deal was.

Russ chuckled. "You sound like Mona." He shook his head. "Maybe not, but if someone thinks this assignment is worth it for your career trajectory, and the PD has something on their hands—they need extra personnel with a particular skill set—then maybe it'll be worth it in the long run. Maybe we need you to fix something in Benson."

Addie pressed her lips together to keep from saying words she would regret.

"Spit it out, baby girl. This old man can take it."

Maybe the point was that he shouldn't have to, but she said it anyway. "I don't want to get stuck here. I mean, how long is this assignment for, anyway?"

"Worried you'll start to like it?"

Addie wasn't worried about the location so much as her attachment to the people here. She preferred being somewhere that emotions didn't need to be a factor. Like her entire relationship with Matt Zimmerman. It might've been a mistake or a diversion at best. A way to release the stress of the job. Even if she'd never admit that to Russ.

There were far too many feelings attached to the places here. The people. The church. The longer she was here, the less she'd be able to ignore that still small voice.

This case might take from her everything she'd tried to build in fifteen years. All her reserves and strength. Digging into this would break it all wide open. Instead of working past her history, she would wind up destroyed by it.

The whole assignment was going to be a nightmare.

14

Thankfully Naomi was still on the front desk when Jacob walked into the retirement home the next morning. Some of the snow outside had melted, and he'd been held up by construction on the freeway offramp. Ordinary things that weren't inconveniences reminded him he lived as part of a community.

That was all he allowed to cross his mind. Not anything about a murder or a police investigation. After all, that had nothing to do with him. Jacob had plenty to do. And okay, his thing had a *bit* to do with murder. But Mr. Harris and his issues weren't something he wanted to take on board.

"Good morning." Naomi smiled, but it didn't illuminate the dark circles around her eyes.

"Morning." Jacob slid over the sign in sheet.

"Mr. Harris?"

"Worth a try, right?" He wasn't going to tell the man's story in a book, but could he give someone closure? Whatever he found out, he could pass to Hank.

"He's doing better this morning. Sorry about yesterday. The doctor sedated him after what happened at breakfast."

Jacob shrugged off the fact he'd asked for this yesterday. "No problem. Past couple of days have been busy anyway."

She nodded. "The police sent over a list of people they want to talk to. They're coming by after lunch is over."

For a second, he thought she would say the police wanted to talk to him. Instead, they were coming to the retirement home. Not right away, but days after the body was found.

Jacob didn't want to grumble out loud, but the victim's coworkers were being interviewed later and yet the captain had brought the town's new federal agent to his apartment on the same day she was discovered?

He didn't want to be disgruntled, but what else was he supposed to do with that? It wasn't like it was at all fair.

"Have you talked to them?" She tipped her head to the side. "Your name wasn't on the list. But maybe they don't know you were…what is it they say?" She frowned. "Like you're acquainted with her, or whatever."

Jacob shrugged. "I'm just praying they find whoever did it. No one wants a killer on the loose."

Especially if the town, and the entire police department, thought it was him who did it.

She nodded again. "That's the truth."

If it got out that he was questioned his life would get even more difficult. He'd go from victim to possible perpetrator. Interviews he had scheduled would dry up. Clients would cancel. The cops were single minded in the pursuit of justice. It wasn't a bad thing, except that they never considered the fallout to a person's reputation when those in blue accused someone of a crime they hadn't committed.

Sure, he wanted them to find out who had killed Celia. But did they have to destroy his business in the process?

He knew the chief had a problem with him. The guy had it stuck in his head that Ivan Damen had an accomplice or an apprentice all those years ago. Which was a completely terrifying thought.

Jacob hadn't seen or heard of a second person being there when he and Addie, along with Hank and Becca, had been taken. Neither had Hank. And it certainly wasn't Jacob, as much as the chief might want to believe otherwise.

No matter how many times he told the chief that, the guy just wouldn't let it go.

"I'll buzz you in."

"Thanks." Jacob headed for the entry door that led to the hallway where the residents lived.

He passed a busy common room where a community bingo game was in progress. Most of the residents looked like they were half asleep, but the perky fitness instructor type woman on stage at the front either hadn't noticed or didn't care.

The hallway smelled like overly floral perfume.

Mr. Harris had a room in the middle of the hall. Even though Jacob had decided to drop the guy as a subject, he still wanted to see if the man would tell him anything more. Maybe he could pass the information to Hank. The cops would get the idea he wasn't the kind of person who hurt others.

What if the older man had killed someone else, and Jacob was able to provide answers to a grieving family who needed closure?

That made him think of Addie and the life she had built —the career she'd gone after, like Hank. Maybe it wasn't so hard to understand why she'd become an FBI agent with a focus on criminal profiling. She gave voices to those whose stories remained silent, in a similar way he did. Except she solved murders that otherwise would've gone cold.

He was incredibly proud of the woman she'd become.

Even if he didn't know her all that well, part of him would always love her and consider her family. Seeing her again had reminded him of the bond they shared.

Maybe she didn't feel it. If she did, then she'd have acted differently in his apartment. Right? He didn't know how to tell.

Jacob was about at the door to Mr. Harris's room when the woman herself walked out of a room across the hall.

They both stopped. Silence stretched between them for a second.

"Hey."

She seemed to shake herself out of the paralysis of surprise and crossed the space between them. "Jake."

She looked good, FBI pantsuit with a wool coat. Hair braided. Professional. The kind of person who got the job done in a compassionate way. Why was she working with the police department? Right now the only ones he trusted were her and Hank. To an extent, Russ and the pastor. Then there was the counselor he met with on occasion.

"How's it going?" She glanced into the room beside him.

He wasn't quite sure how to take her question. "You mean what am I doing here?"

"Fine." She didn't smile, just kept that snooty, professional expression on her face. "What are you doing here?"

"Working on that book I told you and the captain about." He refused to cross his arms, though he wanted to. It would look defensive to her. Like he had anything to hide—from her. They'd been through too much together to have secrets between them.

Still, this wasn't exactly what he was doing here. The book was done—at least as far as Mr. Harris was concerned.

He ran a hand through his hair. "What do I need an alibi for now?"

Her face flashed with hurt before she squashed it and her expression blanked. He saw it all in her blue eyes. Holding her attention until she blinked first. "Look, I'm not going to talk to you about an ongoing investigation. I'm not working Celia's murder. I have cases of my own, and there's enough work to keep me in Benson for two years. Although, I hope that's not how long it takes to catch this person."

He frowned. "Who?"

"I can't talk about it." She shifted, so he got a look at the badge on her belt. "Those are the rules, and I'm not going to break them. Not even for you."

Jacob wanted to ponder that statement. He'd have to do it later, though.

"Please tell me you don't believe I had anything to do with Celia's death."

He didn't realize until he'd said it how important that was to him. He needed to know that she believed he was innocent, probably more than with anyone else in the world. God knew, but if Addie trusted him then that was at least one person he could rely on.

Someone on his side.

"I have a lot of work to do." She glanced away. "A pile of cases that's growing every time I look at a single page of one file. If I want to get through this assignment, I need to work." She winced, but he didn't know why. "Leave the investigation alone."

"When I'm in it? I'm probably the prime suspect. Which means the real killer is going to go free."

"So you'll stick your nose in, and it'll look even more suspicious. Or you'll jeopardize my standing and compromise what I'm trying to do here."

"Sorry, I didn't realize your reputation was more important than my freedom."

"That's not—Jake."

He turned back, three steps away already. "It's Jacob. It has been for years, but you weren't here."

She shook her head. "I don't want us to be enemies."

"We don't get to be allies like this." He wanted her in his life. But was she going to keep the law between them, just to keep herself safe?

It could be that was exactly what she was doing. Playing it safe, so she could guard her heart as it were. Staying aloof to keep things business so she didn't have to get involved. Meanwhile he drowned in his feelings for her.

"It's messy, it always is," he said. "There's no avoiding the fact that feelings get hurt. It's a part of life. At least you have feelings. That means you care about someone."

"Feelings were never the problem. As much as I might wish otherwise." She sighed. "Apparently fifteen years and a lifetime apart hasn't done anything to cure that problem."

"So I'm an illness you suffer from?"

"Whatever it is, it's chronic."

They stared at each other until Jacob said, "You're unbelievable."

"I thought it was funny." She rolled her eyes. "What's that saying, laugh to keep from crying?"

"That's terrifying." They'd both pushed aside their feelings and relationships, to keep themselves safe. "But maybe it's time to embrace the fear."

He moved closer to her. Slow, to gauge what her reaction might be.

"What do you say we live dangerously? See what happens?"

Addie bit her lip. Considering his words. "You're going to be a bad influence."

"As I recall, that was you back in the day."

"Yeah, you were a real choir boy."

Jacob grinned. "I still go to church now."

"Seriously?"

"Maybe you should try it." If this developed into something, they'd have to establish how things would be different this time around. He wasn't making any assumptions, but he lived differently now than he had in high school when he thought he could do whatever he wanted with no consequences.

"Russ wants me to go with him on Sunday." Addie shifted her weight from side to side. "I think I might. I still believe, but…it's been a while since I went to actual services."

"Church is free. Therapy costs money."

"I'm completely sane, I'll have you know." She squared her shoulders and looked down her nose, but he saw the gleam in her eyes.

Jacob grinned. "Me, too. Of course." He winked.

"Of course." She gave him a wry smile.

"Have dinner with me."

"Is that a question?"

"Please," Jacob added.

"Where? And don't say your apartment."

He didn't know why she needed that qualifier but didn't mind if she wanted neutral ground. "There's a place on the corner of Broadway and Ninth. It's called Luce Del Sole. I'll call for a reservation and let you know?"

She nodded. "I'll be there. Just tell me when."

"Thanks, Addie."

She sifted her stance. "How do you know I'll be there to spend time with you, and not so I can build a profile that pins murder after murder on you?"

She worried he'd lump her in with the police? He didn't

even do that with Hank. "My circle might be small, but you've always been in it."

"Why now?"

"You're here." He wasn't sure how to explain it. "You've always felt to me like a 'once in a lifetime' sort of thing."

Her expression softened, though he wasn't sure she was aware of it.

Jacob lifted his chin. "I'll let you get back to work."

She crossed to him and kissed his cheek. Jacob didn't move. He just enjoyed the closeness. The memories wrapped up in the present.

She practically stopped his heart, if he was willing to entertain yet more sentimental thoughts about her. Usually that only happened at three in the morning, daydreaming while he stared out of his windows at the city skyline.

Not the dawn. Looking at the dawn was too painful.

"Soon."

"Yeah." He choked the word out. "See you soon."

15

Addie tried to tell herself the cabins were on her way back to the office. The truth was, she was nowhere near the highway route she'd take to get back to downtown Benson.

Instead, she'd turned onto the freeway that ran east.

The conversation she'd had with Thea Ackerman's aunt at the retirement home had been a bust. The woman had declined quickly after her niece was murdered. She was unlikely to recover. Still, they'd had a nice conversation. Addie had asked her plenty of questions but hadn't learned anything to help her investigation.

Eight miles later she saw a bright sign for Second Chances Rental Cabins.

Addie hit her turn signal and got off the freeway.

She stopped at the bottom of the off ramp. Instead of checking the way was clear and turning, her foot didn't move off the brake.

She stared across the street at the on ramp to get back on the freeway—in the wrong direction. She'd end up heading toward eastern Washington, farther away from Benson.

Who knew where she would end up?

A car behind her honked, long and loud. Addie hit the gas and turned toward the rentals. The car sped up and overtook her.

She didn't look to see if they flipped her off. Otherwise she'd be tempted to pull them over just for being a turd—if this car had lights and sirens, which it did not. Yet. Or she could call the license plate in to the police, but that wasn't exactly the professional impression she wanted to give the cops about her.

Addie didn't overthink about where she was going. The signs were nice. She liked the idea of second chances. Was this what she thought it was?

Years ago, after their abduction, they'd been brought out here. Locked in cabins the killer had retrofitted with all kinds of terrifying things she still had nightmares about. Had someone seriously turned the whole place into a resort of vacation rental cabins?

Why anyone would want to sleep in a killer's playground, she had no idea.

Everyone who lived in town knew where it had gone down. There had been so many people there when she and Jake were rescued. Cops. Feds. Reporters. Spectators. Her mom. What kind of person knowingly stayed here now?

Maybe they were super cheap to rent, and people ignored the history. The owner might have burned them all down and rebuilt them from scratch.

The other option was curious people. The morbid, and those obsessed with true crime. Probably looking for a leftover artifact they could keep as a souvenir. Or they wanted a selfie where a murder had taken place.

All kinds of reasons for all kinds of people.

As Addie pulled under the wooden sign over the road,

she realized she did have a reason for coming here. Even if it was only to prove that she could.

Jacob might have lived in Benson ever since, but it didn't mean he hid any less than she did from their history. They'd survived something horrific. Still, sometimes she felt like she carried it with her everywhere she went. A backpack she couldn't seem to set down. One that weighed on her shoulders and pulled her down.

Addie pulled up in front of the cabin with an Office sign above the door. She got out and looked around.

The temperature had dropped, so she buttoned her coat. No point letting everyone who saw her know exactly who she was. If they knew the town, they'd put it together, and she'd get into a conversation about how she felt being here.

The only person she wanted to talk about that with had just invited her to dinner.

Worst part? She *wanted* to go with him.

She also had a whole lot of work to get back to.

Addie looked around at the serene cabins and the peaceful landscape.

Why did you come here?

Sometimes it was as though she worked up a profile on herself. She probed to find the reasoning behind a word or action. A way to bring understanding.

Usually there was none.

"Good afternoon." Tall and blonde, a young woman emerged from the house and came down the porch steps.

The woman was sorority beautiful. She wore jeans, a denim jacket, and Timberland boots. In her hands she held a pair of suede working gloves. "Are you looking to check in?"

The question was probing. She probably didn't have an open cabin, given the cars beside almost all of them, and wasn't sure why Addie had shown up out of the blue.

Addie tried not to look at the cabin at the far end of the cul-de-sac that fanned the cabins out in a semi-circle. "I was just in the area, and it's been a while. I haven't seen this place since it was fixed up."

"Oh, great. Well, you're welcome to look around as long as you don't disturb any of the residents. If you'd like to see inside the cabins, there's a portfolio of photos on the website. I can give you a card with the address and my email. Just in case you have any questions."

"All the cabins are currently occupied?"

The woman nodded. "I'm Lyric Thompson." She shook Addie's hand. "And yes, we're currently full. Next open booking isn't for three weeks."

"That's okay." She waved the woman off. "I'm Adelyn Franklin."

Lyric blinked bright blue eyes.

"Yeah, that's me. Addie is fine."

The name Lyric suited the woman. She seemed tough but given how striking her looks she could be mistaken for fragile. Or something to be shined and put on a shelf by the kind of guy who had a woman on his arm only for the way she looked.

Maybe that was why she lived out here.

"Addie. Well, it's nice to meet you." Lyric shifted. "I hope it's okay with you that this place was repurposed. It wasn't fun seeing it the way it was, but I gutted everything. It should look nothing like it used to inside. I'm hoping if you did decide to stay here it wouldn't bring back any bad memories."

"I hope it wouldn't as well." Addie finally let her gaze flit over the cabin at the end. It had been painted lavender. Lyric was correct, it looked nothing like what it resembled the last time she was here.

Snow had been shoveled to the edges of the lane that curved at the end and came back this way. Brown now given how long it had been since it fell. The place looked rustic. Plenty of floral design. A gazebo. Swings for kids in a play area. A bridge over the creek. There was likely a profusion of flowers everywhere in summer, all wild like the land around this place.

"It looks great."

"Thanks. Took a lot of work, but I wanted to take something…" Lyric paused. "To make beauty out of ashes."

Addie nodded. "It's lovely. You did the right thing."

"Thanks. It's great to hear you say that." Lyric flushed pink. "All the cabins back onto the land, so you can sit on the porches and watch the deer roam in the morning. I've even seen a couple of badgers late at night. We have wolves, and a guest saw a brown bear once, but I've never seen it."

Addie smiled. "How long have you lived here?"

Lyric shrugged. "Almost four years. This place has been up and running about three."

"Thanks for letting me intrude. I won't take up any more of your time." Addie started to head for her car. "If you're downtown and you want to grab a cup of coffee, I'm in the police station. Go in the main doors but hang a right instead of left. The sign says, FBI."

Lyric gave her a blinding smile. "I'd like that."

Addie shook the woman's hand, looked once more at the cabin, and headed for her car.

She pulled out. Found the freeway. Headed back toward Benson and the office, and the pile of work. The death. The evidence. Suspects. Theories. Profiles.

Things she buried in the same place she'd buried memories of that time. The last few days she'd spent with Jake before they'd decided in the aftermath, they couldn't be around each other anymore. She didn't want to think about the role her mom had played in that.

The man who'd asked her to dinner had forgotten that they'd both screamed. Scarred and bandaged. In pain, physical and emotional. Psychological. They'd taken that pain out on each other.

Not the right time to decide something so life changing as separation. But the fact remained that in the heat of the moment they'd agreed they would never see each other again. Because her mom thought that was for the best.

Now it seemed like he thought she might be his only ally.

Or he still had feelings for her.

She had to admit what she'd had with him was a once in a lifetime thing. Just the way he'd said it. She felt it as well, and there was no point denying that. Then, and now, he'd been everything to her.

Could they make beauty out of those ashes the way Lyric had?

Life had taken them in two different directions so that now they were so far apart there was no way to bridge the gap.

But if they could?

They would never know unless they put their hearts on the line and tried.

As she drove, she studied the scenery. Jagged mountainsides. She spotted four deer wading the river beside the freeway. Life moved on. She didn't have to dwell on the aftermath of when it abruptly ended. Not every day of her life. She could consider the living instead. The wonder of creation. The way things seemed to keep moving. Even in the stillness she could find signs of life.

Until reality intruded and she realized the white pickup behind her was far too close.

Addie kept both hands on the wheel and followed her lane around the curve. She dug her phone from her purse but quickly saw she had no signal.

Probably the mountains on either side. It would be spotty until she reached city limits, which would happen in about fifteen minutes.

The truck did nothing as each second ticked past with the rhythm of the trees.

Addie got to town limits. Since nothing happened, she didn't call for a patrol car to escort her back to the office. She had planned to call Sarah and get some dinner. A milkshake sounded good after visiting the cabins, and that middle of the night meal hadn't happened yet. Their schedules hadn't aligned, but it hadn't been more than two days since their phone conversation.

The half her attention she had on the rearview noticed he moved. Addie held the wheel and watched the rearview.

He was getting closer.

She was still two exits from the one that would take her downtown. She reached for her phone. The pickup slammed into the back of her car.

Addie squealed. The car swerved and she dropped the phone on the floor of the passenger side. Out of reach. Far enough it might as well be in another galaxy for all it was useful to her.

Her car shuddered. Addie gripped the wheel with both hands again and held on. He came around her left side. She spotted him in the side mirror and drifted right. He kept coming closer.

Addie tried to stay in her lane.

Right before the exit he side swiped her. A nudge, but she fought to keep control of her car.

The exit coming up was on the outskirts of town but was

her best bet finding aid right now. If this guy planned to push this, she either had to turn the tables somehow or get to a spot where she'd have help. A police or fire station. Something.

She took the turn at the last second.

As she careened down the off ramp, she spotted him swerve into the lane behind her.

Addie ignored the light and took the corner with a wince. Someone honked at her, but anyone watching would see the pickup in pursuit.

She waited for a lifeline. A spot she could pull into.

The pickup overtook two cars and narrowly avoided a collision with a semi coming the other direction.

He raced up behind her and nudged again.

Addie changed lanes.

He came behind her again—another bump.

Her head slammed back against the headrest. She hissed out a breath. In front of her, she saw a sign.

"Jacob Wilson Photography."

Like a sign from the heavens, Addie veered toward it and turned at the last second into a cracked parking lot. Potholes of iced-over rain. She bumped into one and winced as her undercarriage scraped the asphalt.

She threw the car in park as soon as she could and raced to the door with her purse. Addie dug inside as she went. She'd left her phone in the car and the door open. She drew her weapon at the door and spun to watch for the truck.

16

Jacob heard the screech of metal and the clunk of a car hitting something. He emerged from his office just as the studio's front door flung open, and Addie raced in.

"Call 911!"

He moved to her. Reached for his phone as he did. It wasn't in his pocket. "What's going on?"

His phone had to be on his desk. Or in his backpack. He couldn't remember how long he'd been here, but he hadn't retrieved it yet.

She had her gun out but kept it angled down. Protecting herself. Not from him, though.

"Addie."

She moved to the window and pulled the blind aside. "He's out there. The white pickup truck. He followed me and ran into me. I dropped my phone, so I need to borrow yours." She glanced at him, and he saw more than relief in her eyes.

"Who is it?"

"I don't know." She looked out again. "Maybe you'll recognize him. I never got a look at his face."

Jacob peered over her shoulder out the window. Her car had a crumpled back left corner, but he couldn't see any other damage.

"Where's your phone?"

Jacob moved to the front door and locked it, so no one came in and caught them by surprise. "In the office. I'll lock the back."

"No." She shook her head. "Stay with me, so that I don't have to worry you got jumped."

She nudged him ahead of her, and he led the way to his office. She seemed rattled. But as jumpy as he'd imagine an FBI agent might get. Which meant the overriding feeling he got from her body language was that she had a handle on any fear, and now she was aware. Alert. Ready for what might happen next.

"You think he'll come in here?" Jacob's desk phone was probably easier than his cell at this point. He lifted the handset.

She kept her attention on the door, her stance loose. Prepared to defend both of them. He had a gun in his safe at the apartment but didn't figure she'd think she needed help.

Jacob put the phone to his ear.

There was no dial tone. "Huh." He pressed the button the handset pushed in, then tapped it twice. He dialed anyway. "Nothing's happening. The phone was working earlier, I got a call on it."

"What about a cell?" She shifted her stance, as though any moment now someone would bust in and attack. She had to be ready.

Jacob went for his backpack and found it. "You want to talk to them? They're more likely to come with guns blazing if it's you in trouble." He dialed and moved to her so she didn't have to leave her spot. "They'll want to help a fellow cop."

She said nothing about that, just took the phone and held it to her ear while she kept her gun and all her attention on the door.

It didn't seem like anyone was coming in.

"This is gonna be great." She sighed, then quickly perked up again. "Yes, this is Special Agent—"

Before he could ask why she stopped, she handed the phone to him. "I think the call dropped."

Jacob looked at the screen. "There's no signal. That's weird. It was working a second ago." He moved to the window and held the phone up in case he could get bars by the wall. "Come on." He tried to dial again, and nothing happened. The desk phone was still silent. No dial tone. "What's going on?"

She shifted, and he figured she was getting antsy from the inactivity.

He looked out the window and didn't see anyone. "Maybe whoever picked up for a second on the other end at dispatch will send someone here to check our GPS location, just in case."

He figured it was more likely they'd assume he was responsible for some crime, and she needed help to take *him* down. Not whoever was outside. "I want to check out the front. See if there's someone out there."

The police might not see it, but she'd come here to take refuge with him. That meant something to Jacob. Knowing she saw him as a lifeline—even if it was just because she happened to be driving by. She hadn't gone anywhere else. She'd stopped here and come to him.

He checked all the windows, locked the back door, and found her in the middle of his studio. Watching his back without being right in his face and giving orders like a lot of cops would.

Addie turned in a circle. "No one is coming in, are they?"

"The truck is still there." Jacob had seen the vehicle but no driver. No one was walking around out there, either. "Could we make a run for it? Maybe take my car and head for your office?"

Addie worked her mouth back and forth. "I thought I was being attacked."

"It's okay."

"Why did he do that?" She shook her head, tension he didn't like seeing in the set of her shoulders. Before he could answer she continued, "He could have killed me, running me off the road. Or hit me so I flipped into a ditch."

"You made it here, where you're safe. That's what counts."

She frowned. "I did make it here."

"What?"

"He herded me here." She rolled her shoulders. "Maybe that was the plan all along."

"From the freeway?"

"I walked right in."

He wasn't so sure it was possible to control someone to that extent. Not without them realizing they were trapped. The two of them knew that firsthand. He knew precisely what her eyes would look like the moment she realized there was no escape. The point where she knew death was inevitable—at the end of who knew how many hours of terror.

Right now she didn't have that in her expression.

She struggled, but she had control.

"Let's figure it out. We can wait for the cops, and you can

tell me everything in the meantime. We'll work out what happened."

Instead of responding to that, she looked around. "Do you have a security system? Maybe we can see what he's doing outside."

"We'd know if he was trying to get in." He didn't want to placate her. That wasn't his intention. But getting through this together would help both of them.

He held out his hand. "Let's go sit. Wait this out, and if the cops don't show up in a few minutes we can face down whoever it is outside and go find them."

She eyed his hand like it was a trap. "I could go out there right now. Figure out exactly who it is."

"And leave me unprotected?"

Her gaze flicked up to his eyes. "Because you're helpless?"

"I don't like the idea of you going out there by yourself." Before she could get mad at him, he said, "I know you're an FBI agent. You're trained. But my gun is at the apartment, so I can't watch your back if you try to track down this guy."

Eventually she relented. "Let's go try the phone again."

He thought she might not and was about to drop his hand. She slipped hers into it and they held onto each other. They'd tried doing it in that cabin. They'd both been terrified kids with no idea how to handle what was happening.

She'd pulled away eventually when things got too scary.

He didn't blame her for that. Not when he was too busy blaming himself.

She squeezed his hand as though she knew a little of what he was thinking. Not for the first time, Jacob recognized the fact she understood him in a way no one else did. Or ever would.

In the office, she lifted the handset. He looked out the window.

"No dial tone means the line was cut. No signal means he's got a jammer."

"There's no one outside on this side of the building." He frowned. "But why leave and ditch the truck here?"

"Maybe it's stolen, and he doesn't need it anymore?" She glanced around. Her attention fell on the framed photo on the wall. The one he liked to look at when he was working. "Did you take that?"

"Do you want to talk about my photos, or do you want to figure out how we're going to get to one of our cars if there's someone outside waiting?"

"Give me a second."

Jacob figured that was fair. "That's my grandfather."

Her eyes widened. "You found him?"

He nodded. "A couple of years after…" No point going there out loud. That would only give a voice to things that had power if they were spoken. "It spurned the first book. He introduced me to his people, and I got to tell his story."

She studied the photograph he'd taken of an elderly Native American man. Bison was Cherokee, and he'd handed that blood down to Jacob.

"I said you had Native American in you."

He found a smile. "You were right. Though it took time for my mom to admit who her father was. Didn't exactly fit her narrative, according to my dad."

Jacob hadn't fit either of their ideas of what he should be.

They were happier in Florida, though no less dysfunctional from the sound of it. He just wasn't between them to witness it—and find himself a target.

"But you got to know him?"

"And as many of his tribe who wanted to get to know me." He'd absorbed it all and done his best to document the stories Grandpa told him. The unique experiences Jacob could never understand.

"The book is amazing."

"Thank you." He didn't know what to say.

Not when he'd wondered for years if she'd seen it. If she knew it had blown him away how popular one simple coffee table book had become. He'd searched into his history and been able to give voice to people who might not have been able to tell the world their stories otherwise. That first book about Grandpa had become a whole series.

He'd published the book under his real name. Part of the success was down to his having been a survivor of Ivan Damen, but not all of it. That was a comfort, at least.

"I'm going to look out the front door, okay?"

She held out a hand. "I'll do it. Since I have the gun."

Jacob nodded. "I'm right behind you." He even locked up the office and grabbed his backpack, putting both straps over his shoulders. Might as well be ready to make a run for it.

He put his cell phone in his pocket.

It still didn't make sense that he had no cell signal here. Why would there suddenly be a problem with his phone *and* the internet? It was like something had blocked it all so they wouldn't be able to contact the outside world.

Addie stepped to one side of the door. "Okay, here's how this works."

He perked up at her commanding tone. Had to push aside the flash of attraction that had always been there, for her. She had become a strong, skilled woman. He was no less drawn to her now than he had been before.

"Are you paying attention?" she asked.

He scratched his jaw to hide the smile. "How does this work?"

"I stand here. You open the door, and I go first."

He nodded. "Okay, sounds good."

"Stay behind the door until I say it's clear to come out."

Again, he felt the flash.

"Got it?"

Jacob cleared his throat. "Understood."

Her gaze flickered with confusion for a second.

Jacob motioned to the door. "Let's get out of here."

After that, they could talk more. He wanted to take her to dinner still. But if there really was someone outside waiting, they both needed to focus.

Jacob flipped the lock, but it wouldn't move. He twisted the door handle.

Nothing.

"We locked this." He tried again. "It's stuck."

"We can try the back."

He nodded. They both turned to the room, and he stopped. "Is that smoke?" He put out his hand reflexively, and she grasped his arm. "It's pumping into the room from somewhere."

At the far end of the room, flames whipped under the door to the back hall.

Jacob sucked in a breath. "Fire."

17

"Fire." She whispered an echo of his word.

She couldn't believe it. Except it was undeniable when smoke rolled under the doorway to lick at the floor as it rose into the room. Orange flickered under the door, visible in the gap between the tile and the bottom of the door.

The tang of smoke laced the air. It caught in the back of her throat so that she had to cough to get a breath in.

"We need a way out." Jacob turned. "But the fire exit is that door."

He pointed to the source of the smoke, then moved toward it. Instead of going for the handle he touched his hand to the wood. "It's hot. The fire must be burning hot in the hallway." He touched the metal handle, just a tap of one finger. "No go on the back door."

Addie spoke aloud as she thought it through. "He cut the phone lines. Then he locked the door and started a fire in the only other exit?" She glanced at the front. That wasn't counting the fact she now suspected she'd been herded here.

How was it possible the person outside had set this up? That seemed crazy.

With Jacob behind her she realized he didn't need to see how completely terrified she was. All her training went out the window when she was the victim. Not something she thought she would ever get used to. Even with a badge on her belt, she felt like that scared teen again.

Most of the time on the job she could push it aside and focus. Assuming she wasn't flirting with burnout. And yet, since she'd been back in Benson, things she'd successfully buried for years had shown back up, close to the surface. She'd dreamed nearly every night—nightmares really. And after going to the cabins today she couldn't help thinking about it, even just seeing them fixed up and covered in snow didn't matter.

That, coupled with the adrenaline of being followed and harassed in her car, meant she was having a hard time keeping her cool now.

Jacob frowned. "I'm guessing it's some kind of quick-set epoxy. Squeeze it into the lock, it sets in minutes. We can't get out."

Addie winced. "So he did the doors, then set the fire, and now what? Is he trying to burn us alive in here?"

"That's not going to happen." Jacob crossed the room, went into a closet, and came out with a spray can in each hand. "They came in a pack of two. Lucky us."

"What is it?" She took one. "Oh, a fire extinguisher. In a spray can?"

"Easier than an extinguisher you have to have checked every year, or whatever the rule is now." He moved to the hall door, took a knee, and sprayed under the door. "We can keep the fire at bay, but we need a way out if we're not planning to stay in here and just hope someone shows up."

All she had was a gun and the can he'd given her. Only

one of those things was helpful in a fire. If it got big enough, even the can wasn't going to be able to neutralize a legit blaze.

She should've paid better attention in that ATF seminar.

Instead, she was reduced to looking at the ceiling for a sprinkler system. Shouldn't a building like this have one?

Not only that, but the phones didn't work. "You're right. We do need to get out of here."

For the first time she saw a flash of fear on his face. "What if he's out there, waiting to pick us off the minute we step outside? Clearly this guy means business. He got to work straight away, and now we have only minutes before we succumb to smoke inhalation."

Addie moved to stand in front of him. If she'd had a free hand, she'd have set it on his shoulder. Or taken his hand like she had when he'd held it out, inviting her to connect with him in that small way.

Addie wracked her brain for ideas. "Is there another way out?"

He winced. "It won't be easy to use. And how do we know he didn't bar that way as well? Or he's got a gun and we get shot the second we leave?" He coughed. "We could be headed to our deaths."

"Sometimes the chance is worth it." It gave her strength to realize this was what they did. In times of fear, they shored each other up. Supported each other. The way she worked with her FBI colleagues as part of a team.

The way Russ had taken her camping and let her carry some of their stuff. Helped her to make a fire to cook dinner. She'd tried to do it by herself, but it never worked.

Being part of a team was so much better than flying solo. "We have to try."

"What if the fire draws a neighbor to call 911?" Jake asked. "He could've given us a way to get rescued rather than face certain death. This might actually be a good thing since we can't get out without risking our lives. Setting this fire might be what saves us from whatever else he has planned."

He was worried, so it was her turn to comfort him.

Any second now those tables could turn, and she'd be the one in need of reassurance.

"You'd rather sit around and wait to get rescued, assuming a neighbor will call 911?" Her stomach knotted, because even if she was focused on him that didn't mean she'd lost all her fear. "Last time it took two days for anyone to find us. I'm guessing we don't have that long here." She got close to him. Looked for that solidarity she'd been trying to find with someone else since they parted ways.

Had he ever found it with anyone?

Now wasn't the time to ask him and try to find out. Addie still wasn't sure she wanted to know if he had. "Does your security here connect to the emergency system, or the company you bought it from?"

He shook his head. "I have an alarm for the door. It only alerts me if it's disconnected or set off, nothing else."

"Okay, so that's a no on that." She had to cough. The air was beginning to get thick. "Bathroom? Or a kitchen?"

"For what?"

"If we can wet some towels, we can tie them around our faces. So we're not inhaling chemicals and smoke." She remembered that, at least.

Maybe it was more that she'd seen so many episodes of that fire department TV show. Not that she watched it for the fire safety tips. There was way too much relationship drama for that.

"Oh." His face fell. "That would be down the hall that's on fire. I have waters, though." He went to a cabinet under the coffee pot. Moving swiftly. Edgy. Still, there was familiarity even in those movements, coupled with the realization he was a man now—where before he'd been a boy who believed he was one.

When he opened the door, she realized it was a minifridge. "Here."

She didn't move.

"What?"

Since now wasn't the time, Addie shook her head. "Nothing."

She set the fire extinguisher spray down rather than holstering her gun. Still, he had to unscrew the lid for her so she could take a long drink. "Okay. That's better. Now we…" Movement across the room caught her attention. "Jake."

"What is…" He turned.

Moved in front of her.

Backed up, so Addie had to move as well.

Insects crawled through the vents. Poured into the room. Some took flight, filling the room with a buzz over the sound of flames burning the structure of the hallway.

Addie choked back the noise that wanted to emerge from her throat. She jumped up on the counter even though there wasn't enough room to sit.

"We can't…" Her mind blanked, and there was only terror. It licked with icy fingers at her spine and made her want to shake with fear. "Jake." Everything in her wanted to pray. It was just like before. "Jake."

"Easy."

She had to swat away a fly. "He…"

Jacob spun around. "Look at me."

She shook her head. Look at him? If she did that, she

couldn't see if any of the bugs were headed for them. She wouldn't know if something was trying to crawl up her leg.

None of them were big enough to shoot. What did she have to fight them off with?

Memories of all manner of creeping and crawling creatures running up and down her skin stuck the air in her throat in a lump.

Addie coughed. "I swallowed one. I breathed one in."

"No." He shifted, and she realized he'd set his water down when he touched her cheeks. "He's trying to scare us, that's all."

"It's working." She didn't want to lose it. She wasn't a scared kid anymore; she was a grown woman. An FBI agent. But that didn't take the fear away.

Nothing did.

Jacob touched his forehead to hers. "You aren't tied to a chair. You can move."

She let go of the gun and clutched at the shirt on his sides. Hugged his elbows with her arms. Held on tight.

"Good. Hold on to me, Addie."

He'd said the same thing to her before, fifteen years ago.

She squeezed her eyes shut. "We have to get out of here." But she couldn't move. There was no way she could get off this counter and walk across the floor knowing there were bugs everywhere. It was too much like before.

"There aren't that many." He shook her, just a fraction. Enough to get her attention. "Look, Addie."

She shook her head as best she could when he had those warm fingers on her cheeks. Nothing had ever felt the way he did. He was her lifeline.

Only she'd relied on him entirely too much. Even before they were rescued, he'd pulled away, and she had no idea why. Some kind of recoil when he'd hit his limit and been unable to handle it—along with trying to be there for her the way she'd tried to for him. Then after they were rescued, he walked away completely.

He might be familiar, but it wasn't a place she could be sure of.

"Look."

Her eyes fluttered open. She shouldn't have squeezed them shut so hard. Now everything was blurry. Or was that the smoke in the room?

She stared at the insects dispersed across the floor. "That's your idea of not that many?" She wanted to tuck her feet up on the counter with her. Curl into a ball as tight as possible and pray nothing came anywhere near her.

Bugs were the last thing she wanted to deal with.

She looked back at Jake.

The expression on his face was something like yearning. She stared at those eyes. Saw in them everything she'd ever needed. A whisper of promise that she was worth sticking around for.

Until it all went wrong.

He moved closer, just a fraction. She felt the warmth of his breath on her cheek.

"Jake."

He was going to kiss her.

Addie needed to figure out if she wanted that. Even while she considered the fact she always would. *It's always been you.*

No matter what else happened, that would be true until the day she died. No matter who else became part of her life.

"I feel it too." But he didn't kiss her. Instead, he moved away an inch.

Out of reach.

"What's happening?" Addie asked him. "This is too bizarre. Too similar." Ideas wanted to coalesce in her mind, but there was too much terror to sort through it.

Maybe they would always have crazy chemistry. It didn't mean there was anything between them after all this time.

"Whoever is outside wants us trapped. They know how both of us feel about bugs." He shuddered. She felt it under her hands, even though she was squeezing the life out of handfuls of his shirt.

She tried to unclench her fingers. "Tell me about that way out you have. I don't want to be in here. We need to be outside." She gasped. "I can't breathe."

Even though they were going to walk across the floor covered with skittering bugs. Swat away the ones that flew around trying to escape the smoke.

One flew toward her face, and she made a noise in her throat she wasn't proud of.

You're an FBI agent. Act like it.

But those old fears reared their heads and drowned her good sense.

"The alternative is waiting for someone to call the fire department, and we don't know how long that will take." He kissed her forehead. "We might not have enough time to wait. Even if going outside could mean we get picked off by a bullet."

"Okay." She winced. "Let's go."

If they were up against a bullet, that wasn't nearly as terrifying a prospect as insects everywhere. Touching her.

She shivered, and he shifted, so she hopped off the counter. "Let's move fast."

"I'll warn you now"—he pointed—"you might not like this way out."

"We can't stay here."

There were already two insects on her shoe. She didn't want to look close enough to know what they were.

She took his hand. "Lead the way."

18

"Right here." Jacob crouched at the back of the dressing room and shoved a rack of shoes over. He flipped the latch at the bottom of the wall, then stood and slid the bolt that secured the door shut. "Used to be a loading bay entrance, back when this place was a restaurant before I bought it. I was thinking of using it for storage. I just didn't get to it yet."

He looked back at her. "It's been two years."

The edge of a smile curled her lips, but it did nothing to extinguish the look on her face.

"Come on."

Inside the door it was cramped. A few crates and a pallet, just junk mostly, littered the room. In one corner he'd had them install the new water heater. Jacob heard a rat scurry down one wall but didn't react to it. Neither of them needed to acknowledge more living creatures in here with them.

Especially not after those insects had poured into the room, through the heating vent.

He wanted to shudder just thinking about it. The only reason he got through it this time was knowing she needed him to be strong. Talking her past her fears helped him reason it out. The last thing he'd wanted was for those bugs to be anywhere near him, but he'd worked hard to get over that particular fear.

The past wasn't going to have him in a chokehold. Not that he blamed Addie if her history did. After all, she faced down killers. Something he would never want to do.

He didn't want anything to do with crime. Or law enforcement.

The fact that she did impressed him. Even if it was about overcoming her fears and going after what drove her. He did the same thing, just in different ways.

For that matter, so did Hank.

Addie closed the door behind her. "Is there a way to get outside?"

"They boarded up the entrance, but it's only two-by-fours. I can kick one out." Jacob went to the exterior wall and pressed on one of the old boards. He could see out a gap between two of them. Only the air outside was so cold it hurt to stare out. All he got was a flash of light. Maybe a tree. "As soon as I kick one…"

She finished for him. "He'll see."

He pulled out his phone. "Whoever it is."

"I'll go first." She was right that she should. After all, she was the one with the gun and the training.

"One sec." He held the phone up by the exterior wall. Like the gap between the boards would let in a signal. It did give him enough to call out, maybe because there wasn't concrete between him and the signal…he didn't know enough about it. Or whatever tech had been used to jam his signal before and kill the phone line in his office.

"I'm gonna call Hank." He put it on speaker so they could both hear.

Hank answered on the first ring. "Hey, I'm kind of busy, but what's up?"

"Addie and I are trapped at my studio," Jacob began. "It's on fire, and we don't know if we can get out. We think whoever set the fire is still outside."

"I'll call it in. But I'm across town. It'll take me some time to get there, but I'll get a patrol car and fire to your location." Hank paused a fraction. "What's the address again?"

Hank knew where the place was and what street, but Jacob gave him the number. The quicker help could get here the better.

"Tell them to hurry." Addie's voice shook. "If he's out there, I want him in cuffs. There's also a white pickup in the parking lot. I want an officer to take a look at it."

"Copy that."

It hit Jacob that there existed a shorthand between them. Some connection they had because both were cops.

Jacob wasn't jealous. He didn't envy the job they did.

He was just out of sorts, and this situation was far too weird. It made no sense. He liked his life, and he understood what'd happened to him by processing it through his camera lens.

The quicker Hank could get help here, the better.

"See you soon." Hank hung up, and Jacob stowed the phone. "Anyone else you want to call? Russ, maybe?"

Addie shook her head. "I'll call him later. I don't want him to worry."

Jacob nodded.

"What about your parents?"

He frowned. "Later is good. Not sure I'll actually tell them, though. They live in Florida." He shrugged, antsy for the fire department to get there already. "They moved there a few years ago."

They also hated each other, and even though they were back together they'd made a point to ensure he knew he was the reason they broke up. Now he was out of their lives, they could make a go of it.

He was destined to be a point of contention between people he cared about. His parents. Hank and their coach. Addie and her mom. Hank and Addie.

"Have you been?" she asked.

Jacob blinked.

"To Florida?"

"Once, for Christmas." He shook his head. "Eighty-two degrees on Christmas Day? That's just wrong. It's unnatural."

She grinned, not lost in it but he'd succeeded in distracting her at least.

"Thanks for being here with me."

"You like being in this situation?" She shot him a look.

"Of course not." Did she really think that? "What I'm saying is being here with you is better than being alone."

The truth was, he'd felt like he was alone for a long time. Years. Maybe ever since she left town, and took a piece of his heart with her.

Addie moved to him and hugged him. It was a surprise, but it warmed him that she closed the gap between them.

In the distance he heard approaching sirens. "I guess the cavalry is here."

She stepped back with her cheeks flushed. Probably from the heat and the gathering smoke rather than any other reason. "I'm glad I'm not alone, either. Even if it was planned that I came here." She shook her head. "Though that sounds crazy. I'm not sure anyone will believe it, even if it is true."

Jacob nodded. "I'm sure you and the police can figure out what happened."

He watched the gap between the boards. When he heard a couple of firefighters come around the corner, Jacob kicked out a board in the middle of the wall. Not enough for them to get out, but it was enough to get the firefighter's attention.

"Hey!" The two of them rushed over, and Jacob recognized one. "Zach, we need help."

Zach Peters was a fire department lieutenant. He grabbed his radio right away. "Chief, they're on the D side, halfway down. We can get them out." To Jacob, he said, "Either of you hurt?"

Jacob shook his head. "How did it go with your sister and the doc?"

Zach hesitated a second as though Jacob had surprised him. Then he shook his head.

Jacob winced. "Sorry, man. That's rough."

"Um, you guys wanna get out of there?" Zach glanced between them.

"Yes, we do." Jacob felt Addie's hand on his back.

Zach spoke over his shoulder. "Let's get them out!"

He gave a couple of orders to his firefighters, and they all started to move. Like coordinated actions they'd rehearsed until each strike of a tool was anticipated and each man—and the woman Jacob spotted—knew exactly what to anticipate.

They pried the boards away and cut the rest. Made a hole big enough for him and Addie to get out.

"The cops showed up, too, right?" Addie glanced around. "We believe there might be an armed man around here. He's the one we think set the fire."

"A shooter?" Zach asked.

Jacob motioned to her. "This is Special Agent Adelyn Franklin. FBI."

Zach's eyebrows rose.

"Yeah."

Addie turned to Jacob. "What does that mean?"

All he could think to say was, "Zach and I are in the same Bible study. It happens online, so we can call in from wherever."

"Like the firehouse." Zach held out a hand and helped Addie out.

Jacob left after her.

Zach motioned to the front of the building. "Let's get you two to the EMTs, get you checked out."

Jacob nodded, though aside from the smoke inhalation, the rest of their issues were internal. In the sense that, as much as they might want to believe it, they weren't as past what had happened as either of them thought.

Before she got back, he'd have said he put it behind him a long time ago. Now it was clear he hadn't. The moment Addie showed up it was like everything he did to convince himself it wasn't a factor seemed to shatter and their shared history came back in full force.

Hank rushed around the corner. "Jake! Addie!" The detective jogged over and the three of them hugged as a group. "You guys!"

Jacob winced at the volume of Hank's voice right by his ear and pulled back. Hank tugged Addie under his arm so that her shoulder was wedged right by his duty weapon holstered there.

"We're okay," Jacob held out his hand for Addie. "But we need to get checked out by the EMTs. Make sure we aren't hurt."

Addie took it, and something inside him slid into place. Hank walked with them so, Jacob reiterated everything to his friend. They were given oxygen masks and told to sit. Hank kept him talking about everything. When the detective started to ask the same questions in different ways, Jacob said, "Is this an interrogation?"

Addie shifted beside him, sat on the back step of the ambulance.

Hank ran his hand over his head and back. "Sorry. I just can't believe this." He motioned to the side and looked at Addie. "Your car? You could have died. Both of you could have died in there. Your livelihood is ruined."

Jacob shrugged.

Addie tipped her head to one side. "Aren't you upset?"

"Neither of us is hurt badly. It's just a building." But he knew for sure when he renovated after the smoke cleared, he'd be upgrading the safety features—and security. "I'd rather focus on who that was, and why they did this."

She said, "Is there a plate on the pickup?"

"Reported stolen yesterday."

Addie sighed.

Jacob glanced between them. "It could've been anyone?"

Hank frowned. "If you had security, we'd have his face on camera."

Jacob tried not to feel that as a jab from his best friend, but it stung anyway. "Someone tried to kill us. Pretty sure it's not my job to figure out who that is. I'm not the one who's a cop."

He meant Hank, but Addie reacted as well. She handed the oxygen mask back to the EMT and stood. "Guess I should get to work, then."

"Addie—"

She walked off and didn't look back at him.

Hank shook his head. "You're out of practice."

Jacob had his backpack. He didn't need to get in the studio until tomorrow when the scene would have been cleared. "I should find out if I can go home."

Hank held up a hand. "Hold up. The captain isn't going to let you leave."

"That guy who stood in my living room and asked me for an alibi on Celia Jessop's time of death when the investigation had barely begun?"

"Why do you think he did that?"

"Because I might incriminate myself by answering wrongly?"

Hank motioned Jacob to go with him, away from Addie's direction. It was the last thing he wanted to do but followed anyway. One glance told him she was talking to the fire chief. He was still worried about her—even if he wasn't a first responder. It wasn't like he'd ever be the one responsible for her safety, though he could help.

"Jacob."

He turned to Hank and realized Captain McCauley stood there. Beside him was Alan Lachlan—lieutenant when they had been kidnapped, now the police chief. "Gentlemen."

"You need to come with us," McCauley said. "We have something we need to talk to you about."

Jacob gritted his teeth. "What's going on?"

The chief's expression hardened. "In the car, Wilson."

19

The fire chief's attention drifted over her shoulder.

Addie turned and saw two uniformed cops usher Jacob into the back of their car. He wasn't cuffed, so clearly he wasn't being arrested. Giving him a ride? She frowned. Something was going on, and she had no idea what it was. Addie wasn't used to being out of the loop. Which begged the question of how long it was going to take for her to feel like she was part of law enforcement here instead of being an outsider.

She was guessing about twenty years. Even with her having grown up here.

Too bad she wasn't planning on staying anywhere near that long.

She turned back to the fire chief. "I'd love to see the source of the fire."

He nodded. "Let's take a look."

Addie followed. As they walked, she said, "I haven't worked really any fire investigations. Not my wheelhouse, I'm afraid. But since someone tried to burn me alive in this studio, maybe I should get familiar with it."

"I understand." He gave her a look she often gave victims. Not that he was placating her, but she was processing what had happened and he'd give her some time to work out how she felt about it.

There was still the question of if he would try to manage her, or if as soon as the call was over, he would go back to his firehouse and never think on this scene again—once his report was written.

Getting to know people here would take time. For now, all she needed was a functional relationship that meant she could do her job without roadblocks popping up in front of her every time she needed something.

"I know this was arson, but what's the procedure for that kind of thing?"

The chief glanced over. "You saw someone set the fire?"

She shook her head. "Whoever tried to run me off the road kind of…herded me here." She knew it didn't make complete sense, but things often happened with no explanation. The fire chief had to know that.

"Any idea who it was?"

She shook her head again. "No cameras. The police are searching for him, right?"

"I believe so."

She thought as much, but given the department's higher-ups had ushered Jake to that car and driven away, it had to be the foot patrol officers searching the area. Plenty of them had turned out in response to Hank's call.

Maybe they would find the person responsible.

Addie was going to have to make a statement to the police. She'd have to admit she was receiving hang-up calls and had been since before she left Virginia. The man outside the window—she didn't know if she should mention what might be a figment of her imagination.

Being run off the road was *definitely* not the symptom of a lingering nightmare. Her car had the damage to prove it.

So at least she knew coming home hadn't resulted in some kind of mental break. She wasn't going to wake up in a psych ward and be told she had cracked. Because Addie faced the fact that was everyone's nightmare. And anyone who said that wasn't a deep-seated fear was probably lying to themselves. No one was completely sane.

"Okay?"

She nodded. The fire chief seemed like a nice guy. "I won't take up too much of your time."

"The fire started here. The blaze spread so fast it's hard to tell." The chief motioned to the wall. "Given there's a gas can right here, it's not hard to figure out the source."

"But he only burned this end of the building." She frowned. "Instead of pouring it all around and killing us quickly when the whole place went up."

The chief shrugged. "We could surmise all day, but all we'd be doing is guessing at his intentions. Or hers."

She nodded. "It wasn't designed to go up fast, though. Right?" Just enough to freak them out. To *herd* them to one end, so he could push insects to the main room and leave them trapped.

It had taken minutes—and seemed like much longer—before they got to that spot where Jake could call Hank. They could so easily have died but found a way out and they were rescued. Not because they'd managed to save themselves, though.

The fire chief studied the damaged exterior wall. "I'd say whoever did this had a strategy. What it was, might only be answered when we can question them about why."

"Addie!"

She spun around so fast her head swam. Russ strode over,

a thunderous look on his face that other people would assume meant he was angry. He was, but only because he was mad at being scared.

He moved to her and kept coming. Until Addie was enveloped in a hug that choked her up.

"I'll give you two a minute." That was the chief, but all she could see was the collar of Russ's jacket that her face was smashed against.

His hold was like being grabbed by a bear. After being abandoned by a mother who chased romance to and fro across the country, Russ's hugs had been a comfort. But then, anything would've been. As much as she didn't appreciate what that said about her being starved for affection, she figured it was okay given he was her uncle. They cared about each other.

Russ shifted. "The chief told me what happened."

She couldn't help frowning. "Did he tell you Jacob was behind the whole thing?"

Russ flinched. "Was he?"

"No." She shook her head. "That's my point. He was with me. He didn't do any of this."

Of course, it could be argued he might've had an accomplice. But as with Ivan Damen, she still didn't think that was likely. After all, one had never turned up after Damen was arrested fifteen years ago. Whoever saw a second person, it wasn't Addie or Jake.

It seemed like everyone thought Jake had criminal intentions. The captain had gone to him first for an alibi for that girl's murder. Celia Jessop hadn't even been autopsied before they were demanding to know his whereabouts.

She couldn't help but think they all had it in for him.

Since Addie was predisposed to be on his side because he was her first love and everything they'd been through—even if their relationship hadn't ended on the best of terms. It was hard not to jump in all the time and defend him.

She was supposed to be a professional here, which was why she'd left town. So she could make a life for herself that wasn't all wrapped up in her history and her emotions.

"Come on." Russ slung his arm around her shoulder. "I'll give you a ride, and we'll sort out your car later."

Addie grabbed her phone. She ensured the police were good with her leaving and then told Russ, "You can drop me at my office. I have work to do."

She'd missed her whole lunch break at this point.

He frowned over the hood of his truck.

"What?"

"Nothing. Toss that stuff in the back."

Addie saw what he meant when she opened the door. She didn't throw the box of shotgun shells, but she did put them on the back floor. His heavy jacket on the seat. She wasn't sure what to do with the one sock and the bag containing half a sandwich.

"Wanna finish that?"

She handed it to him. "I'm good."

Her throat was still raw from the smoke inhalation. Was Jake's? Maybe she shouldn't care so much when there was plenty of work to do. The police would find whoever set the fire. She had her job, and it didn't involve doing theirs and getting distracted. Whether this was one in a series of coordinated attempts to hurt or scare her didn't matter.

But the idea she'd been herded to Jake's studio stuck with her.

If someone could do that and be so planned about their attack, what else had they caused her to walk into unknowingly?

She shivered in her seat.

Russ cranked the heat and pointed all the vents at her.

"I'm good. I just need some hot tea at the office."

"Good idea." He hit the gas and peeled out of the parking lot as though the building were still on fire. Except that was the way he normally drove. "Word to the wise?"

He always phrased that statement like it was supposed to be a question. Addie said, "Sure."

"Be careful how vocal you are about standing with Jacob."

"Because of how the police view him?" She shifted in her seat. "Has he committed some crime I'm unaware of?"

Russ said nothing, but she saw the shift of his throat.

"Spit it out, Russ."

"They're hauling him in for questioning over the death of Celia Jessop."

She opened her mouth to tell Russ there was no way Jacob did that. "Someone just tried to kill us. They're choosing *now* to bring him in?"

"It's just questions. He isn't in danger or under arrest."

Addie wanted to text him and tell him to ask for a lawyer, whether he was under arrest or not. Still, she couldn't get in the middle of this if there was even a hint that he'd had anything to do with it.

No way it would get far if this was only a case of police prejudice. Hank would make sure they moved on if it had no weight, and no prosecutor was going to take a case with no evidence.

She had a lot of faith in people she didn't know well, some of whom she didn't know at all. That thought only made her want to push her way into the police department and ruin her tenuous relationship with the cops here. Justice was one thing. But whoever wielded that gavel had to be blind otherwise bias entered the equation.

They weren't going to put up with her for long if she stuck her nose in what they thought was their business.

She had her own cases to work, and someone targeting her. "Whoever set that fire"—she glanced out the front window—"they knew what Jake and I went through. They knew exactly what triggers to pull."

Russ glanced over.

"And there's a killer in town. He's been operating for years, working on his skills. Figuring out how to cover it up. Escalating. Learning."

Not that Russ didn't already know all that. She'd walked him through a lot of it when he visited her office. Still, maybe she needed to remind herself. Even though she'd nearly been run off the road, there were things to do. She wasn't going to let some guy with an agenda to hurt her and maybe Jacob also, distract her from doing what she'd been brought here to do.

Especially if that was his intention.

"You think it's the same person?"

"It would be a serious coincidence, but I'm not about to rule it out."

"Good." Russ lifted his chin. "If you need a hand with all those files, I'm happy to. Just as soon as I talk to Mona."

"What's up with Mona?"

He shrugged one shoulder. "Gotta pick her up from school. She got suspended this morning, but I made her wait when I heard you were hurt. So we need to swing by the school."

Addie blew out a breath. "What happened?"

"Punched the head cheerleader. But they've been beefing for a while, so…"

"Let's go get her."

He frowned. "I'll do it after I drop you off. You need to work."

Addie shook her head. "I can go in later. This is important."

It had been clear from the outset there was a reason she was here. Maybe more than one now that she'd been here for a minute. Sure, she had at least a dozen cases to read, but Mona was her little sister. It didn't matter what was happening at work, her family needed to come first.

Addie hadn't been here for years.

But she was here now.

20

Jacob could feel the simmering rage behind him. He didn't turn, and the cop at his back didn't shove him into the room.

But it was close. "In here."

Jacob was surprised they didn't shackle him to be paraded through the police station like the criminal half the cops in Benson thought he was. Didn't matter which precinct they took him to, the reception would be the same. But they used the main station downtown—the building with headquarters upstairs.

The one with Addie's office at the front, across the hall from the police reception desk.

Too bad they brought him in the back entrance so he couldn't see it. Was she still at his studio? None of them had told him, and Hank didn't get in the car.

Jacob looked back at the hall but didn't see his friend.

Captain McCauley paused in the doorway. "Detective Maxwell won't be conducting this interview." An officer handed him a paper file and McCauley shut the door. "Take a seat."

Jacob was tempted to lean against the wall and not sit, just to be contrary. Instead, he pulled out the chair and settled across from the captain.

He wasn't interested in Hank getting in the middle of this. His friend didn't need to have his career marred by an association with Jacob. At least not any more than it already was.

Still, a little solidarity wouldn't have been a bad thing.

Hank's hands might be tied so that he couldn't step out of the boundaries of procedure and the oath he'd taken. Jacob didn't want him to do that. He wanted any cop to be someone people could rely on to be honorable. That meant Hank not bending the law—even just to reassure him.

Jacob was on his own here.

"What can I help you with?" He figured he might as well begin as though he was doing them a favor. Not that he wasn't well aware they'd love nothing more than to trap him into confessing to some crime.

Celia Jessop's murder.

The captain opened his file and studied the contents. Probably waiting in the hope Jacob started talking just to fill the awkward silence.

But Jacob didn't see silence like that. There was usually some noise, some sign of life, if you listened closely enough for long enough. His cats. Traffic on the street below his apartment. He could hear officers in the hallway and a phone ringing—signs of life that were probably reassuring to the captain to know his people were close by.

All designed to make Jacob believe he was on his own in here.

Which he didn't need to be. "Do I need a lawyer?"

McCauley looked up. "You aren't under arrest."

"So I'm free to leave at any time?"

McCauley's expression shifted a fraction. Jacob wasn't sure if that was supposed to be an agreement or if the guy was displeased Jacob knew that.

"You know, you guys are the reason I have to keep apprised of my rights."

McCauley lifted a brow. "Because you feel the police victimize you?"

"What do you think?"

"Criminals often feel targeted by the police. Mostly I've found it to be down to guilt of the wrong you know you've done." McCauley shrugged. "You go to church. I'm sure you've heard the pastor talk about conviction."

"And you've heard him talk about unjustly judging someone." Jacob couldn't help but fire that back. He didn't have the energy to hold his tongue, probably something he should put that mention of church experience to work dealing with.

He was just about to pray over that when McCauley said, "So how about you go over your whereabouts at the time of Celia Jessop's death one more time. For my records."

Jacob considered his words before he spoke. The captain would try and get him flustered and reacting before he thought. That was the last thing Jacob needed to do, even if he had nothing to do with Celia's death.

Jacob shrugged one shoulder. "When did she die?"

"Tuesday night."

"What time did you say?"

McCauley paused. "Between one thirty and three thirty."

Jacob blew out a breath. "The last time I saw her and we talked was a couple of weeks ago."

"That was the conversation the boyfriend"—McCauley looked at his notes—"interrupted?"

Jacob nodded.

"Guess he sure got the wrong end of the stick."

Jake didn't like the tone. He'd have fired something back, but whatever it was didn't matter. McCauley had already decided he was guilty and lying about it.

Though the town was contending with a killer who kidnapped high schoolers once a year. The police had everyone convinced they had the man in custody two weeks before Jacob and Addie went to theirs. It turned out that wasn't the guy—and they were taken. He hadn't been the accomplice either—just some guy designed to be a red herring.

Then Becca Cowell had been killed.

The police in Benson had been trying to repair the public's trust in them ever since. Whether it was working or not was hard to say. A couple of outfits in town did private security work—one, Vanguard, was all women. He didn't get involved in a lot of it.

Jacob liked his solitary life.

He realized the captain was just staring at him.

"What?"

McCauley stared. "Where were you when Celia was killed?"

"Oh." He frowned. "Sleeping, like I told you at my apartment. So why do you need me to tell you again?"

He could think of a few reasons, and none flattered the captain and his ability to do his job. More likely McCauley had been there the other day to ask this same question with the express purpose of throwing Addie into Jacob's private space and seeing how he reacted to her.

Maybe McCauley figured he would snap. Kind of like right now.

"New evidence has come to light."

"Oh?" Jacob frowned. "What's that?"

"Nothing you need to worry about right now. What you

need to worry about is telling me the truth. It might help explain this new evidence." McCauley sighed. "So how about this. When we look at your computer—which we will soon enough—are we going to find photos of Celia Jessop?"

"You get that I'm a professional photographer, right?" Jacob frowned. "Or do you think that's just a cover so I can give in to some dirty secret you're so certain I'm hiding?"

"I guess we'll find out as soon as the warrant comes through."

They were going to tear apart his entire life. "How about I save you some trouble?"

"How's that?"

Jacob leaned forward slightly. "I. Didn't. Kill. Her."

"I can see why you might want a judge to believe you were cooperative, so they can take that into account when murder charges are filed."

"Because you think all I'm trying to do is look good?" Jacob said. "Because I'm so guilty?"

"You tell me."

The truth was, Jacob didn't feel the need to plead his case. He could scream and cry over the injustice of being accused, but there would be no evidence he'd killed that girl. How could there be when he didn't do it?

"I was asleep." Jacob shrugged one shoulder. "How could I have killed her when I didn't leave my apartment?" He paused a second to wonder how diabolical the police thought he was since Hank was at his place for breakfast when Jacob had come back from the gym.

"That only leaves the onus on me to prove you did."

That didn't sound like a happy invitation. "I guess it does." Jacob had to wonder—again—why they brought him in suddenly now. "Unless there's some evidence I don't know about."

McCauley nodded. "When you're arrested, you'll want to talk to your lawyer about trying to explain how your fingerprint is on a clear, sticky residue affixed to the victim's abdomen."

"My fingerprint?"

He nodded again.

"On like, glue?"

"You tell me." McCauley paused. "It's your print. A partial one, anyway."

"So not a print, but a bit of one that you think is mine?" That sounded inconclusive at best. "I haven't seen Celia for two weeks where I was even close enough to touch her. Why wouldn't she have taken a shower since?"

"That might be an angle you want to take up with your lawyer. When you need one." McCauley's eyes flashed. For a second he looked pretty smug. "A partial match is still a match."

Jacob stood. If that were true, they'd have a warrant for his arrest already.

All he wanted to do was go to Addie.

Considering McCauley was right, and he would need a lawyer if the cops kept up with this, he should probably get on that first. Maybe Russ knew a good one—someone he'd hated as a former federal agent. Whoever it was would be a quality shark who might manage to keep Jacob out of jail.

He needed to face the fact that was where the police wanted this to go. The place where he'd end up convicted of a crime he didn't commit.

And yet, the only person whose opinion he cared about was Addie. As long as she knew he hadn't done it, that would enable him to face anything.

"Don't leave town."

Jacob turned back at the door. He wanted to jump on

that comment but knew it was better he didn't. He hadn't lost it yet, but only barely. "And you're going to take apart my whole life?"

"That's the plan." McCauley leaned back in his chair. "If you didn't do this, then I guess you have nothing to worry about."

"Sure. After all, no one innocent ever went to prison for a crime they didn't commit."

McCauley stood. "Are you besmirching the good name of—"

Jacob didn't wait for him to finish. He pulled open the door and stepped into a busy hallway. All he needed was air, and he'd be able to think this thing through. That had always been what he needed. Ever since freedom was taken away from him and he was locked in that cabin with Addie.

Don't leave me.

He couldn't decide if she'd said that today, or years ago. It all blurred together in his mind. History melded into the present, and all of it washed with pure fear. The idea he might never see the light of day again.

Trapped with no way out. A victim, but this time at the whim of the same people who had rescued him from Ivan Damen years ago.

Jacob hit the bottom step of the precinct almost at a run and nearly slammed into someone.

"Whoa." Hands grasped Jacob's shoulders.

He shoved his arms out, dislodging the grasp before he realized it was Hank. "Hey." Jacob squeezed the bridge of his nose and tried to push out the panic.

"Did it not go okay?"

"My fingerprint is on a dead girl's body." Jacob made sure to keep his voice low. "How do you think it went?"

Hank winced. "I try to be the voice of reason, but they know how close we are."

"I know." Jacob couldn't feel the reassurance, though. "Thanks."

"You think I'll ever not have your back?"

He shook his head. Still, Jacob couldn't get rid of thoughts of Addie. Where was she? Had the smoke made her throat as raw as his? He should be going home to hibernate until he got his energy back. Recharge his battery, as it were. Find a lawyer who would help him beat a murder rap.

He squeezed his eyes shut. All he could see was Addie. "I just hope the one tiny part of McCauley that's wondering if maybe I *didn't* do this gets enough airtime that a killer doesn't get away with it because the captain is so busy trying to pin it on me."

21

Addie stared at the papers she'd hung around her office, cast in yellow light from the lamps. It was too late in the evening to turn on the fluorescent overheads. That much whitewash would keep her up for hours and give her a migraine.

On the whiteboard, the photo in front of her was a close-up image of the bug bite this victim had received. A killing from several years ago, but not the first batch. Just looking at it made her shiver, but she wasn't going to let her fears keep her from doing her job. Working this case could be the thing that cured her.

At least, she had to entertain the possibility.

She still felt, to an extent, the way she had when she left DC. Despite the sleep and the fact she was only working on one investigation, things hadn't been restful. Her sister Mona would barely speak to her. Russ was just Russ. The times she'd seen Jake were about death, and the two of them had nearly been killed.

The week she'd spent in Seattle at the FBI office had been a lot about convincing them why she could do this only if she had a whole team. Trying to explain why she had been picked for the assignment here instead of one of their local agents when the truth was she had no idea.

The assistant director in Seattle had been as unhappy about it as her. He could only spare agents if she for sure needed backup. Addie wasn't about to ask just because she felt like a self-fulfilling prophecy on a good day and a whole lot worse than that on a bad.

Given what Zimmerman had told her about this giving her a clean slate to get promoted, she figured if it was true then that meant she could move on from here when it was done. If she succeeded.

Probably she'd be fired.

Either way, Addie didn't have to get stuck in Benson forever. That would be a nightmare when her history was around every corner. Ready to rush at her when she least expected it.

But this investigation—and her own history that seemed to be related somehow—was a serious hurdle.

"Wow." Dr. Carlton stood at the door in a skirt suit and heels, a trench coat over her arm and a briefcase in hand. "This is a lot of cases."

"Hey, Sarah." It was nice to see a friendly face.

Jacob had been hauled in for questioning by the police, and no one updated her on how that had gone. She'd kind of thought Hank would come by. Not yet though. Were they questioning Jake still?

Addie needed to focus on work, or she would realize it was hours later and all she'd done was think about Jake. That wouldn't be good. It made her long for DC, where she'd rarely been distracted by personal stuff. Even with Zimmerman, and their relationship.

Which made her wonder if she'd had feelings for him or

if it was simply about connecting with someone? She knew how Russ felt about it—because the first book he read every day was the Bible. What about Sarah? Maybe Addie needed to figure out the answer on her own as to the kind of person she wanted to be here or anywhere.

Focus.

Addie turned to the ME. "I have a question."

"Hit me." Sarah put her briefcase beside the coat tree and hung up the trench.

"Was there anything from the autopsy on Celia Jessop that I don't know?"

"There's always the unexpected." Sarah folded her arms. "She was stabbed twice, and there are some shallow cuts."

"Methodical?"

Sarah nodded. "Clean and precise. But I don't think the killer had medical training and the blade had a serration close to the handle. Maybe a pocketknife or small hunting knife."

Addie had three other similar cases. They didn't look like torture, which was why she'd settled on experimentation. It was more common than she wanted to see in cases where the killer had no empathy.

Sarah frowned. "So you believe this was the first death this year?"

"Unless you have anything." Addie shrugged. "All the others were in a series of two or three, over two months. They're spaced a few years apart each time. Each killing season, as it were, shows a pattern. The first kill is opportunity and looks like desperation. The others are more methodical, like he's testing things out in some cases. But there are always a few common elements."

"Like the bruise?"

"I'd noticed that. I wasn't sure what it indicated." Addie

frowned. "Mostly because I've been distracted by the bug bites. It's on my list to tackle next."

"Can I show you something?" Sarah unfolded her arms and pointed to one of the victim photos. That one had a broken hyoid bone and petechiae around the eyes.

Strangulation.

Addie figured she knew what this was. "Sure."

Sarah moved around behind her. "Each of the victims shows swollen skin around the neck. Not exactly bruising, but pressure was applied. This one that has a broken hyoid bone? Celia had the same thing when I took a look at the X-rays. I'm wondering if you've got more than just these two, and it was overlooked because of the other injuries. I think he's right-handed. And I can tell you he's over five eleven but not taller than six one."

Sarah's arms came over Addie's shoulders, she bent her right elbow and grasped her wrist with her left hand. The inside of her wrist touched Addie's throat. "If I apply enough pressure, it squeezes off the carotid. You'll pass out because blood backs up in your brain."

Addie's mind spun with the implications. "And the bruise by the throat? The broken hyoid?"

Her arm constricted against Addie's throat. Addie patted Sarah's forearm. The ME lowered her arms. Addie felt the pieces click together in her mind. "It's a chokehold."

"He pulls. I think a watch may be responsible for the break."

"But it's not on all of them. So maybe he doesn't always wear it." Addie walked along the row of whiteboards and looked at each victim. "Or he didn't have a watch for a while, but he wears one now and didn't account for it."

The killer could have DNA from the victim on a watch

he still wore. Testing it could nail their suspect—when they figured out who it was.

Did Jacob wear a watch?

"Martial arts, maybe. Or police training, though holds like that are illegal now. He isn't going to care about that when he's gotten away with this for so long. He believes he's above the law."

Addie went to her notebook and jotted down several things about the knife and the hold. "Seems like some of the things he does are instinctual. Others are methodical. He lives his life and when the urge to take a life grows to where it's undeniable, he finds someone. After he kills again, he can suppress the urge for a year or two."

If there was another death before Celia's it could be that the death wasn't even listed as a murder. Or it was considered solved. This guy could be working outside of the local counties for all they knew, especially if the first one was a trigger kill—where he snapped. It could have happened somewhere else if the guy suddenly found himself unable to control the compunction to end a life.

Sarah sank onto the edge of the desk. "I'll look in my files. It's possible someone was overlooked."

"Thanks."

"I should go." Sarah glanced at the thin gold watch on her wrist. "I'm supposed to meet my dad for dinner."

"He lives locally?" Addie had no idea where her mom was these days. Or who she was in a relationship with. It was too hard to keep track when it changed so frequently.

Sarah retrieved her things. "He moved here a few years ago. Persuaded me to do the same."

Addie lifted her chin. "Thanks for coming."

"Anytime." Sarah waved and headed for the hall.

Across the way, the police department had their lights on.

She could see the front desk sergeant typing on a computer, the phone between her shoulder and cheek.

Still no sign of Hank.

Addie didn't know if she was supposed to bug them for an answer on Jacob. Everyone knew about their history. It wasn't as though it would be a shock to anyone if she came across as concerned—which she was.

It would be naïve to believe without a doubt that he hadn't killed Celia. Or any of these women. She couldn't know without a shadow of a doubt without solving the case.

Whoever sent her here might not have known just how tightly connected she was to each of these crimes, but they knew she would have to jump the hurdle of her issues. The drive she had to understand every evil person and why they did what they did would fuel her. Enough to overcome her fears? She wasn't sure, given her reaction to those insects.

Maybe she would always have those triggers.

But having fears didn't stop her from being an FBI agent. If it did, no one would qualify. Still, she felt the need to prove she actually *might* be able to do this alone.

No one in her life would think she could.

The lure of achievement tempted her. Even if the odds were so low she would no doubt fall on her face.

That drive to believe in hope that amounted to a mustard seed had also led her to get burned out. To find a cause for evil, when instead there were too many instances where no explanation existed. Some people were damaged, in certain cases—usually coupled with a particular psychological profile—a person targeted others for no reason at all other than that they could.

But Jake?

She just couldn't believe him capable of something like this. Multiple murders spanning years?

Then again, didn't people who knew—and sometimes loved—serial killers often say they had no idea the person was capable of those horrors? It was why this killer had managed to get away with all these deaths. For years.

Addie put more detail onto her profile. There were still a lot of questions, but she was beginning to be able to fill in the gaps on this thing. That put her a few steps closer to cuffs on a suspect and filed charges.

If he truly had nothing to do with it, Jake would be free.

She didn't want to be doing this for that reason. At least not that reason alone. She was an FBI agent who had every intention of fulfilling the oath she'd taken to operate with integrity and honesty—and no bias.

Addie made a note to find out if any of the others had a broken hyoid. They could have all been choked as a method to subdue them. Then there was this insect bite, always a different creature.

That was some research she didn't particularly want to get into, but maybe the police department or the crime lab had an expert in that stuff, and she could draw from their knowledge. Get a support team going.

Addie sent a couple of emails. She'd had a stilted conversation with her SAC earlier after she missed her meeting because she'd been trapped with Jacob in that fire.

No, don't think about him.

Her mind was like a broken record.

Or she was an addict in her own way, looking for a fix.

Considering her history with alcohol, she might have replaced one vice for another. Her personality hadn't changed, she just found something less obvious to obsess over instead. Yet another thing she needed to fix about herself.

Sometimes it felt insurmountable. She would never be

the person she wanted to be because she had too many issues that had to be fixed.

Not for the first time she considered quitting the FBI to save them the embarrassment of her not being a good agent. Maybe every agent felt like they didn't measure up. But she'd met plenty who thought they were God's gift to the bureau. Given the confidence she'd had in herself that got her crowned homecoming queen had been the same thing that led to her being the victim of a deadly killer—and nearly losing her own life? Addie wasn't all fired up to think she was all that. Not ever again.

Her cell phone rang.

She grabbed it and looked at the screen, but it wasn't Jake. It was that same unknown number. She steeled herself, then swiped to answer. "Special Agent Franklin."

Silence greeted her.

"It's you, isn't it?" She exhaled.

Was she assuming the same killer was whoever tried to run her off the road and then burn her and Jake in his studio? She couldn't prove it was, but she had a theory.

"Nobody has noticed, have they?" She needed him to answer her questions.

But he never did.

She gripped the phone. "You *want* me to find you."

The line went dead.

Only the ticking of the clock and her own exhale could be heard.

22

Jacob's phone buzzed. He had a coupon for the local sub sandwich shop, valid tomorrow. It was after midnight, so he didn't want a sandwich. But he was food shopping. The grocery store wasn't empty. He sidestepped a couple headed for the chips, and went for the freezer section at the back.

It wasn't hard to assume the stares he was getting from staff and customers were about the fingerprint. Except the police probably hadn't released that information. Not much different from the normal attention that came with his high school yearbook photo, enlarged and currently on a book display by the registers. He never used self-checkout, just so he didn't have to walk by it.

Then again, Addie was on the cover right beside him, along with Hank and Becca.

If he wanted to see his friends, maybe he should go look at the book. It was the easiest way to feel that connection and not deal with the drama. As if the dust jacket on a book was anything close to a relationship.

Jacob blew out a long breath.

His life had been fine for years. He'd been content with his work and his quiet home. Why would that be a bad thing? Except it left him wide open for someone to plant his fingerprint on a body and frame him for murder. As if he should be the type of guy to spend the night with some woman he wasn't married to, just for the sake of an alibi. The police understood that he was single, didn't they?

Addie was the only woman he'd...another sigh.

That wasn't worth dragging up in his memories. Church had shown him that he didn't need to feel guilt or shame over the choices they'd made simply because they thought that was what they were supposed to do. Because it was what everyone else did. Instead, there was a better way. One they'd had no clue about, but he did now.

The last thing he wanted was to fall back into that old trap and those old ways of thinking.

This whole situation would test his resolve not to be that guy who relied on his emotions far too much. He wasn't perfect now, but he had the resource to be at peace and stand firm even when he was being accused of murder.

His phone buzzed again. Probably another sandwich coupon. But it was an incoming call, one he answered. "Addie?"

Silence greeted him for a second. "You sound better than you did earlier."

"From the smoke?" He headed down the aisle where coffee was located and added a pack to his basket because he forgot some when he'd been shopping with Addie. No point in ever risking running out of that life-saving brew. "Or the police interrogation?"

"Please tell me what that was about."

"They aren't telling you anything?"

"They know we're connected." Addie sighed. "It's not

that they're deliberately shutting me out, but I'm not one of them. I'm federal. Add that to the connection between us..." She left that statement hanging.

"Maybe everyone else thinks that's bad." He perused the tea even though he wasn't going to buy any, this time or any other. It wasn't as though his mother ever visited his place. "But *I* like the sound of it."

"Me, too."

"I don't have a lot of connections." He hoped she understood what he meant. "Not since you. It's nice to know it's still there."

"It is, isn't it?"

"Do you wonder if it ever left?"

"Sure." Her voice softened. "Maybe we should've done better. Figured it out and stayed together."

"You figure we'd be married with four kids by now?"

"And a dog."

"Ha." He barked a laugh. "No way, two cats. That's non-negotiable."

"Maybe it wouldn't have worked, and we'd have wound up another statistic of divorce. Given your hardline stance on pets." He could hear humor in her voice.

Jacob found himself smiling. Considering the day he'd had, that surprised him. After his livelihood was damaged and almost destroyed, he was labeled the suspect in a murder. Now Addie had him laughing.

He could hardly believe it was possible.

Thank You, Lord.

Her being back in his life might have changed things, but maybe they weren't all for the worse. Some might have been for the better.

He found himself saying, "I guess we'll never know."

He figured there was a chance still that they might find

out. If she stuck around. If they worked at it, and this developed into something. Sure they had chemistry. That was basically all their relationship had been before. Now, if they were going to get into a relationship, he wanted more substance. Except with a murder charge between them, was that likely?

It could be too late for them or just the beginning of something new. With a shadow of what-always-should've-been.

She said, "Hmm," then changed the subject. "Are you okay, after the interview?"

Jacob told her about the fingerprint on the body.

"I hadn't heard that." Her tone wasn't one he could read. He'd need to see her face for the truth.

"I guess the onus is on me to prove someone else planted it there if the police aren't going to investigate anyone else. Maybe they'll just pile all the evidence they have on me, so it looks like I did it." He squeezed the phone, now hot against his cheek. "They might not ever find the real killer. They're so determined to put this on me."

"I'm sorry."

"I know you'd help if you could." Maybe that was an assumption, but he figured it was true enough.

"I should just walk in tomorrow and pull jurisdiction." She hesitated, purposely *not* saying something to him. "Make it my case because it is."

She was investigating cold cases, according to Hank. Jacob didn't know why they'd be related to a murder that only happened a couple of days ago.

"That's sweet, Addie. Thank you for wanting to help. But it'll look too obvious that you're trying to save me if you do it."

"It'll look obvious when I put cuffs on the right guy." She went quiet for a second. "Maybe I can help you."

"How?"

"Let me worry about that."

"Because you know for sure I didn't do this?" Maybe she had proof he could pass to his lawyer. If she disclosed it to him.

Jacob was gauging the kind of special agent she was. He didn't know how far Addie might go to uncover the truth. Did she follow the rules to the letter, or go renegade when it was necessary? Or did she fall somewhere between, depending on the circumstances?

"Jacob." She said nothing else, as though everything he needed to know was contained there.

Maybe it was.

She sighed. "You probably want to get some sleep."

"Are you still at work?"

"For a little longer. You turning in?"

Jacob frowned. "I'm at the store."

"But we already…" There was a long moment of silence and then, "Ah. Pizza night?"

She knew what it meant. Jacob felt that connection buzz like a surge of power in an electricity line. He was a photographer, so he didn't exactly know how that worked, but he'd seen the effects of excess energy that needed to be discharged.

He got two pizzas instead of one. Just in case.

"You had a rough day."

Jacob pressed his lips together. He didn't want to talk about it. That's what pizza was for.

Addie said, "Pepperoni with the cheese in the crust?"

"Is there any other way?" He felt the curve of a smile on

his lips and turned for the middle aisle so he could go check out.

"So it was bad, then. Talking to the cops?"

"Given the fact they found my print on her body?" Did she think he'd be able to just brush that off? "I have to be able to explain it. Someone is framing me, but I can't even say as much because they probably hear that like once a week."

"You kept your head. That's good." Addie said, "The truth will come out."

"Hopefully not after I've served years of a sentence for a crime I did not commit."

"I'm praying for you." She paused. "I'm a little rusty on that front, but desperate times."

He almost stopped in the middle aisle the memory hit him so hard. "Thank you."

The two of them huddled in that cabin. They'd cried out to a God neither of them was sure they believed in back then —not in those dark hours when they'd felt abandoned. But what else did they have to do? It was either accept death or try anything they could think of to figure a way out.

Rescue had come.

Even if he didn't understand why Becca died or why they were the saved kids. The killer had been put in prison—a place the police wanted to put him now as well. Life didn't always make sense.

He just tried to minimize the surprises and disappointments. At least as much as he could.

With Addie here now, he wasn't sure how to do that.

"Want to come over?" Maybe it wasn't a good idea, but the question was out. "Share some late dinner."

She said, "I haven't eaten. I was waiting to hear what happened with you."

"Meet me at my apartment? We can forget about everything, just eat and watch TV." He had a guest room if she ended up there late and didn't want to go home. He'd let people think whatever they wanted. What Jacob did with his life, and the principles he chose to uphold, were his business and no one else's.

Or that was the pizza night talking, and he was just over other people's opinions.

Murder or something illicit. It wouldn't matter that he'd done neither.

He was too tired to fight right now.

"Addie?" He walked through the automatic doors to the outside air, where an icy wind blew. There was no new snow and nothing in the forecast, but it was still freezing enough he had to flip up the collar of his jacket. He'd never been entirely comfortable outside at night but wasn't exactly going to admit to being afraid of the dark.

"Let me wrap up here and text Russ. I'll come over."

"Great." He headed for Grandpa's truck parked in his spot. It reminded him of that first night he'd seen Addie. When she'd nearly died in a hit-and-run, and he'd scurried away like a scared rabbit when the cops came.

He wouldn't be doing that anymore. It was time to stand up for himself and figure out how to get the truth out so he could prove this was a setup.

"See you soon?" Her voice sounded hopeful. Jacob wasn't about to disrespect that. They'd probably have to talk about the morals he'd acquired in the last few years. Get some ground rules.

Did she even want to start something with him?

No doubt it was a terrible idea that would only end in disaster. Given last time, probably not the right path. Still…

A rustle behind him had Jacob spin around to meet whatever it was.

"Jake?"

The dark figure rushed toward him. At the last second, he spotted the glint of a blade.

"Hey—"

The man slashed out and slammed into him. Jacob whipped his arm around. The bag of pizzas and all he'd bought slammed into the man's shoulder.

He was so focused on combatting the attack that he didn't realize what had happened. Not at the first second.

The man drew back.

Jacob heard Addie's voice from a distance. "Jake! What's going on? Jake!"

He stumbled. Fell against his truck and started to slide to the ground. Pain sliced through him like a whip. Branded. Fire. Ice. All of it tore through his abdomen.

He looked down and saw the knife. The blood.

"Addie."

23

"The grocery store. That's what he said," Addie yelled to the interior of her car.

The dispatcher's voice came through the speakers. "An ambulance is already on its way. They'll be there in two minutes."

"I'm already here." Addie swung her wheel to the left and bumped over the incline in the curb into the parking lot.

She hung up the phone with a jab of her finger on the dash screen. Jake's truck was parked in "his" spot. She thanked the man upstairs that Jake had a favorite place to park so she could find him.

But where was he? Addie drove around the front of the truck. No one was inside.

Her foot slipped off the brake. There he was.

She stopped the car with no thought about the white lines or whether she would be blocking traffic. Almost no one was out here, but someone had been. And they'd left Jake for dead on his backside, leaned against the truck.

She nearly fell out of the car but scrambled up and raced

to him. "Jake." A prayer brushed across her lips as she fell to her knees beside him. "Jake, can you hear me?"

The knife stuck out of his abdomen. Blood everywhere.

Don't take it out.

The words rolled through her mind, and she realized that was right. She had to leave the blade there because it plugged the hole in him right now. A surgeon needed to be the one to take it out, preferably in a sterilized room at the hospital.

She realized she'd reached for the handle but held her hands over it without making contact. "Jake." She touched his cheek. "Maybe you shouldn't wake up and feel this. But I do want to see your eyes."

An ambulance siren cut through the night.

Jake let out a groan.

Addie waved over the ambulance so they could get here as quickly as possible. The ambo pulled up, and two uniformed EMTs got out. One was a tiny African American woman with braids pulled back who grabbed a duffel and raced over. The other was a blonde man who retrieved a yellow backboard.

"Hurry."

The woman got to Addie first. "Hey, you found him?"

"He's my friend. We were on the phone when someone —" The cameras. Addie's head whipped around to the light pole with the device mounted to it. Whoever did this would be on camera.

The woman lifted the stethoscope from Jacob's chest and wrapped them around her neck. "I'm guessing he was stabbed."

Her colleague knelt on the other side of Addie.

The woman waved them into action. "Let's pack this and get him to the ED."

Addie frowned. "Don't you mean ER?"

The woman tore open two packs at once. "They don't call it that anymore. It's the emergency department now."

"Oh." Was that really the point here?

The EMT held gauze down on either side of the blade. Her colleague handed over more. Then they taped the gauze down tight so the blade wasn't going to move around while they loaded him in the ambulance.

"He's going to be okay, right?"

The woman frowned. "You did good calling us so fast, getting us out here. The rest is up to him, the doctors, and the Good Lord."

"That's true, I suppose," Addie said.

Her partner's jaw flexed. "Whatever."

The female EMT shot him a look. "Let's get this guy loaded." She looked at Addie. "I'm Freya."

"Addie Franklin." She figured it wouldn't hurt for them to know. "FBI Special Agent."

The guy whistled, but she wasn't sure he wasn't being sarcastic.

Freya motioned. "That's Trey. He's always like this. It's not just you." She reached for the yellow backboard. "Time to roll."

They slid Jacob onto the board, and the two EMTs loaded him in the ambulance. Freya called out, "Meet you there!"

The doors slammed shut.

Addie looked down at her hands and realized there was blood on both. She lifted her arm and used the sleeve over her bicep to wipe the tears on her face. *Jacob.* Back in her car, she couldn't quite get her fingers to turn the key without slipping off. She hissed a breath and let some more tears fall.

What did it matter?

She couldn't help Jake. The hospital staff had to do that.

She hadn't been able to stop the cops from taking him in for questioning. She couldn't prove—yet—that it wasn't him who'd murdered all those women. She hadn't been with him here, on a grocery store trip where she figured the last thing on his mind was that he'd be stabbed.

Who had done this?

Addie pulled the keys out and put them in her pocket. She retrieved her gun in its holster from her glove box, and her badge and credentials. Jacket from the backseat.

She suited up just as a black and white pulled into the lot. Addie knew how close to the edge of breaking down she was, so instead of waiting for them to get out she strode for the front doors of the grocery store.

The beat of feet on the asphalt raced up behind her. She was so mad she didn't even turn around.

"This seems familiar." He tugged on her arm, although it was pretty gentle. Little more than a suggestion.

Addie spun around.

"Oh." Officer Hummet blinked. He looked down at her hands, then back up to her face. "Your friend who ditched you last time?" His eyebrow rose, as though he was unimpressed.

"Turns out he was right to, since your *captain* is trying to pin a murder on him."

Hummet didn't even blink. Beyond him was another officer, older, who'd only just caught up. Eric lifted a brow. "And your role here?"

"To see if whoever stabbed Jake is on the security cameras."

"That would be our job." Hummet motioned to his partner. "On account of we don't need to be at the hospital until your friend wakes up so we can get his statement."

"I'm not a bad person because I want to check the cameras first." She folded her arms. "We need to know who did this."

Hummet nodded. "Okay. You're welcome to observe."

Addie opened her mouth to argue.

"That's my final answer." He studied her. "Don't make me call you ma'am."

"Come on." Addie spun to the doors and found the same office where they'd looked at the feeds what seemed like weeks ago but was actually only a couple of days.

Hummet went inside the office to talk with the security guy.

His partner, who didn't give her his name and she couldn't read it on his shirt as there was a smudge of something yellow on it, stood in the hall watching her. Eating an apple pie he'd acquired from somewhere.

"So you're the fed?" He took a bite that amounted to a third of the pie.

Addie said, "That's what they tell me."

Thankfully Eric exited the office then.

"Well?"

Officer Hummet's expression had darkened, his young face like someone who'd seen too much. *Not good.* "Can't see his face, but we'll run with what we've got."

"Or, the second you report this it's going to get handed to some detective with six open cases on his desk. And the victim is a suspect in a murder?" She could guess who had the motive to do this, but her and Jake's lives had never been that simple.

"I'll make sure this is looked into. All of it above board."

Officer Apple Pie didn't seem to think that was a good idea. Or he just didn't care because it would cut into his lunch break.

Addie figured that meant she needed to leave. Before she said something that would get her in even more hot water with the PD. "Find out who did this."

Hummet didn't promise anything, but she knew he couldn't do that. Some cases went unsolved. Others, an FBI agent specializing in profiling who knew the local area and some of the people who lived here, were called in.

She headed for her car, all of it and the adrenaline racing through her mind. Her body wanted to break into a run to get rid of the excess energy. Her hands didn't stop shaking.

Someone had ordered her sent here. But the second she got here, those hang-up calls and heavy breathing silences turned into actual attacks. Like the same person was responsible.

He'd herded her into danger.

Had he done the same to get her back in Benson? The FBI had sent her, officially, so how was that possible? She couldn't help but wonder if it was the case. Whoever wanted her here so all this could happen was likely also responsible for the murders. Though, she needed proof if anyone else was going to believe her. She had to figure out who it was.

Could she find out who had been involved in persuading the FBI to send her here? Or they'd faked the request.

She needed more information.

In her car, Addie sent Zimmerman an email he would get first thing tomorrow asking for a name. Who had requested her to be reassigned to Benson? It wasn't the Seattle office. Even with the mayor's brother being a senator, the mayor and the cops here didn't have that much pull. The answer seemed more than that. Someone in DC had to have put it through, pulled the strings, and done this.

And how did they connect to a string of local murders?

Then she called Russ.

He answered on the first ring. "Hey."

"I figured you'd be asleep."

"What happened?"

Of course, he knew something was wrong. Addie explained, then said, "I'm headed to the hospital now so I can be there when he wakes up."

"I'll call Hank and meet you."

"Yes." She hadn't even thought of Hank. "Good idea. See you soon."

Ten minutes later, she pulled into a spot at Benson General and raced for the front desk in the emergency department. "I'm looking for information on Jacob Wilson. He was just brought in. Stab wound to the abdomen." She flashed her badge.

"I'll let the doctor know you're here." The woman picked up her desk phone.

"Thanks." Addie paced the waiting area. Avoided the pockets of people looking exhausted and distraught. Two people at separate corners seemed like they needed to be in bed on an IV bag, not out.

Someone had sent her here. Walking her right into a killer's hands.

Her and Jacob.

The doors swished open, and Hank raced in. "Addie!" He hugged her, and she gave herself a second to let go of her composure.

"Officer Hummet checked the security tapes at the grocery store. He said there wasn't enough to identify the person who stabbed Jake."

Hank squeezed the bridge of his nose. "This is unbelievable."

"Yeah? A retaliation crime on the same day Jake is questioned for a murder?"

"You don't know that's what this is." Hank frowned.

The doors opened again, and Russ entered, followed by Mona. Her uncle squeezed her shoulder while her sister hung back.

"You wanted to come?"

Mona shrugged.

Russ frowned. "She doesn't get the responsibility of being at home alone right now."

"If we have time, you guys can tell me about that."

Mona rolled her eyes.

Russ nodded. "I could use a good cop for this routine."

"I doubt you'll get that from me right now." She needed good news. Then she'd be able to relax.

Mona rolled her eyes. "Whatever."

"A friend of mine was stabbed. He could die." Addie shook her head. "Maybe you could have some compassion."

Mona wandered to a chair and sat but didn't pull out her phone. Grounded from that as well?

"I'll talk to her." Hank headed over.

Russ didn't back down. "It'll pass. Soon as she gets it out of her head that a twenty-five-year-old isn't dating a seventeen-year-old that lives under my roof."

Before she could respond that she agreed, a doctor walked over. "You're here for Jacob Wilson?"

24

She sat by his bedside with her head tipped to the side, asleep on the chair. He watched her until he felt the need to shift his legs and adjust his position.

Jacob realized immediately that was a terrible idea.

A groan slipped from his lips. He tried to complete the move anyway, so he didn't end up awkwardly tipped to one side. It didn't get any better. He practically had to Lamaze breathe through it, unable to think about anything else for a second.

"Hey, hey." She touched his arm. "Easy. You need to take it easy."

He let his body slump where it was, totally spent. "Addie?"

She pushed hair back from her face, and he saw the dark circles under her eyes.

"Hey."

She frowned. "I should tell the nurse you're awake."

Jacob stalled her with a hand on his arm. There was a tube in his arm. "What happened?"

He didn't want to think about it. His abdomen burned

like fire, but the last thing Jake needed was to contemplate the origin of all that pain. He didn't even know what time it was or what day.

"You don't remember?"

He tried to squeeze her hand, but his grip remained as weak as a newborn kitten's. "Say it."

Addie leaned on the rail at the side of the bed and leaned down. "You're safe, and you'll heal."

He stared at her face like he could drink it in. Was she going to kiss him? He wouldn't mind, but his mouth tasted like he'd licked the bottom of his running shoe.

"You were stabbed." She touched his cheek. "I found you a few minutes after, and I'm happy it wasn't worse than it is." Relief washed over her face. "The surgeon sewed you up, inside and out. All that's left is to rest and heal."

She leaned down and touched her lips to his forehead.

"Addie." Her name was a groan, all he could muster.

"I know. I'll be back in a second."

Jacob drifted back into sleep. All his energy drained.

He roused for a short conversation with the doctor, where Addie held his hand and kept looking at him with those reassuring glances. As though she fully intended to take care of him.

He figured he owed her the chance to do that if it was what she wanted. He'd never take that grace for granted. The idea that after he'd broken things off with her, following the worst time in their lives, she'd give him the honor of wanting to be with him again. Even just as friends? Jacob was willing to take whatever he could get.

The light in the room had dimmed when he opened his eyes again.

A dark figure stood by the window.

Jacob's head swam. "Who…?"

Where was Addie?

Panic rolled through him. Too many crazy things had happened lately for him to be at peace when he couldn't help himself. He'd have no choice but to pray and ask God to protect him and Addie.

Jacob tried to gather his strength enough to say, "What do you want?"

The man turned.

He tried to see the face. Was it the man who stabbed him?

Jacob's world descended to black, and when he woke again the room was washed with light.

"Addie." He blinked the room into focus. "Addie!"

The door flung open, and she rushed in, a paper cup in her hand. She set it on the side of the bed.

"Hey." She leaned down close.

"I need water."

"Okay." She found a cup with a straw, and he drank the entire thing. "The doctor is coming in soon. They were going to uh…disconnect you from some things. And check you over."

He felt its sensation and didn't want to talk about his bodily functions with this woman. Or any woman. Or any doctor, but he figured he'd have to come face-to-face with reality while *someone* was in the room.

Jacob frowned. "Someone was in the room."

Addie looked around. "It's just me."

"No." Jacob shook his head. "Someone was here. In the dark."

Her expression shuttered. "Do you know who it was?" The question had a guarded tone.

Jacob didn't have the mental capacity to analyze it. He just liked looking at her.

"Jake, who was here in the dark?"

"I don't know."

She squeezed his shoulder. "I'm going to get the nurse again and talk to the officer on the door."

He did not want to see the captain. "McCauley?"

"Eric Hummet."

"I don't know him."

"He's good. We've made friends."

Jacob frowned.

Addie kissed him with her smile. "I'm not being naïve, but I'm trusting him."

"Okay." Didn't mean he had to like it.

"I'll be back soon."

Jacob watched her go.

The longer she was gone, the more he tried not to grumble about it. The doctor came in. He was given more instructions, and they reiterated everything done to put all his innards back together. Maybe he would remember.

The nurse did her thing so he could pee in private again.

Addie didn't come back in for that, which was good. When someone left—or showed up—a couple of times, the door opened, and he caught a glimpse of her in the hallway.

He didn't want to think about that man in the dark of the room.

Or the one in the parking lot.

He wanted to be in the light today and worry about the rest later. He was going to worry about *all of it* later. When he could move without nearly screaming. When cops didn't factor in his life—except one beautiful one.

"Hey." Her face swam in front of his. "You're pretty out of it."

"You're just pretty."

He heard the exhale that accompanied her smile. "Jake?"

"Yeah?" He reached up with his hand not tethered to meds and touched her cheek. Ran his hand into her hair.

"Did you see who stabbed you?"

He shook his head. "Don't talk about that."

"Jake, I need you to tell me."

"Don't remember." That was a good answer.

"Is that true?"

He pressed his lips together.

"Tell me."

He said nothing.

"The police are going to bring in whoever it is. We can't have someone who would hurt another person like that, leave them to bleed out on the ground…" She cleared her throat. "Walking around free. It isn't right."

So much pain. Not his, but the grief of the man who had done it.

Jacob had seen it in his eyes as the knife went in. Not anger, just pain.

"Who was it?"

He swallowed. "Celia's father."

Instead of rushing out to tell the police, she touched her forehead to his. "It's going to be okay."

"Tell him I didn't kill her."

"I know, honey." Addie kissed his forehead.

Jacob shut his eyes. She slipped away and he heard the door shut.

Even though he wanted to think of nothing but her—not the pain, not anything but Addie. Still thoughts crept in like those bugs in the vent. He felt them come and couldn't help the burn of tears at what Celia's family had suffered.

Sure, they were convinced he'd killed her. The fact he hadn't didn't mean anything to them when their daughter was dead.

Jacob felt the tear roll down his face, swiped it away, and realized he needed to shave a couple of days ago. Still, thoughts of that man's eyes right before the knife slid into Jacob's stomach.

The nightmare was worse.

Days later, when they released him, Jacob didn't see Addie until he was wheeled outside to the curb. The sun had set behind the high rises of downtown. A siren blazed past, and an ambulance pulled into the corner bay at high speed.

"Ready?"

He glanced over at her. She'd gotten some sleep after he sent her home, so she didn't spend the night in that awful chair again. Jacob nodded. "Where's Hank?"

Addie helped him out of the chair. "No one's seen him. He didn't call into work, but the consensus is he's out looking for the guy who stabbed you. Or the guy's wife, because she packed her things, and no one has seen her either. We think they're together."

He concentrated on her voice so he didn't have to think about how much it hurt to walk. Maybe they shouldn't be letting him go home so soon. He was useless. All he could do was lay in bed. Doing that at home was preferable to hospitals full of noise and people twenty-four seven.

"Okay. Legs?"

Jacob lifted his feet and folded them into the car.

"We can fill your prescription on the way. Get you the pill you'll need in…" She looked at her watch. "Two hours."

He could wait that long. It would hurt, but he could do it. He just needed a distraction. "Tell me what else has been going on."

"Home front first." Addie pulled out of the pickup lane and headed for the exit. "Mona and Russ got into it. Her boyfriend is twenty-five. Can you believe that? She's seventeen. It's crazy. Anything you can imagine; she's been doing it." Addie made a face. "Russ is *so mad*. He's taken away her phone, her car. He drives her to school and work, then home."

Jacob winced.

"Yeah. That was a fun couple of days."

"What else?"

"The field office in Seattle sent a team of two agents over yesterday. I've got backup, and they're hot on the case."

Jacob glanced at her.

"Okay, so they don't like me, and they don't like Benson. Apparently, they want to be in the *big city*."

"Okay."

She smiled. "Doesn't matter. I want this thing solved, and I'm done with either of us being strung along in the middle. So it is what it is, and I took two personal days. Who knows what the two of them will have figured out by the time I'm back in the office in a day or two? Right now, I'm here to help you. Work can take care of itself."

"Is that a good idea?"

"It's the right idea. I don't care if the FBI disagrees." She gripped the wheel with both hands. "You were *stabbed*."

"Is Hank really missing?"

"I'm sorry." She winced. "I even pinged his phone and got nothing."

She pulled into the garage in the basement of his building. Jacob thought about standing in the elevator for long enough to get upstairs and wanted to stay in the car rather than do that. It sounded exhausting, and he was ready for a nap at this point.

Addie pulled to a stop beside another vehicle. Russ got out of his truck.

Jacob quickly realized it was *his* truck, not the old marshal's.

The graveled older man pulled a wheelchair from the bed of the truck and set it beside Jacob's door.

He was pretty proud that he got into it by himself without crying.

Addie wheeled him to the elevator, and Russ hauled his stuff. They piled in, and Addie used his key to get them into his floor.

As soon as the doors opened, he knew something was wrong.

Russ stepped out first. "Door's open."

Addie shifted. "We can see that, Russ."

Jacob just stared. Addie pushed him over, and he nudged the door.

Addie let out a long breath. "The whole place is trashed."

Russ frowned. "PD?"

"They'll need to get the crime lab up here to dust for prints. Figure out who did this." She shifted. "Jacob?"

He could only stare at the mess. His home. His private space. Someone had come in and tossed it.

She laid a hand on his shoulder. "We'll pack a few things, what you need for a couple of days."

Jacob swallowed. "Where am I—"

Russ leveled him with a look. "You're staying with us."

25

Addie eased the door open and looked in. She'd been staying in this room but brought Jacob in as soon as they got here. He wasn't going to sleep in their home office, and neither was Russ. Addie on the other hand fit fine on Russ's thinking couch.

She watched for a second and tracked the rise and fall of his chest under the blankets. The guy had been wiped out by the time they got a few things from his apartment, dealt with the cops, and drove here from downtown.

"He good?"

She eased the door closed. Russ stood in the hallway. She followed him back to the kitchen where Mona made coffee. "He's resting at least."

The teen glanced over her shoulder at them but didn't interrupt.

Russ pulled out a chair and eased into it. One day, it would hit her that he was getting old, but there was something timeless about his age for now. He didn't look or act much different than he had before she left town the last time.

"What did the cops say?"

Addie dropped Russ and Jake at the house, turned around, and went straight back to the apartment. "Signs that the lock was picked or whoever had a key missed the slot and scratched up the chrome. Security says Jake's key card was used to access the floor from the elevator, but they also told me there are a couple of copies of the card floating around. One spare, and at least one that Jake lost at some point."

"Anything stolen?"

"Nothing obvious." Addie paused while Mona sat at the table. "But he'll have to go through everything and see what's missing."

"Good call getting his things for him, not wheeling him through there. He didn't need to see that."

Addie nodded.

"Who do you think did it?" Mona's question was soft, and for once without that tone of adolescence that crept into her words.

Addie shrugged. "That's an excellent question, and I hope the police figure it out."

Mona shifted. All of Addie's cop instincts flared. She had to go about this gently, or the teen would shut down.

Carefully, Addie said, "Is there anything you want to talk about, Sis?"

Mona stared at the table. Ran her thumb nail back and forth across a grain in the wood.

"You can tell us anything. I want you to know that." Addie paused. "I'm not a cop at this table. I'm more like your lawyer or your therapist. There's a confidentiality clause."

It might be a privilege that she needed Mona not to abuse, but that was a bridge they'd cross if they had to. All depended on what her little sister wanted to tell her.

Addie fought the temptation to keep talking. To apologize for being absent so much, try to convince Mona that things would change. Since Addie didn't know how long she would be here, she couldn't make promises.

She wasn't about to spout a bunch of stuff that sounded nice but would amount to lies. The teen didn't need more of that when their mother was an expert.

Addie wondered when their mom had visited last.

"I do need to tell you something." Mona focused on Addie.

This was about her? "What is it?"

More thumb across the table. Addie was just about to prompt her when Mona spoke quietly. "It's about Austin."

Russ made a noise in his throat. He really didn't like the boyfriend.

Considering the guy was eight years older than the high schooler at the table, Addie was inclined to agree. She'd already planned to have a talk with Austin when the case was done.

Maybe it couldn't wait.

Mona chewed on the words for a second. "He knows all about what happened. To you and Jake. Back in high school." She stiffened in the chair.

"It's okay." Addie wasn't going to jump on the girl. That would only cause Mona to shut down, and Addie didn't need her sister to be gun-shy about talking to them.

Russ kept his mouth shut, thankfully. They all knew well how he felt about the boyfriend. He was a little more trigger-happy with getting mad.

He'd cut his teeth on raising Addie. As far as she was concerned, he'd done the best job he knew how. Raising Mona was something he'd done since early in her life, unlike having teenage Addie dropped on his doorstep for weeks or months at a time while her mom traveled around with her latest boyfriend. Eventually around middle school they'd sat her mom down and told her Addie wasn't going with her next time.

Mona winced. "He's kind of obsessed with what happened to you. He has newspaper clippings and photos. Stuff I don't think he's supposed to have. Like pictures of that girl Becca, you know…after she was dead."

Addie glanced at Russ. That wasn't right. "Any idea where he got them from?"

Russ just lifted an eyebrow. He hadn't gotten anywhere with the girl and was leaving this to Addie. Something she was grateful for.

"He wouldn't say." Mona shrugged one shoulder.

The coffee pot beeped now the carafe was full, but no one got up.

Mona shifted in her seat. "He's weird about it. I don't know why, but it's like that's all he thinks about. He's supposed to be taking classes to finish his degree and he calls in sick to work all the time. He doesn't even care he'll probably get fired."

Addie figured that was why Mona had so many days of missed school. The lure of a relationship was powerful, especially when you were seventeen and controlled by hormones.

She knew that as well as anyone. She'd made those same mistakes.

Maybe it was in the blood they got from their mother.

Rather than assuming she'd learned from missteps, Addie was only willing to admit she'd pushed all that aside when she left for college. When she joined the FBI. The fling with Zimmerman had been the closest thing to a real relationship since Jake. And she'd hardly even allowed her emotions to get involved.

Just every other part of her.

She had begun to realize those choices weren't the most constructive thing if she wanted peace or hope for the future. It was far too easy to let her life self-destruct for a few moments of happiness.

The most challenging part was figuring out how to do things differently.

Russ would tell her to go to church. If she was honest, he wasn't often wrong. Probably she should give it a try at least. It seemed like going back to service was a good start.

As soon as she had the time to attend. Maybe Jake would go with her, or she could go with him—since he attended.

Mona glanced at Russ. "I didn't know how to break it off. Austin was getting kind of…smothering. Then he was spending a lot of time with his ex. I wanted to end it, so thanks for forcing me to get out."

Russ squeezed her hand. "It's what I'm here for."

Addie didn't need them to get off track. "Any idea where he is?"

"I knew you were going to do this." Mona's eyes flashed.

Addie figured there was no way to sugarcoat it. "I was nearly burned alive by someone with knowledge of what happened to Jake and me. If he didn't do anything, then he has nothing to hide with me asking a few questions."

Russ lifted his chin. "Want some backup?"

Addie shook her head. "I need someone here to make sure nothing happens to Jake."

And Mona, but the girl would bristle if she thought Addie was purposely "taking care of her." Which, of course, she was, whether Mona knew it or not.

"Take backup with you." His tone didn't invite any argument.

Mona leaned back in her chair. "And if I don't tell you where he is?"

"It'll take me only slightly longer to find him."

The teen pressed her lips together.

"Where is he?"

"Fine." Mona blew out a breath. "He stays at that cabin sometimes." She winced. "The one where you were held."

Addie tried not to react, but this guy was a real winner. Mona had fallen for it. Not that Addie could blame her, since poor choices about men happened to every woman at some point in their life. Especially the women in their family.

"That's where he is now?" Addie asked.

Mona shrugged. Nodded.

Addie pulled out her phone and opened her email. She asked Mona a few more questions and got his last name, date of birth, and phone number. She sent all of it to the two agents who'd shown up from Seattle—Kyle and Stella.

Addie pushed back her chair. "Got any to-go cups for that coffee?"

Russ stood as well. "I'll get you one."

They met at the front door, and Russ handed her a thermos.

"Thanks." Addie slipped on her coat.

"I was serious about that backup."

Addie kissed his cheek. "I'll make some calls on the way."

He watched her drive away. Addie used her dash screen to call Hank. It rang for a while, then went to voicemail. She left him a message to call her but didn't tell him where she was going. Maybe Hank didn't care. He was busy looking for Celia's father.

Both were missing, along with Celia's mother, as far as she was concerned.

"What are you doing, Hank?" Addie sighed, then called Captain McCauley.

He picked up before the second ring.

"Busy?"

"Too busy to talk to the FBI? No, ma'am." For a second, she wondered if he'd been drinking. "Especially not when every time I turn around, something has happened to you. It's definitely been an interesting couple of weeks."

"Nice change from the normal pace?" she asked.

"Sure, as long as things go back after."

Addie wasn't sure that would happen. She told him where she was headed and why, and McCauley said, "I'll be there in fifteen. I don't live far."

"Sure?"

"You gonna go in alone if I don't show up?"

Addie wasn't going to answer that.

McCauley got the idea. "Exactly. So it's good you called."

"Russ made me."

McCauley snorted. "I'll be there."

"Copy that."

The gate was open when she pulled in two top 40 songs later, making her wonder if Lyric ever closed it. Did she leave it that way so customers could come and go as they pleased? Addie didn't spot the captain's car.

Addie turned the volume down on her music. She flipped off her headlights so there would be no glare on the cabin windows to wake anyone and eased toward the structure.

Close enough to see that the door was ajar.

Addie parked and sent a text to McCauley. He still had a couple of minutes before he would get here. If someone were inside and hurt, they might not have time for her to wait. Addie needed to at least look.

She pulled on a vest from her trunk and fastened the straps, then slid her gun from the holster on her hip. A badge on display. Just in case anyone had a question about who she was—or her reason for being there.

First was to listen.

No sound came from inside.

Addie used a free hand to ease the door open. The creak cut through the dark, quiet night. Inside, the cabin looked normal but like it needed cleaning. Not the destruction that had been evident at Jake's apartment. This place hadn't been ransacked like that.

Still at the door, she looked everywhere within eyeshot without going in, which she would do with McCauley when he got here. She didn't see anyone, and there was still no sound. No one cried out for help.

Addie had to hold back for now and wait.

She started to turn and look for McCauley's car when someone rushed from the house and slammed into her.

Addie fell back, stumbled off the porch steps, and hit the ground.

A dark figure jumped over her and ran.

26

Addie rolled over on the ground. Arms stretched out on the ground in front of her. She aimed at the fleeing figure, her finger on the trigger.

A door opened across what amounted to a cul-de-sac. An older man in a bathrobe stood with light behind him, silhouetted in the glow from inside his cabin. Addie moved her finger off the trigger of her weapon.

The guy who'd shoved her off the porch raced between two cabins and disappeared into the dark.

"Special Agent Franklin!"

Addie winced. She clambered to her feet, the gun at her side.

In jeans and a hooded sweatshirt, McCauley came over to her, one hand on his holstered pistol, a thunderous expression on his face. "What just happened?"

"He shoved me and ran. He's fast." Addie touched the back of her hair and winced.

"You need an ambulance?"

"No." She didn't shake her head. Instead, she turned to the cabin.

McCauley's hand landed on her shoulder. "Ready."

Addie stepped into the cabin and swept left to right.

The place was one open-plan living and dining area with the kitchen in the left corner. One door at the far end. "That was locked."

It had been. She and Jake had tried to get out during a time where they'd been free—not tied to chairs.

She shook her head, dissipating memories. "Clear."

"Clear." McCauley motioned to the door secured by padlock the last time she was here.

Addie avoided the memories that tried to surface when she looked around and grasped the handle. McCauley stood ready. She opened the door and covered him while he went in first.

"Clear."

She stepped after him into the room. "Bathroom?"

He nodded. They repeated the sequence where he opened the door and her going first, which meant she got hit with the smell before he did. The sharp tang that meant fresh blood.

McCauley shifted behind her. The proximity made all her instincts fire, but she shoved off the tension that would only get worse. "We need the ME and the crime lab. Officers to secure the scene."

"Copy that."

Addie took a step back, out of the bathroom. She checked under the bed and in the closet, unwilling to deal with any surprises from anywhere. There had been far too many of those since she got back.

Captain McCauley seemed like a decent guy and a good cop—except he hadn't pushed back when the finger of suspicion pointed at Jake. But she didn't know him. Couldn't trust him.

She grabbed her phone and sent Mona a text. Asked for a photo of this Austin guy she'd been seeing. Addie tried to feel sympathy, but when the guy was a messed-up predator at best and at worst something far darker, she wasn't exactly going to get upset he could very well be the man dead in the bathroom.

The text came back seconds later. A shot of Mona and the guy Russ had restricted her from seeing.

Addie winced.

"What is it?"

She enlarged the picture to show only Austin and turned the phone to McCauley.

"You know this guy?"

Addie moved into the bathroom. Holstered her gun as she went. The bathtub was full, though the level remained four inches from the top. The occupant's identity had yet to be confirmed.

"Nasty."

Addie agreed with McCauley's observation. "This needs to be confirmed by the ME, but it's him."

The man in the bathtub had his head and shoulders out of the tub, the torso covered in cuts and slashes. Defensive wounds on his forearms, where the knife had cut him as he lifted his hands. Tried to fight off the attacker.

Blood-soaked water had spilled on the floor and tracked onto the rug.

Addie crouched. "Might be a footprint."

"You gonna tell me this guy's name at least?" McCauley set a hand on his waist.

She wasn't sure how to answer without making it clear someone close to her who knew Austin. Her association with Jake hadn't helped either of them.

"I have an informant." They'd find out soon enough it

was her sister. "That's why I knew this guy was obsessed with what happened to Jake and me."

McCauley said nothing.

Addie turned to get a read on him just in case she needed to protect herself. But the look on his face was something else. "What?"

"Just figured you're probably counting it a good thing there's no way I can pin this on Jake."

"Do you want to?" The guy was laid up in bed with stitches in his belly. Both her and McCauley knew there was no way he could've done this.

"Honestly? It depends how long this guy has been dead."

Addie bit back what she wanted to say. Was it worth telling him that Jake didn't do this in no uncertain terms? She doubted he'd believe her even if he couldn't have—considering his injury.

The police in Benson would consider her compromised by her association with Jake. Maybe they already did.

Okay, fine. They *definitely* did.

McCauley worked his mouth back and forth.

"What is it?"

"Fine." He sighed. "We think the fingerprint was planted on Celia's body. It didn't get there by accident."

Addie wondered how long she should wait before requesting the Benson Police Department offer Jacob an apology.

She'd figure it out later. Right now they had a dead young man to deal with. "This guy wasn't killed too long ago."

"How'd you know?"

"Aside from the fact that guy shoved me off the porch? Most likely the killer, and not an opportunist." She let that hang like a question even though it hadn't necessarily been one. "The water in the bathtub is still warm."

McCauley's head snapped around to the tub.

Addie walked from the bathroom with a satisfied grin on her face. She'd seen the steam coming up from the water, which apparently the captain hadn't. No way could they pin this on Jake. Not if Austin had been killed recently enough, the water in the bath hadn't even had a chance to cool.

That made her feel better than anything else had in a long time.

Jacob would recover. Hopefully, by the time he'd done that, she'd have cleared up who the real culprit was for Celia Jessop's murder.

Or the rest of her team would have.

She had to at least admit to herself that this was far beyond personal. Stella and Kyle, the two agents who'd been sent over from the field office, would be taking the lead.

The string of as-yet-unsolved murders were cases she would work like a professional. The only issue was that anything even remotely connected to Jake was a blind spot of personal involvement where her emotions had no anchor and simply jumped to his side of things.

Her mind might be able to consider logic and reason where he was concerned. Her heart? Different story.

The FBI agents who'd been sent to help her could keep things grounded. She didn't need to be at the forefront in this. No matter what that did for her prospects of a promotion, or coveted assignment, or whatever this whole thing was about.

That stuff wasn't even on her radar, not when she was back in Benson. This place enveloped everything. It was why she'd left in the first place.

She wandered to the fireplace. The flames were low,

headed for a smolder. The corner of a printed page lay in the ash, partially burned. Addie pulled a pen from her pocket and used it to shift the page over. Beneath it was a photo—her photo. The image of her that occupied her personnel file with the FBI.

"Anything?"

Addie straightened out of the crouch. "Yeah, the crime lab will need to see what they can salvage."

"You think it's connected to Celia and the open cases?"

She scrunched up her nose for a second. "Doesn't fit the MO. It might turn out there are enough correlations it's the same guy, but I'm guessing this wasn't planned." She could rule him out as the accomplice. "He would've been a kid when Jake and I were seniors."

"We can find his phone, pull his call history and the messages we're able to salvage. Dig into his social accounts. See what we can find."

Addie circled the room again to see if the killer might've taken something of Austin's. Cleaned up yet more evidence. She doubted it was Austin who set that fire, but it might not be possible to tell either way.

Addie lifted the couch skirt and looked underneath. The crime techs would search every inch of the cabin, but she didn't like standing around doing nothing until they showed up.

"Anything?"

She settled into her crouch and pulled her phone for the flashlight. What was illuminated gave her the answer. "Yes."

"Gloves?"

She turned to him. "You have some on you?"

McCauley handed over a pair. "Grabbed them from the car when I called it in. Reinforcements should be here in a few. Then how do you feel about searching for whoever ran off?"

"Not sure how far we'll get. Whoever they are, they're probably long gone by now."

"Worth a look. Maybe they dropped their wallet."

Addie tugged the phone from under the couch and straightened. "That happen to you a lot?"

McCauley shrugged. "I've been a cop a long time. You'd be surprised."

"Were you on the force when…" She didn't even want to say it aloud. Not when things were so fresh.

They always looked different in the light of day. But standing here in the same cabin? She had to fight the shudders even if it looked nothing like the same one where they were held. The walls were different. The floor, the kitchen and all the furniture. She could almost pretend she'd never been in here before.

Except for the window.

Addie couldn't fight it off anymore and shuddered.

"You found a phone?"

She handed it to McCauley. "Not sure what we're gonna do if we need his fingerprint to unlock it."

"How about your informant? Maybe they know the code."

Addie sent her sister a message. "Just so you don't think I'm hiding anything from you, this guy is my little sister's boyfriend. Russ made her break up with him a couple days ago."

"You think she'll consent to an interview?"

"Ask Russ. She's seventeen."

"Understood."

Addie's phone buzzed. She deciphered the message. "Show me the screen." What came up was a grid of dots to draw a pattern. She slid her finger across in the way Mona had described and the phone unlocked. "Guess it's his."

She moved so she could see the phone over his shoulder.

McCauley pulled up the messages. "Not much that's recent except the ones from 'Mom.'"

"What about calls?"

He tapped the phone icon and pulled up recent calls in and out. "Huh."

One was from tonight. "What is it?"

"That prefix is usually PD phones."

Addie used her own phone to dial the unlabeled number in Austin's phone. In hers it came up assigned to a name. "Hank Maxwell." She registered the time of the call and looked up at McCauley. "Any reason your detective would have direct contact with a victim in the last hours of his life?"

"Could be several reasons."

"Tell me the last time you saw Hank Maxwell."

McCauley hedged.

"You have no idea where he is."

"Doesn't matter. Whatever he does, he's covered."

Addie figured that was a brotherhood way of operating as cops. But if the person in question had committed a crime, how far did they go to keep it under wraps? Perhaps years, and the offender had a list of people he'd murdered when the urge overcame him, and he couldn't avoid it any longer.

Red and blue flashing lights lit up the front window and open door.

Addie lifted her chin to convey everything McCauley needed to know in her expression. Cop to cop, if that phone disappeared or Hank's number was suspiciously absent from the call list when it was logged as evidence? They were going to have more issues between them than they already did.

"Thanks for coming out here with me. I appreciate the backup." Addie could see she'd surprised him with that but didn't drag it out.

She took a step toward the door. "I'll go wake the owner. Let her know what happened."

27

Jacob didn't care how much it hurt. He needed coffee.

That didn't mean he planned to stand for much longer than it took to walk from the bedroom Addie had used as a kid to the kitchen.

If he pulled up a chair to the counter, he'd have to stretch to pour a cup. That wouldn't be a good idea unless it was a stool.

This was far too much thinking.

One hand braced on the hallway wall, Jacob shuffled old man steps to the kitchen. The coffee pot light was on, and the pot was half full. He felt the hot burn of tears behind his eyes and told himself it was only about needing another dose of meds soon.

Jacob leaned his side against the counter. He braced his weight with one hand as though the granite was a crutch. He got a mug, and slammed it down too hard on the counter. Pushed out a breath.

"Sit." Russ's gruff voice echoed across the kitchen. "Let me do that."

Jacob wasn't sure he could make it to the chair. Thankfully, Russ caught his elbows and helped him lower his behind into a chair. Jacob hissed out a breath.

"There you go. Milk?"

"Black." Jacob cleared his throat.

"Sugar?"

"Half, please."

"Coming right up."

Jacob sniffed again. This was ridiculous. He felt like a baby. "Thanks, Russ. For this and letting me stay here."

The older man turned and set the mug down. "Seriously?"

"I appreciate it."

Russ pulled out a chair and sat with a mug of his own. "The kind of man who wouldn't invite you into my home like this, or at any other time? That's not the man I want to be."

Jacob nodded. He started drinking the coffee and wound up gulping half of it in one go even though it was hot. He looked at the clock.

"Said she'll be back soon."

Jake didn't bother acknowledging that. "So, what's new?"

"You really want to talk about me?"

"I want to talk about *anything* that doesn't have to do with murder or attacks."

"Fair enough." Russ swigged from his own mug. "I'm working with a couple of friends. More like acquaintances, since they were referred to me by…" He trailed off and cleared his throat. "That's not important. They're looking for somewhere to house people who need a safe place to hide."

"Like federal witnesses?" The guy had been a Deputy US Marshal before he retired. Maybe this had to do with that.

"Not exactly." Russ tipped his head to the side. "It will be to keep them safe because they're in danger. We'll be giving them a chance to live their lives."

"How many?"

Russ blinked. "Why?"

Jacob shifted enough he could get his phone from his pocket. Thankfully he wore sweatpants, so he didn't have to lean too far. Leaning *hurt*. Then again, basically everything hurt so what difference did it make?

He thumbed through to the file in his emails and set the phone on the table between them.

Jacob flicked through the images. "This is the artist's rendition of what the fourth floor of my building will look like when renovations are complete."

"The fourth floor?"

"Russ, you know I own the whole building."

The older man shook his head. "That's not why I told you this. You asked what's new with me, and…"

He hesitated long enough Jacob could jump in. "I don't think you're trying to get something from me. I'm saying we didn't open for applications yet."

"How many units?"

"Fifteen."

Russ blew out a long breath. "I'll pass that to my contacts." He nodded. "Thanks, Jacob."

"Whatever you need." Because what Jacob wanted right now was to talk about anything *but* murder and blood. This was a great diversion. Helping people and making a difference in their lives? He'd take that any day.

"No one anticipated when I did that first book, the one with my grandfather and his people, that it would hit as big as it did. I gave a lot to the tribe. Scholarship funds, and medical programs. Then I built myself the haven I needed."

Except it had been trashed, and the privacy he'd had was gone now even if he put it all to rights.

Jacob swallowed. "Being able to do that for other people would be another gift I can give."

"They'll pay rent." Russ lifted both hands. "This isn't about freebies."

"Sure." Jacob rotated the cup. "I'll charge them fair prices."

Except rent in his zip code was nuts, so he'd lower the prices however far he wanted. At least enough to cover taxes and utility bills. After all, he owned the property outright.

The front door opened, and he heard it close. "Russ?" It was Addie.

"Kitchen!"

Jacob started out of surprise in the middle of twisting around to look for her. To get a glimpse. Which would've been fine if his abdomen hadn't been an angry mess of stitches.

"Sorry."

Jacob shook his head. "Don't worry about it."

He swallowed some coffee to keep from hurling while Addie rounded the table and crouched in front of him.

"Hey." She set her hand on his knee.

Jacob put the coffee down. "Hey."

Russ's chair scraped across the floor. He was halfway to the door when Addie said, "Hey." Russ turned back.

"Austin…"

"What?"

Addie shook her head.

"I'll tell Mona."

Addie bit her lip. Russ left the room. He didn't want to get into inane small talk. But as with Russ, the last thing he wanted to talk about were her case details. They had to, though. "What happened?"

Addie tugged a chair over.

"There's coffee."

She nodded but didn't move for it. "I'm not going to sleep anyway. I'll get some in a sec."

"What happened since…all of it, I guess."

She squeezed his hand. Jacob didn't let go.

"Well, I found Mona's boyfriend, the kid who is obsessed with us. He's dead, but I have no idea yet if it's the same killer."

"I wasn't sure this could get more complicated, but apparently, it has."

"I'll head to the office shortly and get an early start." She shrugged. "We'll figure it out."

Jacob couldn't help thinking something was coming. It was like watching a storm gather on the horizon. "Will you promise me you'll be careful?"

The last thing he wanted was for her to get caught up in something that was even a flavor of everything they'd been through. Especially alone.

"Maybe I should have become a cop."

Addie tipped her head to the side. "You think that's the only way to protect me from the dark?"

Before he could answer she squeezed his hand. "I don't need a cop, Jacob. There are plenty of those in my life, and it's nothing like what we have. Right here."

"I'd kiss you, but I need a shower and I don't think I'll be leaning forward for a month." The words were out before he could call them back.

Instead of getting the brush-off, he watched her cheeks pink. She lifted off her seat. He figured she was going for coffee to break the moment, but she moved to him and leaned a hand on the table.

She smiled a second before she lowered her head. Touched her lips to his.

It was nothing like what they'd had before, but there was a familiarity about it. Like déjà vu in the best way. An old familiar sweater on a cold day.

Then he lost all thought as she shifted, turned her head, and the kiss deepened.

Jacob reached up and touched her cheek. Tasted the promise in her. The hope that existed between them that he'd never found anywhere else.

She leaned back, and he heard her breathy sigh. Jacob opened his eyes, aware of the tug of a smile on his face.

Addie felt the same on hers. "Definitely not a cop."

Jacob cleared his throat and finished his coffee.

"Need a refill?"

Before he could answer, Mona rushed in with tears rolling down her face. "What happened?"

Addie shook her head. "You don't want the details. And I can't give them to you when it's an open investigation."

"You have to tell me what happened!"

"I can't tell you."

Jacob shifted his lower body around along with his upper body. "You could sit with us and talk it out."

The teen knew their friend Becca had died in the same incident where they were taken. Hank's girlfriend had suffered and died at the hands of a demented killer.

Jacob had been pushed to his end and nearly broke. Only the arrival of the police had saved their lives otherwise they would have been buried with Becca.

Would Hank have gone on without them, believing it was

his fault they were dead and he was the only survivor? Maybe he believed exactly that about Becca's death.

"You know that we know what it feels like to lose someone." Jacob couldn't push out those thoughts about Hank.

Where was his friend? He needed to ask Addie.

Hank didn't cope well when he was pushed to his limit. Jacob had learned that the hard way when he'd tried to get Hank to open up to him about exactly what happened when Becca died.

Jacob couldn't imagine, but he knew why Hank didn't want to talk about it, ever.

Mona spun around and walked out. Russ went after her, following a silent but heated conversation between him and Addie. No words spoken out loud—but a lot had been communicated there.

Jacob was in too much pain to decipher it.

When it was just the two of them again, Jacob said, "What was that with Russ?"

She sighed, her hips back against the counter. "He parents differently than I would. But neither of us is her actual parent. Life just sucks sometimes." She glanced aside. "She needs her mother, her father. And yet, it's better that neither is here."

"She has support and love. Why would she need anything else?"

Truth was, Jacob didn't know anything about raising children. He'd barely managed to keep himself stable over the years. He would much rather be alone than wrapped up in other people's feelings. When it came down to it, he sucked at relationships.

"I'm sorry." When her gaze came back to him, Jacob said, "For how I broke things off."

"We were both in pain, and my mom's comments

certainly didn't help anything. She threw her weight around, making those snide comments about you and me. Putting us both down. We didn't know how to deal with any of it."

Neither of them had mentioned the elephant that'd been in that room before now. The one who looked an awful lot like her mother.

He said, "Ever feel like you still don't know how to deal?"

Relief washed over her face. "Yes."

Jacob wouldn't mind another kiss, but if he stayed out here much longer, he wasn't going to be able to walk back to the bed. He'd have to sleep out on the kitchen on the floor. Or have Russ drag him down the hall.

He shifted to get up. Addie moved one arm over her shoulders and supported his weight. It hurt, but she wanted to help him, so he figured it wasn't worse than going by himself and falling.

"Bed?"

Jacob's gaze met hers.

Her eyes widened. "I didn't…"

He wanted to laugh, but it would be too painful. "It's fine. I'm damaged goods now."

They made their way slowly into the hall.

"That's not why I reacted." Addie stilled. "I would never think that about you. It's just that. This time…"

"You'd want to do things differently."

"I think that means I need to go to church and figure some things out first."

Jacob smiled through the pain. "I think that's a great idea. Especially if I can take you. We can go to lunch after." No way could it be construed as a date, but he wanted to spend the time with her.

"That sounds good." She helped him not fall onto the bed.

Jacob gritted his teeth and tried not to let her know how much his stomach hurt.

"Sorry. Sorry." She fussed with the blanket.

"I feel useless."

"You need to heal."

"You just tucked me in." He frowned.

"Please don't worry about anything."

"I'll call Hank. Find out how I can—"

Addie stiffened. "Do me a favor, Jacob?" She avoided his gaze. "Let Hank go for right now."

28

Addie slipped off her coat and hung it on the tree by the glass entry doors.

"Morning."

She smiled at Stella, one of the two agents sent over from Seattle. "Hey, how's it going so far?"

"I've been here about ten minutes more than you." Stella had a pixie cut, high cheekbones, and the figure of a woman who did spin class six times a week but ate enough to fuel her life. She was muscled and glowed.

"How was class this morning?"

Stella made a sound akin to "phew," and sipped from a smoothie. Yet another normal thing that made Addie glad for the time she'd spent with Jake last night. A sweet moment, even in the middle of all this.

"You know," Stella said, "I wasn't all fired up to come to Benson, but it's not bad here."

"Yeah?"

Stella nodded. "Maybe it's just not as bad as I *thought* it would be."

Addie chuckled.

Kyle strode in. He waved, so she waved back. "Stella tell a knock-knock joke again? They're usually terrible."

Addie shook her head. "She admitted Benson might not be so bad."

Kyle made a face.

"It might grow on you as well."

"I guess anything is possible." He headed for his desk.

They'd established a certain working rhythm, but it was still new. She had no idea if they would stick around after the case was done. She wouldn't mind if they did. She was used to working with other agents, and she'd discovered an empty echoey office wasn't her favorite thing.

She checked her email, dealt with the immediate stuff, and headed for coffee.

Kyle met her at the coffee bar she'd set up. "How's your sister? And your friend?"

Since Stella didn't drink coffee, Addie filled two mugs and handed him one. "It'll be a long process for both of them."

Kyle was older, maybe nearly forty, but a newer agent. He'd joined the FBI from a career as a police detective and had an excellent eye for inconsistencies. "I can't imagine."

"Mona is still pretty upset, but so is Russ. It's hard to put the hammer down on the teen antics when she's grieving. She can't blow off steam in unhealthy ways because she's grounded." Addie winced. "I'm just glad she's not the one who found him, and she was nowhere near when it happened."

Stella nodded. "Me, too. Poor kid."

"Jacob looks better, and he's moving around." She realized she hadn't referred to him as "Jake" that time but wasn't sure what it meant. "When he's up to it, we'll get him back to his apartment and clean up there."

The cops didn't have any leads on who'd broken in or why. Nothing was taken. There were no signs of forced entry, and the security system hadn't noted any anomalies.

Neither she nor Russ was all fired up to kick him out, though. Even if Russ's couch was uncomfortable and her sleeping on it meant he couldn't spend all hours at his desk working on that thing he said he didn't want to bother her with. Because apparently, Jacob was helping him with it.

Addie shoved away that irritation. She probably didn't have the bandwidth to worry about peripheral stuff right now. Russ likely made the right call there.

"Where are we at with all this?" Addie motioned to the whiteboards.

Kyle waved a hand out. "The way you organized it cut out hours of work trying to correlate all the details. We were able to find two additional cases in PD files. Except we believe they're the *same* case."

"Tell me." She tried to phrase it not like an order because she wasn't their boss technically. And they were here doing her a favor.

Stella brought over a tablet. "Two victims. One male, one female. Both show the same injuries, though one was strangled and the other has slit wrists."

"Murder-suicide?"

"They were found two weeks apart on different sides of town," Kyle said. "But we believe they're connected."

"Decomp was different, but I think that's down to weather conditions and the environment they were left in." Stella swiped the screen of the tablet. "The strangled female was dumped up river, we think, and washed up on the shore of the lake that's east of town."

Addie nodded. "I know it. We used to go out there every

Friday in summer, and everyone would sleep on the beach after."

Stella scanned the screen. "The male is the apparent suicide. Aside from cause of death, his injuries are almost identical. He was left in a storage unit, inside a freezer. Discovered when the unit was auctioned off. But the investigating detective didn't find anything on the previous renter."

"What were the injuries?"

Kyle took the tablet and ran his thumbs over the screen. "Bug bites over sections of their bodies but concentrated on the legs. Cuts and scratches on the hands and arms, possibly defensive wounds."

"Ruptured eardrums?" Addie's stomach flipped over just saying it.

Stella nodded. "Yeah, that was listed on both."

Addie stumbled to a chair and sat. She took a long breath and blew it out slowly. "Anything else?"

Stella and Kyle glanced at each other, then looked at her. Stella lifted her chin. "How about you tell us what you're thinking?"

Addie didn't want to say it.

"This is about what happened to you, isn't it?" Kyle spoke with a measured tone.

She could only nod.

"These deaths occurred two months ago."

"He's doing it again." Addie swallowed. "But it makes no sense. Why kill Celia?"

"You think it's the same guy, some kind of copycat?" Stella shifted to sit on the edge of a table.

"An apprentice." Addie winced. "There were indications, but no one ever figured out if it was true that he worked with someone."

"None of you ever saw a second person?" Kyle sighed. "I wish we could ask Detective Maxwell."

Addie hadn't heard from McCauley whether or not Hank had been found. "He's still AWOL?"

Stella nodded. "It isn't looking good for him."

Addie wanted to jump to his defense. The way she did with Jake.

Hank wasn't the friend she'd known.

Not even the Jacob she knew now was the same boy she'd been so in love with. They'd all lived a lifetime since the last time they were together.

Things with him might be familiar, and what seemed to be there between them had a hint of the easy thing it had been. Yet there was a whole lot about it that was new.

Addie felt the same about being back in Benson. Who she had been in the FBI was a person she'd decided on. Maybe she needed to be to move on from everything that happened. Someone who analyzed and took a step back to look at things from the outside rather than getting involved, and it ended up messy.

Who she was in Benson didn't quite match up. Someone wanted her back here, and just in time for Ivan Damen's apprentice to begin his work again?

Addie fought a shiver. She got up and grabbed the phone from the desk, punching in the numbers to call SAC Zimmerman.

He picked up. "Calling to ask for your job back? Or some other reason?"

Addie pressed her lips together. Did he think she was going to cry and plead for another chance at their relationship? They lived on opposite sides of the country, and he was back with his wife, wasn't he? She figured whatever the question, Kyle and Stella didn't need any more reason to believe her emotions were clouded right now.

"Well?" Zimmerman sighed.

"Who pushed for me to come here and take this assignment?" Addie asked.

"That's what you want to know?"

"I'm sorry, did you think this was going to be a personal call?" She tried to keep the sarcasm out of her tone. "I'm busy with a dozen open cases. Do you know the answer or not?"

Zimmerman went quiet for a second. "I can try and find out."

"Great. That would be…" She'd already said *great* again. "Thanks. I appreciate it."

"Hmm." Zimmerman hung up.

Addie turned to her new colleagues.

"Talk it out." Kyle took a sip of his coffee. "You're the profiler. What are your instincts telling you?"

Addie had hardly put the thoughts together but figured that was a good idea. Sometimes it helped to speak aloud ideas. Even doing that could help pieces to fall into place.

"He's starting again." Addie frowned. "Or he never stopped. He's been developing it all these years, working out how he operates. Now he's ready. He did it with these two victims you found."

Stella said, "And now?"

"There's a reason I was brought back here." There had to be. "How, I have no idea. But why now? It's not like I was expected, so he couldn't guarantee I'd be here. And it's not like he's taking advantage of me being here now. It doesn't feel like that."

"So it could be that he orchestrated your assignment?"

"It brings things full circle with me back in Benson. He

finishes what Damen started, and he can make it his own from there." She thought about all those silent phone calls. "Or he hates himself, and he wants to end it."

Stella nodded. "He could want you to catch him."

Kyle said, "Not the first criminal I've met who wants it to end. Wants to get caught because they don't like what they do."

"But knowing he hates himself doesn't narrow it down," Stella pointed out. "At least not in a way we can track."

Somehow, Addie had to figure out how to marry up the two sides of her. The woman she was in Benson, a survivor with history here, and the FBI profiler she'd become. Both parts of her were going to have to work together to solve this.

"Question is, who in Benson had a hand in getting you back here?" Stella said. "The mayor? The police chief? Isn't the mayor's brother a senator in Washington, DC?"

Kyle said, "That guy might have juice enough he got you assigned here."

"There would be an official request," Addie said. "But who could've pulled strings behind it?"

Someone might have whispered in his ear, and the mayor made the request. She didn't think the police chief was a likely candidate. Maybe someone within the police department.

"We could all go talk to the mayor. Pin him down." Kyle had a gleam in his eye. Like a detective determined to put the screws to someone.

Addie would like to see that. But these two were outsiders. "I'll go."

"Sure?" Stella asked.

Addie nodded. "I'll keep it casual. See if I can get him to open up about how it went down."

"Good," Stella said. "Something is definitely up in Benson."

"At least you didn't use the word *afoot*." Kyle grinned. "While you're out, we'll work on these two new cases."

"Celia's death still doesn't make sense. It fits, and it doesn't, at the same time." Addie wandered to the board that held those case details and studied it again, hoping to see something she hadn't gone over a hundred times already. "If he killed two in the same manner as Damen, then why kill a single girl differently?"

"Could be there's a missing male out there somewhere," Stella said. "Someone we didn't find yet. Or another case labeled differently."

Addie thought about Austin. "Who worked the two cases you just discovered?"

"The suicide was signed off. Not much of an investigation to speak of, and the state police took it because he was found out in the woods." Kyle tapped the tablet screen. "The girl's case was assigned to…"

The door opened. A pale man with dark hair and dark circles under his eyes came in, moving slowly.

Celia Jessop's father.

Addie set a hand on her holstered weapon, ready for whatever might happen next.

The man raised both hands, despair in his eyes.

"I'm turning myself in. I stabbed Jacob Wilson."

29

Jacob had slept for a couple of hours before hunger brought him to wakefulness. He'd hit the kitchen and found ramen he'd been able to make in the microwave. Sitting hurt, he ate it standing up in the kitchen before heading back down the hall, not sure where he was going.

Russ was in his office. Jacob kept on down the hall.

Mona's door was open.

Jacob glanced in and saw the teen leaf through a magazine but not reading it.

She glanced up. "Hey."

"I'm up. Need anything?" He wasn't sure how she felt about him being here or if she cared at all. Jacob was more than aware this wasn't his home, and being around people felt different than having just his cats for company.

Mona shrugged.

"Doing okay? I mean, if you want to talk about it."

Another shrug.

"Okay…" He left one final door open, about to leave.

"Russ took my phone," she began. "But before he did, everyone was talking about how you killed Celia Jessop."

Jacob turned to leave, unwilling to have this conversation.

"I'm glad she's dead."

He frowned. Turning back hurt. He did it, anyway. "I didn't kill her. You think your uncle or your sister would let me stay here and put all of you in danger if I had?"

"Maybe you convinced them you're innocent." She lifted her chin.

Since it was the first sign of life she'd given anyone in a couple of days, he decided to dig in there. See if he could draw her out. "Celia's dad thought I did it. The police seemed to think so—maybe they still do. But I'm telling you I had nothing to do with it, and that's the truth."

She stared at him. The skin around her eyes flexed.

He wasn't going to beg and plead for her to believe him. Jacob didn't have the energy for that. "What did you mean when you said you're glad she did it?"

Sure, it was a clear deflection back to her, but it wasn't like he wanted to talk about him.

Jacob leaned on the door frame.

Mona shrugged. "Celia…she was Austin's ex. Just as crazy about what happened to you and Addie as he was."

"How long were they together?"

Mona made a face. "It's not like they were married or anything. But they talked about it like it was forever." She shrugged one shoulder. "Maybe a few months."

His "chat" with Celia. The one that had turned into an altercation with the guy he presumed now was Austin? It had happened nearly three months ago now.

"That must've been frustrating, with you and Austin trying to make something work." Even though it had been morally questionable, technically illegal, and just plain a bad idea, he wanted to connect with her.

Mona said, "They still hung out all the time. Celia's new

boyfriend didn't know. She bragged about him all the time like he was this big shot."

"Any idea who it was?"

Mona made a face.

Jacob thought back on the conversations he'd had with Celia at the retirement home where she worked. Mostly they talked about patients there he wanted to interview. They'd barely strayed into small talk beyond asking about each other's weekend, like two coworkers on a Monday. Benign stuff Celia couldn't possibly have read into—or anyone else that might've overheard.

But maybe he couldn't be sure of that.

It would be far too obvious for Jacob to ask if Celia had ever mentioned him.

"For a while, I thought she was talking about you." She paused. "Like you were her boyfriend. But we saw you on the street once, and she made this comment."

"It's okay if it was bad." He wanted her to tell him. "I'm not going to get mad."

"She thought you were creepy. I don't get it, but she made it sound like she knew something."

Jacob frowned. "If she did, she kept it to herself."

Why hadn't she come across as nervous or scared of him in person? Had there been an ulterior motive in her talking to him at the retirement home? Maybe it had been about feeling him out. Getting to know him so he let down his guard.

Jacob didn't like the idea he'd been played.

He wasn't the best at reading people and might be better if he didn't spend so much time alone. But he hadn't needed the skill. Now Celia was dead, and he might never find out what she'd been up to—if she'd been up to anything.

"Maybe she was afraid of you," Mona said. "But it didn't seem like it. She was just wary."

Jacob wasn't going to let that go. "You don't have anything to worry about from me. Okay?"

"Like I'm supposed just to trust whatever you say?"

"Russ teach you that?"

"He taught me not to be naïve or make assumptions." She made a face. "Guess it didn't work."

"I'm sorry about Austin." Regardless of the merits of the relationship, she had lost someone she cared about.

"Yeah, me too." Mona sighed.

He wasn't sure what he'd expected. Maybe teenage hysterics? She seemed levelheaded. Or the storm had passed, and another wave might hit her in the future, but she was in a calm spell for now.

He wasn't a cop. "Do you know who might kill Celia or Austin?"

"Aside from her new boyfriend? Celia said he was crazy possessive." Mona shifted. "It didn't sound good, and Austin was weird about it. Asking her who he was. She wouldn't say, but maybe he followed her, and the guy found out. Maybe he killed them both."

Jacob sent Addie a text. Asked if she knew who Celia's mystery boyfriend was. He couldn't remember if she'd mentioned anything about it to him, but it wasn't like they talked through her case.

He wouldn't have anything at all to do with it if McCauley didn't think Jacob was guilty of *something*. Too bad the police captain didn't feel the need to base those assumptions on actual evidence.

He didn't need to get into the middle of a police investigation. But since Celia's death would be pinned on him unless the cops found another suspect—preferably the *actual* murderer—he figured it might be down to him to ask a few questions.

"Does your sister know that you knew Celia?"

Mona shrugged. "Maybe not."

Jacob wondered if the cops knew she was associated with Celia. "Did anyone from the police department talk to you after she died?"

"Geez, questions."

"Sorry," Jacob said. "I'm just trying to get things straight in my head, you know?"

"Cause everyone thinks you did it?"

"The important thing is that I didn't." And yet Celia's dad had been convinced like everyone else, so much so that he'd tried to kill Jake. He swallowed. "Her death can't go without someone finding out who was responsible. That's why I'm asking."

Pretty soon he was going to have to lie down. His energy level was tanking fast, even with the food in his stomach.

Maybe the energy it took in digesting that was more than his body could handle and sleep would claim him again. It seemed like that was all he'd done for days. Sleep and dream of Addie kissing him until he wondered if it had even been real and not just a dream.

"I'd be surprised if the police don't come by and ask you about Austin."

Mona nodded. "I think Russ is making them wait."

"He shouldn't put it off forever. Not when you could help them find out who killed Austin, and maybe Celia too." Jacob wondered if the cops had Celia's phone. Surely that would show them who she was in a relationship with. People used their phones for everything these days, no matter their generation.

It was an electronic record of a person's life, for good or ill.

"Don't you have a friend that's a cop?" she asked.

"I haven't spoken to him in a few days." Jacob winced. "I think he might've gone after the person who stabbed me."

Then again, he had no idea where Hank was. Neither did anyone else. Their guess was as good as Jacob's since Hank did what he pleased. He showed up when he wanted to. They hung out when it worked for Hank since his schedule was harder to plan around than Jacob's photography sessions and the interviews he'd been doing at the retirement home.

It was just how things had gone over the last few years. Not bad, just what they'd fallen into.

Hank would come back around eventually. Jacob could only send so many texts before he had to face the fact his friend could tank his career singlehandedly, and there was nothing he could do to help Hank with that.

Down the hall something clattered, dropped on the floor in another room.

He was about to call out to Russ when Hank stepped into the hall.

"Hey," Hank muttered.

Instinct had Jacob turn and lean the front of his right shoulder on the doorframe. Then he realized what didn't seem right—Hank's hair was mussed as though he'd run his hands through it. Scratches marred his face and forearms where his sleeves rolled up. Split skin on his knuckles.

He prowled down the hall at a slow pace. "Hey."

Hey?

"Is everything all right?" Jacob heard Mona move behind him and lifted his hand back there. Hopefully she saw him wave for her to stay out of sight.

Behind his back she gave his hand a slight squeeze, and he heard a whisper of clothing, then nothing.

"Yeah, yeah." Hank sniffed. "Where's the girl?"

"Addie?" Surely he meant the FBI agent they both knew, and not the teenage girl Hank had no business talking to unless it was as a cop. Hank's badge was nowhere in sight.

"Nah, the sister." Hank wouldn't meet his gaze.

Jacob had never seen him like this. "Mona went out. Needed some air, you know?"

His friend wasn't here to check on Jacob and see how he was doing after the stabbing. Nor was he here for any other good reason. Where was Russ? Surely the old marshal had figured out someone was in the house.

Russ wasn't the type to leave something like that to chance and risk the people he cared about being unprotected.

"Wanna tell me what this is?" He needed a way to contact Addie without Hank knowing. Could he tell Mona to do it, again behind his back? He wasn't sure how to get that done but he'd have to figure it out fast if he was going to make it work. Hank moved toward him.

Kept coming.

Jacob braced. "Tell me what this is."

Hank stopped right in front of him. "You wouldn't understand."

"I think I'm beginning to."

They'd been friends for years, survivors of the same tragedy. Jacob had been blind to the truth beneath the surface all that time. He and Addie had considered themselves patient zero with the ripples affecting the entire community.

Maybe that wasn't true.

It seemed as though the origin might lay with Hank and

the truth Jacob hadn't ever wanted to face. The thing right in front of him.

Hank shifted, then rammed his fist into Jacob's stomach before Jacob could move out of the way. Or brace. Either would have been good. But Hank's power hammered him.

Jacob cried out and doubled over. Pain eclipsed everything. Tears burned in his eyes.

This was wrong. So wrong. "Why are you—"

Hank grabbed Jacob's arm, pulled it behind his back, and slammed him on the floor.

Jacob roared out all the pain. "Mona, run!"

Handcuffs slapped on his wrists behind his back. But this was no arrest.

The pain overwhelmed him, and everything went black.

30

"I'm afraid you're going to have to leave your weapon with us." The bouncer—who was probably "Head of Security" in a place like this with its ballroom and full cocktail menu—wore a black shirt and black pants with an earbud in one ear.

"There's no need to be afraid." Addie flashed her badge. "And no, I'm not disarming myself. But I am going in there."

She stepped around him into the crowded ballroom.

The mayor's assistant had told her that he was here tonight. She'd been two blocks over at a barbecue restaurant with her boyfriend. Meanwhile this black-tie event had a full crowd of people, plenty of brass in uniform and Benson's who's who.

She hadn't bothered changing, but since she wore her work clothes of pants and a white collared shirt under her wool coat, open so the fact she was armed was clear to everyone, she figured she could pull off not looking like a total slob.

She should've changed her shoes. Rich women always looked at the shoes first.

Then again, considering most of her shoes were at her condo, maybe that wasn't an option.

Addie sighed and scanned the crowd for the mayor.

Zimmerman hadn't called back, but he'd emailed her a copy of the request the FBI had. Whoever took down the details hadn't passed along the person's name who wanted an agent assigned to Benson. Multiple people had to have signed off on it, but she wasn't likely to get to the bottom of this on that end until tomorrow.

So she was here to dig on this side.

She found the police chief and Captain McCauley first.

They both knew Celia's father had turned himself in for stabbing Jacob. What else was there to do tonight except party with the big wigs? Certainly not drive to her uncle's house and apologize to Jacob for their assumptions and how they'd treated him in light of him being a victim.

Then again, maybe they still thought Jacob killed Celia.

Addie was bringing her personal feelings into a case where she didn't need that. She recognized that she was a human being—more so here than in Virginia. This place meant something to her, and so did the people who lived here.

She was probably going to battle this the entire time she was in her hometown. But she was also going to do her job, save lives. Bring those responsible to justice as best she could, with professionalism and integrity.

If she got a little wrapped up in it, so what?

Addie walked the periphery until she spotted the mayor and his wife.

She headed for them, and right as she stepped into his circle, she realized the police chief and McCauley had clocked her moving and done the same. *Fine.* It didn't matter, did it? This was going to happen either way.

The mayor frowned.

"May I have a word, sir?" Her voice was tight, but she was as polite as she could be.

He brought his drink but shooed away his wife. "Through there."

The mayor's two security guards followed at a distance as he headed first into a side hallway lined with thick carpet, crown molding on the walls framed with gold color. They passed a table with carved legs. A massive vase out of which spilled a profusion of flowers that exploded like fireworks from the mouth of the china.

The mayor opened double doors on the right side of the hall and stepped into a study lined with bookshelves.

No one sat in the high-backed velvet chairs.

"Care to tell me why you're interrupting my evening?" Mayor Simeon Olivette lifted his glass for a sip.

"I'll make this quick, sir." Addie was aware of the police chief and McCauley behind her but faced the mayor on her own on this one.

Since her question was for all of them, she turned and included the two city cops with the mayor. "I need to know who requested from the FBI that an agent be sent here."

"Me." The mayor shrugged one shoulder.

"Did you ask for me specifically?"

He frowned. "We knew you worked for the FBI as a profiler. Which is what we needed."

She tried to figure out if he was referring to himself in the third person or if he meant himself and others. Maybe Police Chief Lachlan and Captain McCauley.

"We put the request through for help, and you showed up two weeks later."

Addie frowned. It hadn't been an emergency, necessarily.

"That's quick." She glanced at McCauley. "Have you ever known bureaucracy to move that quickly?"

He frowned. "I'm sure we asked for an agent. I figured they'd send someone from Seattle. Maybe a task force. One person shows up, and it's you? Didn't make any sense to me."

But he'd assumed Jacob killed Celia Jessop. Did that make sense to him, even though there was no evidence?

Addie frowned. "So you weren't expecting me." She glanced around. "But someone had to have mentioned my name. To get me pulled off the team I was on and ordered back here."

At the time it seemed like she was being sent to Benson to get over her history and then get a promotion. Zimmerman had all but said as much when he told her she was being reassigned.

"We met about the need for outside help." The mayor motioned to the two cops. "Talked about calling in the state police, or even a private investigator. We heard about this one who works all over—bringing down killers."

"That's just a rumor," McCauley said.

"Fine, *I* heard about her." The mayor sipped his drink. "We also talked about using a private security team from here in Benson and letting them take a look at the case to see if they can solve it. A couple of them used to be cops, or feds, or something. But we don't know them."

"You know me." Addie paused. "Was anyone else in these meetings, or just the three of you?" She glanced at Lachlan.

The chief of police frowned. "And Detective Maxwell, a couple of the times. He worked most of the cases."

"Is he the one who connected them?"

Lachlan shook his head. "He figured there wasn't much to it."

Addie turned to McCauley. "Anything I should know from Austin's phone?"

The captain frowned. "We're looking for Hank."

"McCauley." He needed to stop giving her the runaround concerning the guy.

"Austin sent a series of texts to Hank."

The mayor frowned. "What's this about?"

McCauley said, "The texts indicate Hank Maxwell was Celia Jessop's boyfriend."

Chief Lachlan kept quiet.

"And no one has seen Hank?" Addie said. "Because that's a serious conflict of interest if he didn't immediately tell you he and Celia were in a relationship. He investigated her murder." They had to realize. "He should've been our number one suspect from the beginning. Instead, Captain McCauley is pinning down Jacob Wilson as though he had anything to do with her. Or the captain has any evidence of his involvement whatsoever."

"I was told they knew each other." McCauley sighed. "It was worth a conversation."

"Told by who?" Addie asked. "Detective Maxwell?"

McCauley scratched at his jaw.

Addie turned to the mayor. "Did Hank Maxwell specifically mention me when the request was put to the FBI for an agent to be brought here?"

Chief Lachlan answered instead. "He's the one who mentioned the FBI."

"Even though he didn't believe the cases were related?"

The chief shrugged. "Maybe he figured feds should look like idiots more than us. At least, that's what I thought at the time."

"Seems like a waste of time and money just to prove himself right that they weren't connected. And if he's the one behind it, he's risking the truth coming out." Addie let that sink in. They didn't like the idea one of their own might be dirty—a serial murderer. "Unless what he wanted was for me to come here."

The mayor leaned forward. "Why would he want that?"

"Because this started with me, Hank, and Jacob. I think that's how he wants it to end." In fact, what Addie thought was that Hank wanted to end her and Jake. "There's a plan at work here. Hank has been pulling strings. Orchestrating things for years. Biding his time."

"There's no way." McCauley shook his head.

"Because no serial murderer ever fooled the people he was closest to? Gave them no indication of what went on beneath the surface?"

Lachlan winced. "I was the one who recommended him for the police academy. You're telling me he fits the profile of a demented killer? That would've come out in the psych eval."

Addie scoffed. "You think I wouldn't have noticed that my friend in high school was probably in league with the person who kidnapped us."

"If there was a protégé," Lachlan said. "Then it was Jacob Wilson."

"Because Hank was always your golden boy."

"You don't know—"

Addie cut him off. "Tell me."

Lachlan's face flushed. He moved to one of the chairs and ran both hands down his face, shoulders slumped. It took a minute, but eventually he spoke. "I can't tell you how many calls we responded to at the Maxwell residence over the years. Started around the time he was three. Mom's boyfriend."

Addie's heart sank.

"Hank was twelve when he beat the guy and kicked him out," Lachlan said. "I shook his hand." The police chief frowned. "I'm not giving you ammo to label him some kind of sicko."

"He was my friend." Some patterns existed in the history of sociopaths. They learned how to adapt and blend in. It was almost a game with some. A way to see if they could fool everyone. "We need to find him. Talk to him."

McCauley frowned. "And yet we ignore Jacob Wilson, the misunderstood recluse? He's the one who fits the profile."

"Hank is the one directly involved. I think he was the one who was in a relationship with Celia Jessop," Addie said. "He lied to you guys about it and betrayed the oath he took to uphold the law with integrity. Tell me what Jacob has done, aside from not fit the mold because he chose to live his life *his* way instead of what you thought he should do."

She of all people knew trauma effected the victims in all kinds of different ways.

"We're finding him." McCauley folded his arms.

"If I'm right, he orchestrated all of this. I don't want to believe it's possible a cop could do that, but we can't allow it to cloud our judgment."

None of them liked that.

"This is personal for all of us." Addie shrugged. "But I have two FBI agents in my office working this case, and they have no personal connection to any of it."

She was glad she'd asked for backup. They might be strangers to her, but it could come in handy if she was right that Hank had been orchestrating things. Covering up. Planning, and experimenting.

He might've figured out how to get her back here. For some specific reason she hadn't figured out yet.

"So we just turn it over to feds we don't know?" Lachlan said.

Addie nodded. "It's the right thing to do. So, yes. I'm fully prepared to let them take this and step back if necessary. I did what I could. They can find Hank and figure out his involvement in every death the FBI was handed to investigate. I'm telling you guys the FBI is investigating these cases and Hank is the number one suspect as of right now. Don't get in the way."

Addie's phone rang. She slid it from her pocket, hoping it was one of the agents. Or Hank turning himself in like Celia's father had.

It was Russ.

She swiped her thumb across the screen. "Hey, can I call you back in a minute?"

A low moan sounded across the line. "Addie…"

Her body went cold. "Russ?"

31

Black spots sparked at the edges of his vision. *Don't pass out.*

Jacob tried to control his breaths even though he was shaking in pain. The stitches on his stomach were soaked red. Wet.

He slumped against the wall, hands tied behind his back.

Sweat beaded on his face and down his spine.

His body flushed with heat.

No way could he get up, let alone walk. He barely managed to keep himself upright. But he wasn't going to leave Mona, and he didn't have the strength to get them both out of here.

The room had been cleared of furniture. Living area, kitchen, and dining. Whatever might have once been here had been removed. The inside white, painted that color. Primer on the drywall, but this was no renovation. Floor. Ceiling. Walls. The only color difference was the ancient chrome stove.

Mona lay too far for him to reach her. She was out cold and had been ever since Hank dragged her in from the car.

She had a cut above her eyebrow and blood at the corner of her mouth.

Blinds on the window were down. He could see trees outside between the slats, lit by an exterior light. Jacob had no idea what time it was.

All he knew was that reality was about to hit him like a train. There would be no escaping it when he acknowledged the fact this was so similar to what happened before.

Him injured, though he'd only been beaten by Ivan Damen while he was unconscious from the shot that incapacitated them on homecoming night. Addie had been in a similar state, though he'd had a concussion after the fact. He didn't know if she'd suffered the same because they hadn't talked much after the hospital.

He'd tried, but too quickly they'd argued. Too much pain between them. Stirred up by her mother. It had ended in them parting ways and never reconciling.

Until now.

Jacob sniffed back the burn of tears.

He knew she'd rather be here than her sister. Did she know? Addie would search until she found them. He prayed it wouldn't be too late when she did.

Russ was hurt.

Mona was here.

The door opened, and Jacob knew he couldn't avoid the obvious any longer.

"Hank." The name was a groan from his lips. Jacob coughed. The movement caused a spasm in his gut that tore through him like a laser. A tear rolled down his face.

"Shut up." Hank shook his hands and paced, not looking at Jacob or Mona.

Jacob didn't want to put it together. He didn't want to consider how blind he'd been, how stupid. He'd trusted

Hank. Maybe some sense of self-preservation had him hold back and keep the relationship the way it had always been. Or it was normal because they were two guys. But Jacob had never shared the real stuff with Hank, who had enough going on as a detective.

He'd told himself Hank didn't need his drama. That they didn't need to rehash what'd happened to him continually.

He'd ignored any sign of instability in his friend. Kept things surface level. Held back. Used the friendship as a lifeline and let the status quo stay as it was for years. He pretended he did the right thing, as though what they had when they hung out was about supporting Hank over Becca's death.

Jacob knew what this place was.

"This is what you do when you're 'hunting'?"

Hank glanced over. Anger flared in his eyes.

"This is your cabin, right?" It wasn't the original ones, as those had been renovated. "You told me you were going to buy the ones where we were held, but that you got outbid. I figured you wanted to burn them all down. But that wasn't it, was it?"

Someone there that night, one of the survivors, had been Ivan Damen's protégé. Jacob knew it wasn't him or Addie, and Becca had died.

"Tell me how Becca died."

Hank strode to the wall and kicked a hole in the drywall. Jacob thought it was only a random outburst until he saw behind the sheetrock.

"If you're going to recreate what happened, I'd think you need Addie."

"Next best thing," Hank muttered as he pulled drywall away, exposing a duct normally covered by a vent. The kind of vent that insects had poured out of when Jacob had been trapped with Addie.

They'd both suffered hundreds of bug bites, tied to chairs in the center of the room. After they passed out, they'd woken up untied. No bugs in sight. As soon as both were fully awake, Ivan Damen had pumped music through speakers in the top corners of the wall. So loud it gave them hearing damage even with their hands over their ears.

Until they nearly went mad with the fear.

Maybe that was what'd happened to Hank. Instead of the outcome Jacob and Addie had reached, Hank might have made a deal with the devil to get himself out.

Who knew how he'd reacted? People made emotional decisions under duress. Torture victims said whatever their captors wanted them to say just to make the pain stop.

It could be that Hank was simply a victim like Jacob and Addie—and Becca—who had succumbed to the will of his captor. Damen could've messed with his head, just in a different way than he'd done with Jacob.

Hank had been twisted.

"I'm sorry he hurt you."

Hank whirled around and threw something. Jacob braced. Pain tore through his abdomen, and a knife embedded in the wall beside him.

He didn't even have the strength to reach for it.

"Why are you doing this? We're friends. Mona is a kid just like we were." Hank didn't even look like he was paying attention. "You're going to destroy her life, just like ours were?"

Jacob looked at the knife.

His hands were behind his back. He couldn't even reach over to grab it.

Hank didn't look at him. He just stalked over and pulled the knife from the wall.

"Is this because she knows too much about Celia and Austin?"

Hank had to know the police wouldn't be able to ignore something like this. He was never going to get away with it.

"You want them to find you. Catch you."

Hank stared at the blade.

Jacob figured he'd be dead in a minute, regardless. "It's not too late. You don't have to make this worse than it already is, Hank. We're friends. I'll speak for you. No one knows what we went through except us. That's extenuating circumstances."

"You don't know what I've done. You wouldn't understand."

"Tell me. Talk to me." Maybe they'd have the first real conversation of their decade's long friendship. Shame washed over him. "I'm sorry I never saw it."

"Now you know what I am." Hank lifted his gaze, the knife in front of him. "What I've done. All the people I've killed? You wouldn't understand, Jake. You're not like me."

Jacob's head swam from the pain. His entire body flushed, damp with sweat. But he had to try. "That's what you think? You're so different?"

Maybe he could get Hank to understand they weren't that far apart, no matter what Hank had done—especially if it got his friend to hold off on whatever this was long enough for Addie to find them.

"Damen told you to kill Becca and then yourself, right?" Jacob's mind wanted to hang on to that thought, but he pushed on. "I'm sorry if you believed you had no choice. He wore me down as well. He didn't let up with the torture.

That's what happened to us, Hank. We were *tortured*. Whatever that turned you into, it isn't on you."

His actions were his responsibility—Jacob believed that. But the truth was Ivan Damen had some of the blame if Hank had been broken to such an extent that he carried out what their captor wanted.

Hank huffed. "As if you know."

"The same thing happened to me."

Jacob needed him to understand what he'd never told anyone. Maybe that was the reason he'd held himself back from Hank. He hadn't wanted to admit the truth to himself, let alone tell anyone else what had come over him.

"I know how it feels because I had to face the same thing. To consider what I was prepared to do just to make it stop. That doesn't make you less. Or evil. Not like Damen."

Unless Hank went through with the same thing, using Jacob and Mona—and maybe Addie—as his victims.

"You don't have to do this."

Hank crouched.

Jacob's entire body clenched.

He lifted the knife and touched the blade to Jacob's cheek, scoring a line down that burned.

Jacob felt blood trail down and drip from his chin. He gritted his teeth. "Hank, don't do this. You've done enough. Don't make things worse."

"You think we're the same," Hank said. "But you have no idea."

"You're a cop." And yet, it was clear that his impression of his "friend" wasn't close to the truth. "Just tell me."

The longer he talked, the more chance Addie had of finding them. The more time she had to mount a rescue.

"Talk to me." As Jacob spoke, the cut on his cheek opened. The skin stung.

The last thing Jacob wanted to do was go through that ordeal again, all because of a man who was supposed to be his best friend. Hank knew what they'd been through, and now he wanted others to suffer in the same way. But Jacob had already been there. He didn't need to feel it.

Mona didn't need to.

"The time for talking is over," Hank said. "You have no clue. But you're not completely useless. Someone needs to take the fall."

"You're gonna make it look like it was me?"

"All of it." Hank shot him a dismissive look. "I've been trying to stop you for years. I finally managed to, but too late to bring you to justice."

"You're the one who put my print on Celia's body."

Hank said nothing.

"So now you're gonna kill me?" Jacob felt like his heart was going to give out. He didn't know if it was shame or the heartbreak of finally seeing reality.

"Murder-suicide." Hank's voice had no inflection. No emotion. "There was nothing I could do. After you confessed to Mona's murder and everyone else's, you took your life."

Jacob gritted his teeth. It wasn't just blood rolling down his face. "You think Addie is gonna believe that?"

"She knew all about it. She'll tell me that before she dies."

"I want to see her." Jacob said, "You and I have been friends a long time. Give me that at least. You want to get away with all this, pin it on me? Fine. But I want to tell her goodbye."

Hank straightened from his crouch and stepped back.

He walked to the door and outside. Slammed it behind him so the whole cabin shook. Jacob heard a lock click into place.

Mona blinked her eyes open and sat up. "We can agree he's completely crazy, right?"

Jacob nearly started full-on crying he was so relieved at seeing her awake. At not being alone. Even if it was Addie's sister, and he couldn't protect her in this condition.

He didn't even know if he could stand. Right now, it seemed like she might be able to protect herself.

She bent her legs and stood. "How about we figure out how to get out of here?"

Jacob agreed. "I don't want to know what happens if we stay."

Mona got to her feet. He saw a wince of pain cross her face, but she pushed it aside. The way Russ taught her to. The way Addie would.

"I'm glad you're all right."

Mona looked him over and winced. "This isn't going to be fun."

"But it'll be over."

One way or another.

32

Addie leaned on the rail at the end of the bed. "Are you sure?"

Russ lay in the bed wearing a hospital gown, a bandage wrapped around his head. He didn't have a concussion, thankfully. But he'd been bleeding badly when an ambulance got to the house. Jacob and Mona were both missing.

"Am I sure I saw Hank Maxwell step over me after he clocked me on the back of the head?"

She blew out a breath. "I just have to be certain."

Taking a blow to the head would leave anyone out of it. Enough they could be confused about what they'd seen.

"I know." Russ made a face. "Because I know how this works."

She walked around and handed him the water cup beside the bed.

He drank begrudgingly.

"Did he say anything about where he was taking them?" she asked. "Anything at all?"

Russ didn't shake his head. "I never liked that boy."

Lachlan stood beside the door. When Russ said that, he

perked up. "Oh, so you knew he was a serial killer, and you said nothing?"

Lachlan had been trying to shift the blame ever since she'd made it plain just how wrong he'd been about Hank Maxwell, the decorated detective both he and the chief considered their golden boy. When this came out, the public would raise an outcry about how the police had concealed a killer for years. As if they'd known.

"I said nothing?" Russ shot Lachlan a pointed look.

Lachlan pressed his lips together, silent.

"What's this?" Addie asked.

Lachlan said to Russ, "Your judgment was clouded."

"Because Jacob Wilson is a friend of mine? Not me who got that wrong, or so it would seem." He let that statement hang with no elaboration. Russ didn't waste time over-explaining anything. Especially not when he seemed to think the truth was simple.

Still, Addie was interested in getting out of there to find him, not talking around and around about who made a mistake and who was going to take the blame. "We need to figure out where he took them and what he's up to."

She looked at her watch. "My team will be here in a couple of minutes."

They'd called to tell her they had something. Addie was on the way to the hospital at the time. The plan was to hook up and work this as a team, so she had backup just in case Hank came after her, too.

Addie didn't care about that. In fact, she welcomed it. They could hang back and let him come to her. Then she'd spring a trap on him.

But Hank would expect that.

If he wanted her, he had to have some plan. After all, this had been building for years. She'd have said there was no way he hadn't methodically planned all of this. Except for Austin and Celia. She was convinced Hank had snapped and killed Celia. Then Austin had asked too many questions—or figured it out—and Hank had to kill him as well.

Austin was murdered after Jacob was stabbed. Maybe Celia's father had interrupted Hank's plan for Jacob, and Austin was the death that came as a result. Hank had scrambled. All that pent up need to take a life interrupted by the fact Jacob was taken to hospital. He'd bided his time and later come after Jacob at the house—along with Mona.

There had to be a reason Hank took Mona as well. Maybe she'd decided to fight off Hank to save an injured Jacob, and Hank had to improvise.

She figured Hank was determined to carry out his plan, no matter what.

She just couldn't figure out if he intended to finish what Ivan Damen started or wrap up that part of his life so he could start over somewhere else.

Reborn.

Or something else, entirely.

"And after your team is here?" Russ asked. "What will you do?"

"The FBI is going to find Hank and we're going to get Jacob and Mona back." Addie didn't care if she was making a promise she might not be able to keep.

The promise she made was to herself first and foremost.

She *would* get them back.

Why else was she in Benson again? She wasn't going to accept that it was all Hank's doing. Not if she believed God had ultimate control and He had allowed it to happen.

That meant He was in this whether she was accustomed to acknowledging that or not.

Addie might just be getting a jump on that fresh start.

God, Jacob knows You. He needs You now, and so does Mona. Keep them safe. Help me get them back.

"Addie."

She sniffed back the burn of tears. Looked at the police chief and the captain. "Ideas where Hank might have taken them?"

Lachlan winced.

McCauley said, "He hunts."

"Okay." Did they think she could do anything with that? It seemed like they were scrambling, but maybe also realized they didn't know Hank all that well. It could cost someone's life, and it just might be their fault.

"I don't know where he goes." McCauley shrugged.

"Me either," Lachlan said.

"And you haven't called anyone to have them look it up?" Russ asked. "See if he has property in his name. Or where his cell has been for the last month."

Addie lifted her chin. "Guess what the FBI is doing?"

"Standing here with us?" McCauley fired off.

"As opposed to making a plan so you can save face? I'm just thankful you handed the case to the FBI, or who knows how many more bodies there would be?"

She needed to get out of here.

Lachlan took a step toward to face off with her. "If you think for one second—"

Someone cleared their throat. Loudly.

Addie turned to see Kyle in the doorway, Stella beside him but slightly back. As though he intended to guard her from anything that happened.

"Anything?" Kyle asked.

"I had the same question."

He gave her a short nod. "Let's go."

Addie kissed Russ on his cheek, even though he'd never

liked that. This wasn't a time for withholding emotion. She cared about him. If the worst happened, all they had was each other.

"Find them." Russ winked.

She turned back at the door. "I will." Then she motioned to Lachlan and McCauley. "Let Russ get some rest."

They went with her to the hall, but Addie kept walking. Going with Kyle and Stella until they were outside.

Stella said, "Talk now, or at Hank's house?"

"I could ride with you guys if that's okay?"

They looked at each other.

Addie said, "Hank's house?"

Kyle nodded. They climbed in the car, Stella in the back and Kyle driving. Addie turned to her female colleague. "You guys found something?"

Stella said, "Hank has a house he inherited from his mother. He has no other property in his name, but we did find a storage unit for Becca Cowell."

"He rented it as his dead girlfriend?"

Stella shrugged. "She didn't do it herself posthumously is my guess. It was empty except for a freezer."

That didn't sound good.

"The PD crime lab is there now just in case we missed something in the nothing. They're going to check the freezer for DNA or blood, even if it's been cleaned up."

"Great." Maybe there was something at his house.

Kyle said, "He'd want to keep important things close by, right? Where he could make sure they're safe, and no one finds them."

"That would be my conclusion." Addie didn't know what to think, though. "I can't believe I considered him a friend." She couldn't imagine what Jacob was going through right now. Even just physically and mentally. He was also coping with the fact he'd called Hank his best friend for years.

And now this?

They'd all been blind to the truth, not just the police department.

"Crazy." Stella shook her head. "A cop?"

Addie spotted a flash of something in her eyes. She knew a shadow well because she would see it in her expression in the mirror. Addie glanced at Kyle, but he only shook his head.

The two of them knew each other well. Had worked with each other for nearly two years and clearly had a rapport. One day she hoped to consider them friends as well as colleagues. But she might never be part of the bond they shared.

Addie wanted to hear their story. "Thank you for coming here. Both of you. I appreciate it because I don't know what I'd have done if this happened to me, and I was alone out here."

"Of course," Stella said.

Kyle nodded. "Happy to."

"You guys aren't worried you'll get assigned here permanently?" Maybe they couldn't wait to get back to Seattle.

Stella made a *huh* sound. "It's not so bad here. I think it's growing on me."

Kyle didn't say anything, but when Addie glanced over, she saw a ghost of a smile on his face.

Definitely some history there.

Addie started to answer but caught herself. Would it be so bad? Being close to Russ and Mona. Having Jake back in her life. "I'd love the company."

"You're not worried *you'll* get stuck here forever?" Kyle chuckled.

With the threat over, she would be able to move on.

"We have to find them first," Addie said. "When Hank is in custody and we have this all straightened out, *then* I'll figure out the next step."

Stella shifted. "Bet no one thought you'd figure this out in a week."

Kyle snorted.

"Unfortunately we know now why the police weren't able to put it together."

One of their own had been assigned to investigate most of the cases. A cop had committed the crimes, so he knew exactly what they looked for when they worked a case.

"So why didn't he work to stall you as soon as you showed up?" Kyle asked. "Surely he wouldn't want you to figure it out."

"I'm thinking he has a plan, and I needed to be here for it." Addie tapped her finger on her knee. "I think he did try to throw me off in a way since he pointed me to a victim, and it turned out to be nothing. Maybe he knew she was killed by someone else."

And then there were her other theories. "I also think maybe he wants to get caught and that he *wanted* me to figure out it was him. I think that's why he orchestrated it to get me back here."

Stella said, "Some killers do draw attention to themselves just so it can end."

"And given what I know he went through because I went through the same, I think he might hate who he is and what he's done. I think he might want me to stop him because I understand, and he's so guilt ridden he doesn't want to go on being this person."

She knew it was a long shot. She was concluding with not much evidence and theorizing about Hank's state of mind.

Instead, she needed to sit him down and talk to him—in an interrogation room.

Her office didn't have one, so she'd have to use the PD.

Addie blew out a long breath.

Kyle pulled the car into a neighborhood. Addie waited as he headed for the third street down. The blue house at the end.

She glanced at her colleagues. "This is the house Hank lived in as a kid."

"Guess we're about to find out what horrors await us inside." Stella pushed out the rear door, and Kyle popped the trunk.

"I'll take the back door." Kyle smoothed down the Velcro straps of his vest.

Addie and Stella did the same.

"You guys take the front?"

They both nodded.

"Let's move."

Lord, let me find them. Please.

Kyle disappeared around the side of the house. Stella let Addie go first.

"Not sure I'm interested in announcing ourselves."

Stella said, "Are we worried about explosive devices?"

Addie stopped at the front door. "Well, I am *now*."

Stella didn't smile. "Back up. Let me."

Before Addie could ask why Stella was the one who should put herself in harm's way, her colleague kicked the front door in. Stella hesitated a second.

When there was no explosion or gunfire, she headed inside. "FBI!"

Addie followed right behind her. They cleared each room systematically, but the place had no occupants. "This is the original furniture."

Addie could picture Hank's mother, sitting in the recliner. Smoking and watching *Cops*.

She followed, and they cleared the kitchen, meeting up with Kyle, who said, "Bedroom and bathroom are clear."

Addie stared at the empty kitchen. "Do we have a whereabouts on the mother?"

Kyle shook his head. "Word is she left town years ago, but we haven't found anything to corroborate that either way."

Stella winced. "Basement, anyone?"

Kyle glanced over, and she motioned to a door. "Yep."

"Good." Stella stifled a shiver. "You can go first."

Kyle stepped toward it. "Age before beauty?"

He was through the door before Stella frowned.

Addie followed him down a set of steps. "Any sign they're down here?"

Kyle swept the storage area first. At the end was a padlocked door. He stowed his weapon and found a crowbar.

Stella and Addie held their weapons ready. Kyle forced the padlock off.

The moment the door opened, the smell hit Addie before anything her eyes could comprehend.

Stella muttered something behind her hand.

Kyle said, "I'll call PD."

Addie moved to the open door and looked in. Barely bigger than a closet, a figure sat in a chair. Secured to the arms. She studied the decomposing body until she spotted a centipede moving around.

She turned back to her colleagues. "That's Hank's mother."

"Tied to a chair and left like that?" Stella said.

"We need to find Jacob and Mona. *Now.*" It was more

urgent than ever Addie had to get to them. "Where are they?"

She wasn't sure which of them could answer the question but had to ask it at least. Maybe it was a prayer.

A cry for help.

Addie's phone rang. "It's McCauley."

Stella said, "Maybe he heard already."

Addie put the phone to her ear. "Special Agent Franklin."

"I looked into the hunting thing."

"And you found something?" Addie asked.

"Hank doesn't have any property," McCauley replied. "And his truck doesn't have any GPS we can get into. But I found something."

She wanted to scream at the phone to get him to say it already.

"His stepdad had a cabin he would take Hank to. The chief remembered it," McCauley said. "I looked it up, and I have the address."

"Send it to me. We'll go check it out."

"Remember Austin?" McCauley asked. "I'll send you the address. And I'll meet you there."

Addie wasn't sure about that. "Captain—"

He cut her off. "This guy…this *cop* has been lying to all of us. I'm not going to let him take more lives."

"Fine." She hung up and told Kyle and Stella. Addie prayed they'd find Jacob and Mona. "Let's go."

33

"He's going to kill Addie." Mona paced in front of Jacob. She shook out her hands, her legs a motion of jerky movements.

"We won't let that happen, right?"

He didn't try to move. Blood continued to seep through his shirt. Eventually he'd grow lightheaded, and he wouldn't be able to walk. It wasn't going to take long for him to get to that point. Walking was pretty much out of the question when it would only slow down Mona.

He could get her killed.

Poison to her future, the way he'd been poison to everyone else.

"You need to go." The words spilled from his mouth as a croak.

Mona spun around. "You mean *we*, right? But how do we get out of here?"

"We need Hank to come in." Jacob already knew what he was going to suggest. So did she, given the shift in the expression on her face. Before she could argue, he said, "You hide behind the door. When he's distracted, run out."

It wasn't a great plan, but what other choice did they have? He wasn't going to survive this. But if he could make sure she did, then it counted for something. Addie would know he'd done everything—given everything—for her sister.

For her.

If he managed to take out Hank in the process—again, unlikely—maybe God would look on him with favor and for once Jacob would know he'd done good for someone else. That instead of being a force for ill in their life, he did something to their benefit.

"Where do I go?" she asked.

Jacob saw the scared girl inside the young woman in front of him. "I know it's safer to stay together, but if you can get out, you might be able to find help. Or help will find you. Either way you must try. It's the only way either of us has hope of being saved."

Truth was, Jacob didn't worry about himself surviving this.

He hadn't seen the truth in Hank. All these years of friendship, and he'd allowed his own feelings to cloud his judgment when it came to the detective. He'd always thought Hank was hurt, and maybe jaded, because Jacob made quarterback instead of Hank. Because Addie had survived, and Becca hadn't. Jacob had hit big with that book.

Instead, the truth was far darker.

Mona looked at his stomach, then up at his face. "I'll go get help." She bit her lip. "What do I do?"

"Get behind the door. Wait for Hank to—"

The door flew open and bounced against the wall behind it. Hank stalked in and went right to Mona.

She backed up to the wall.

He put his hands on her throat, a low chuckle coming from him. "You're going to distract me and run?"

The door was wide open. Jacob sat against the wall, unable to get up, let alone go. Mona struggled for breath.

"Hank! Don't do this!" Jacob shifted and tried to stand. Pain tore through his abdomen. "Hank!"

Mona's eyes rolled back in her head, and she went limp in Hank's grasp. Jacob wasn't sure whether she actually passed out or had decided to go ahead with the plan. But either way he was going to do this for her.

"Hank, she's just a kid. Don't kill her."

Hank dropped her to the ground. Mona made no sound, though he saw her face when she landed. The expression of surprise.

Hank came to him.

Good. Mona needed to be able to get out of here.

"What happened to you?" Ivan Damen had to have killed something in him.

The cops had attributed her death to Damen, but in Jacob and Addie's cabin, Jacob was instructed to kill Addie and then himself. He hadn't, and for a long time, he'd believed it was because he wasn't strong enough to do it.

He hadn't been able to save her by letting her die. He'd selfishly made her suffer longer because he couldn't do it. He couldn't let her go.

"Like there's something wrong with me?" Hank lifted his brows, no remorse there.

"What did Ivan do to you?"

"Because I turned into him like he poisoned me or something?"

Jacob blinked. He'd always believed *he* was the poison. Damen had done the same to Hank, but Jacob worked through it. He worked the poison out as best he could and built a life. Maybe it would always lay dormant in him, but Hank hadn't dealt with it.

"What did you do?"

"They deserved it."

Jacob swallowed. "Who did you hurt?"

He was worried about Mona, who hadn't moved yet. She could be biding her time, but he didn't even see her shifting to look, assessing the situation. Maybe Hank had genuinely hurt her.

That meant Jacob had to stall until Addie showed up with all the cops in the county. He wasn't going to think about how she'd know where to find them.

"Some people are just predisposed to evil. Isn't that what Addie would say? All those behavioral studies, trying to understand perversion. As if it can be tracked or categorized."

How much had Jacob missed? Before Damen and after him. It had nothing to do with Jacob's effect on his life. It was all Hank and the choices he'd made. Jacob might have been distracted by his own deal, coping with his own trauma. He'd tried to make his life the best it could be.

Hank had done the opposite. "You want me to tell you it wasn't your fault? That you didn't mean to do any of it. Fine. You were poisoned. You're sick."

That had to be it. Something had broken in Hank. He'd succumbed to the darkness of Ivan Damen instead of running from it the way Jacob and Addie had. Which only made his heart break for his friend.

Hank had fought that demon for years, and there was nothing anyone could've done to stop it.

He'd given in to the darkness.

Hank's lips shifted. "I knew exactly what I was doing with every single one of them."

Jacob had never known his friend could be so calculating. He had to face the fact they'd never been friends. He hadn't known Hank at all, despite being in each other's lives for years.

Hank had kept the truth from everyone.

There was nothing Jacob did to make Hank this way. He'd chosen it, but it had also been the influence of evil on him. Maybe Jacob kept Hank from doing worse. Jacob might never get an answer on that, but he wanted to hold that hope close anyway. The way he refused to let go of the dream of being rescued—like last time.

But this time it would be Addie doing the saving.

The idea he *wasn't* poison poked up inside him like a flower growing through the sidewalk.

A little glimmer of hope from God that he was good. A new creation like that flower. Before, there had been only hardness and dry cement, now there was life.

That gift of God. Like having Addie back in his life, even under the circumstances. What was between them had never died. Maybe it was a forever kind of thing, and they'd messed it up for a while. But there was hope they could make something work.

That he wouldn't be alone anymore.

That he'd find someone to face the sunrise with.

"And now I've got you and Addie here so I can finally finish what Damen started."

Sickness roiled in him that had nothing to do with the fact his blood currently leaked all over the floor around him. Addie wasn't here. Mona was. Had Hank lost his mind? "Were you the accomplice?"

Hank made a noise. Behind him, Mona shifted very slightly. "There was no accomplice," he said.

"Then what were you doing all this time?"

"Learning. Growing my skills and making sure I had what it takes to do this right."

Maybe he thought he was invincible now, better than anyone. Or maybe there was a niggle of doubt.

"Addie put it together. She knew the cases were connected. She'll figure out it was you."

"And I'll be waiting when she does."

"I'm not going to let you hurt her."

"You were going to *kill* her." Hank sneered. "Now you think you can save her?"

No, but God can. And it had nothing to do with whether Jacob was good enough or not. He wanted to throw up, but he needed Hank to keep talking. "Tell me about them."

"Looking for a confession?" Hank scoffed. "I guess it doesn't matter since the cops will pin this on you like all the other deaths."

"I'm surprised you didn't arrest me a long time ago for a murder you committed."

Hank grinned. "That would've been good."

"The fingerprint." He thought for a second that he'd already mentioned it, but his mind couldn't think straight. "That was you?"

"Why else do you think I came to your house for breakfast? Because we're friends?"

Jacob pressed his lips together. *Come on, Mona.* He needed Addie as well. But the person he should be crying out for was God. The one who had held him together all this time, the way He held the world together with the word of His power. God had seen him as good this whole time, a new creation.

Jacob should have seen it before now. He might have realized some other things and saved people from being hurt.

He winced. Poison again, the way he'd always seen

himself. It might be something he would struggle with for the rest of his life.

But at least he knew now it wasn't true.

"Addie isn't coming." Jacob needed to know what would happen next. "She doesn't know where we are."

Hank said, "You think she won't find you? Have more faith in your girlfriend."

"Did you kill Becca?" If there was no accomplice and Damen hadn't done it, maybe Hank had faced the same scenario as Jacob and Addie—and all the others taken—and made his choice. Ended the life of his girlfriend so she didn't have to suffer.

Hank said nothing.

Jacob wanted to know, but he needed to persuade a man he didn't know to trust him. Or comply with the distraction. Or give Hank the space and ammo to stab at Jacob with words instead of a knife.

"Ivan told me to kill Addie."

Jacob stared down a killer and let go of his darkest secret.

"To end her suffering, and then my own. He gave me the knife like he did with all the others he took."

That was Damen's MO. Set up the scene, torture the victim until they were at their end, and give them a way out. Ivan had never directly killed anyone. At least not by his hand. Instead, he had his victims do it—while he watched.

"I would've done it, Hank. I understand what can push you to take a life. I wanted to end Addie's suffering. So I didn't have to see her in that much pain."

Hank had always maintained that his scenario with Becca had been different. But what if that was simply so he didn't have to face what he'd done? So the cops wouldn't think he was anything like Ivan Damen.

Had Hank been hiding that guilt and shame all this time?

"If you did kill Becca—" Jacob looked him in the eyes. "I'd understand because I went through what you did."

"You think you're anything like me?" Something dark drifted through Hank's expression.

"What happened, Hank?"

"As if you'd get what that kind of pain is like."

"Damen hurt you?"

Hank huffed out a breath. "He wasn't the first."

Jacob's throat closed. He was about to speak when Mona scrambled up from the floor and raced for the door.

Hank roared and spun around.

Jacob swiped out with his leg and slammed it into Hank's shin. Hank fell to the floor, still screaming with rage. The sound split the air—and Jacob's eardrums.

Mona raced out into the night, screaming. Her arms and legs pumped as fast as Jacob had ever seen anyone, propelled by fear.

And then she was gone.

Hank got up. He swung his leg around.

Jacob raised both hands, but Hank's boot slammed his head and palms. The blow ricocheted pain through his skull, and he cried out.

Jacob blinked, and Hank was over by the door. His former friend slammed the door shut. Still inside. Hank flicked a lock on the door, then spun around with a sneer on his face. "Now you die."

Fear rushed over Jacob.

Mona was free, but he was right back in the past, smack-dab in the middle of the worst nightmare he'd ever had.

Jacob knew then there was no way he'd get out of this.

God, don't let Addie get caught up in it. He couldn't bear for her to be hurt.

That was his last thought.

34

Addie's stomach knotted as soon as the cabin came into view. It didn't look inviting at all, but someone inside had lights on behind whatever covered the windows. She could see thin strips of light between the boards.

"Whoa." Kyle hit the brakes.

Addie slammed her palm down on the dash as the car sprayed gravel and came to a stop.

In front of them stood a blonde with a look of terror on her face.

"Mona." Addie shoved her door open. "Mona!" She didn't know what else to say. She just gathered her sister in her arms and held on for a second.

"I'll get an ambulance here." Kyle moved back to the driver's door while Stella stayed by them, her weapon drawn.

Addie had never been so thankful to have partners with her.

Stella said, "Cops are here."

They rolled up behind Kyle's car. No lights or sirens. Just the low turnover of engines in a convoy of officers and SWAT.

But one thing breached the surface of her thoughts. "I need to do this myself."

Mona stepped back.

Addie clutched her sister's shoulders. "Tell me what's going on in the cabin."

The story spilled from Mona in fits and starts. Jacob being hurt, bleeding everywhere. Hank acting crazy. "He killed Celia, and Austin. They wanted to know everything about you." Mona sniffed. "That's why Austin broke up with Celia and started dating me. So they could get the story out from me, like I knew anything." Her voice broke on a wail.

Addie tugged her sister in again for a hug.

But Mona shook her head. "Hank killed them both."

"Okay. I know." Addie nodded.

"He kept them close, dating Celia even though her parents hated it. Austin hated it. He wanted to kill Hank. Celia thought it was cool, getting that close to him when he'd been through the cabins and lived."

"And now?" Addie asked. "What does he want with Jacob?"

"And *you*."

Addie shook her head. "He didn't take me. He just took you guys." Not that Mona didn't know it. But maybe she wasn't thinking straight.

She sniffed. "He wanted you in there. He said you were both going to die."

Stella's brows rose. "Murder-suicide?"

"Or he wants to kill us and go to prison for life. Not that anyone is likely to choose that end." Addie was leaning more toward suicide. "But my guess is he hates what he's done, as much as he needed to do it on some level. To prove something or satisfy a part of himself. Or he's just plain evil." And she had considered him her friend.

"The mask came off." Stella turned and lifted her chin to the approaching cops.

"It always does." Addie tugged Mona's elbow. "Stay with Stella, okay?"

"What's going on?"

Addie ignored the question.

Stella said, "I don't like that look on your face."

McCauley strode up, a swarm of cops all ready to take down a dangerous fugitive. One of their own.

She wanted to keep them from doing that more than she wanted them to go first. Addie felt like this had started with her, even if it hadn't.

She set off toward the cabin.

McCauley followed at a fast clip, right behind her according to the crunch of his footsteps on the gravel. "You think we're going to let you go in there all by yourself?"

She should probably have Kyle go in, since he was completely neutral in this.

"Hank is my detective."

"And he was my friend." She'd believed him. Trusted him. He'd been part of this all along, deceiving everyone. Orchestrating it so she was assigned to Benson just so he didn't have to live with what he'd done all these years. So she could tear away the mask and show everyone the truth. So he could be exposed. Revealed.

For fifteen years, all Addie had thought about was her trauma.

She'd never considered anyone else.

McCauley snagged her elbow in a loose grip. Her arm was free in one tug, but his point was made. "You're not going alone. Or first."

"I can talk Hank down." She slammed a hand high on her chest to make her point. "I can. No one else here. I was part of this when it started, just like Jacob. Currently injured, and maybe dead in there because *you* fingered him for a murder that had nothing to do with him."

She saw the guilt on McCauley's face even in the dim light. It didn't restrain her.

"Jacob had nothing to do with this until you dragged him in." *Oh, Lord. He could die.* She was sure she wouldn't survive it if she went in there and he had no life in him. If Hank had killed him, and he'd bled out alone right back where their darkest days started.

"Addie." McCauley reached for her.

She stumbled back and realized tears streamed down her face. "Don't touch me!"

Mona stared. The cops stared. Her partners geared up from the stuff in their trunk.

Addie could have kissed both of them. She strode over.

Kyle said, "Do you want the shotgun?"

"I need to talk to him, not just kill him."

Stella shook her head. "Time for talking is over."

"You *cannot* kill Detective Maxwell." McCauley barreled over. "This department needs answers."

Kyle shut the trunk. "This is a federal case."

Stella motioned to the cabin with a tip of her head. "Let's go, Special Agent Franklin. Time to work."

Addie followed them over to the cabin, moving fast enough they left the cops behind. They were probably setting up to breach and drag Hank out.

She just needed to get Jacob out, and she would be able to take a full breath rather than these desperate gasps.

Jacob was in there. *Breathe.* Jacob was bleeding. *Breathe.* Jacob could die.

Kyle and Stella halted at the door. Kyle raised his fist.

"Wait." Addie touched his shoulder. "I do want a shot at

talking him down. The last thing we need is this turning into a hostage situation."

"And yet," Stella said, "you're going to walk in there and give him a second hostage?"

Addie pressed her lips together.

"You can. We know you could do this. But that's not how it works." Kyle's expression flashed with something dark.

Stella glanced away. "We need to work together."

They were right. She couldn't go off half-cocked on her own. Not with so many cops here to watch her back. This needed to be handled the right way.

Addie nodded. "Okay. Let's do this." She held her gun in front, angled down at a forty-five.

Stella braced, ready to go first.

Kyle turned, lifted his foot, and kicked beside the door handle.

The frame cracked, but nothing moved. Kyle kicked it again. It didn't move that time either.

Stella said, "Barricaded."

McCauley stepped onto the porch. "Let's give SWAT a crack at it. Fire is on their way with the EMTs, so if my guys can't get in they'll give it a go."

Addie nodded. But she couldn't very well stand here and wait. She stalked off the porch to round the cabin and look at the place from every angle. The first window didn't give her a view—not without standing on something.

Her pace grew more desperate as she rounded the back corner. There should be another exit, per the fire code. Surely.

She stared at the back of the cabin.

Jacob.

The last time they'd been in a situation like this, she couldn't imagine what their families had been going through.

Now she could say she did. Except Addie would never react to it the way her mother had, wailing about how Addie couldn't be scarred. She was too pretty.

Fix her. She's broken! She can't be hurt. She'll never get a man!

As though that had anything to do with the situation as the cops pulled them out of the cabin Ivan Damen put them in. As they realized Hank had been taken as well, the same time they were. That Becca was dead and they weren't.

Then in the hospital, her mom had inserted herself into the conversation. He'd looked relieved to see Addie, but her mom demanded to know why he hadn't given his life to save her when her mom had barely been around Addie's whole life.

Addie stowed her weapon in the holster on her belt. She pulled at the back door handle. She braced her foot on the frame and pulled again.

It didn't move.

Fresh tears rolled down her cheeks. She swiped them away, then kicked at the door. Took out her frustration on the fact Hank had secured it shut.

Jacob was going to die in there, and it would be on her. The same way their breakup was on her.

Addie hadn't stuck up for herself. She'd just let her mother say whatever she wanted. The cop who pulled her out of the cabin while her mom wailed had muttered something disparaging. She couldn't even remember the words now, drowned out by her mom's screaming and carrying on. It hadn't been encouraging about the kind of person Ivan Damen targeted.

The kind of person her mom was.

Addie had spent fifteen years being as far from that person as she possibly could be. The same way she'd had nothing to do with her mother.

The way she'd passed off credit to the other members of her teams and task forces, agents she partnered with. Keeping her hair and makeup simple. Not drawing attention to herself.

She wanted to draw Jacob's attention. He was the *only* one she needed.

Addie bent at the waist and took in some longer breaths so she didn't pass out. She'd lost it.

She needed to pull herself together, go back around the cabin and—

The door flew open, nearly smacking her in the face as it swung out.

She heard the distant shouts of police.

Hank Maxwell slammed into her, and they both went down. Addie's back knocked into the ground.

Hank tried to get off her.

She ditched the gun and grabbed his shirt. "You're done, Hank. It's over." And he better not have killed Jacob.

Before he could scramble up, Addie rolled over and pinned him beneath her. Hank added to the momentum, and she was flipped again. Her temple hit something.

Addie cried out.

Hank's hands circled her neck. "Last one."

She saw the flash of his gritted teeth. Her mind screamed at her body to take a breath, but his grasp prevented her from doing it.

Inside the cabin, there was a giant crash and a wave of yelling.

I'm here. I'm right here.

Addie needed to get him off her. She couldn't get her weapon. Maybe he had one.

She patted his waist with her hands. His weight on top of

her. She wanted to vomit. "Hank." The word was barely audible. "Jacob."

"I won't go to prison." His hands flexed. "Not before you're dead."

She kept moving her hands, hoping he didn't notice. She found a phone sandwiched between his front pants pocket and her hip. He shifted, and the rub of hard plastic on her hip *hurt*.

"Hank." She wanted to plead. Beg him to let her live. But what if Jacob was dead? Maybe she didn't want to live in a world where he lay cold in the ground.

Her hands stopped moving.

No, she couldn't quit.

"FBI!" Kyle yelled. "Let me see your hands!"

Addie felt a tear roll from the corner of her eye. "Hank. It's over."

He stared at her, nothing but darkness.

"It's over."

"FBI!" Stella echoed. "Let her go and show us your hands!"

Addie saw the change in his eyes. It began in the darkness and seeped out to permeate every inch of him, to his fingertips.

Hank jumped off her and launched himself at Stella.

Kyle put two bullets in him.

He fell to the grass.

Stella stumbled back but rallied quickly. "Hey…thanks."

Kyle held out a hand to Addie. "EMTs are here. They're getting Jake now. It doesn't look good."

Addie found her balance then let go of his hand. "Like Stella said. Thanks."

Then she ran inside to see Jake.

35

The elevator doors opened, and Addie walked out onto the same floor where Jacob had been admitted after the stabbing.

Her phone started to ring in her pocket.

The screen said *Zimmerman* even though it was after one in the morning on the East Coast.

She swiped her thumb across. "Special Agent Franklin."

"Word coming down the pipeline is a detective was apprehended. Friend of yours."

"That was fast."

"The mayor is all over it." Zimmerman sighed. "Spinning the tale, so he looks like the hero who brought in the FBI. Now he's after police reform in Benson."

Addie winced. She didn't have a lot of love for the police department here, but there were good cops everywhere, and Benson was no exception. "Anything else?"

She needed to see Jacob.

Mona was being treated, and she would hang with Russ after. The cops were cleaning up the scene. Addie would have to write all the reports when she got to the office tomorrow.

Tonight was about Jacob.

Zimmerman said, "William Benning told us where he buried all the missing girls."

"Good." She was glad the team had closed the case.

"You're staying in Benson, aren't you?"

Addie stopped outside the door to Jacob's room. "Things aren't going well with Ellie?"

He was quiet. "I miss you, okay?"

There was no way she was going back to Virginia. She just didn't know if she was staying in Benson, either. Not until after she talked to Jacob. "I've got to go. Thanks for everything."

He had helped her. Cared about her. Now it was time for a new chapter in Addie's life.

She hung up the phone and stepped into Jacob's room.

The sight of him stopped her dead. Pale skin, so pale. Purple lips. Mussed hair. Blankets and beeping monitors.

His voice croaked, "Do I look that bad?"

"Honestly?" She moved to the beside. "Yeah, it doesn't look good."

"Maybe you should kiss it better?"

"Are you on medication?"

"Yes." His eyes fluttered open, and she saw the effects in his gaze. "A lot of that medical…stuff."

Addie leaned down so slowly. She touched her forehead to his and closed her eye. "I love you." She whispered the words on his skin. "You probably won't remember this tomorrow, but I need you to know."

"Love you, too."

She smiled, shifted her face, and touched her lips to one

corner of his mouth. Then the other. "I'm going to let you sleep now."

"Don't…go."

Addie touched his cheek with her fingertips. "I'm not going anywhere."

She'd been determined Benson would only be a short-term assignment. Even if Hank had orchestrated the whole thing, the fact was that Addie belonged here. If Kyle and Stella stayed, or not. If she was assigned to the Seattle office and had to commute, then fine.

Addie was going to do what it took to make a life here. With Jacob.

After fifteen years apart, they had the chance to make up for lost time and get to know each other again. Explore this big town trying to be a small city. Fall in love again, every day. See where things went.

Addie was going to go to church with Russ. Figure out her faith and the place it had in her life now.

Finally take hold of the life she was always supposed to have had.

36

Three weeks later

"Are you sure—"

Jacob cut her off. "If you ask me that one more time…"

"You're going to what?" Addie glanced over. One brow raised. "Because I just might want to see where that threat leads."

"No brownies."

Addie gasped. "How dare you!" The mock ire lasted half a second, then she dissolved into laughter that rang through the predawn valley.

"You'll scare the deer."

"Good. They should steer clear of people."

Neither of them mentioned Hank or his "hunting." In the last three weeks, and since he'd been released from the hospital, his whole Bible study group had shown up to help Jacob clear up his apartment and set everything back to rights.

Hank had left evidence that pointed to Jacob being the

culprit for Austin's murder, which Hank had committed. Jacob hadn't enjoyed hearing how the guy shoved Addie and ran from the scene.

Or any of the rest of it.

Let alone telling any of them what happened with Hank in the cabin—seeing Addie's face.

Russ was alive and home, along with Mona.

Hank was dead.

Carl Harris had passed away in his sleep at the retirement home, but the police were still going to talk to his family members about the murders he'd told Jacob about.

Russ had signed a contract with him for the entire fourth floor of Jacob's building. The first client of what he called, "The Accountant's Office" was set to move in soon. Some guy who'd been on TV a few months ago for turning himself —and a suitcase—nuke into the government. Apparently he'd been cleared of any wrongdoing and was looking for a fresh start.

Jacob had Addie's hand in his, and they were here.

He tugged, and she stopped walking slow up toward Golden Hills Bluff. He didn't want to think about the fact his stomach still hurt. He'd nearly died, but apparently there was more for him to do here on earth because he hadn't been called Home.

"What is it?" She moved close.

"There's nowhere else I'd rather be."

Addie touched her hands to his cheeks and pressed her lips to his. Jacob slid his arms around her waist and pulled her close—as close as they could be. For now.

It was all there in her kiss.

Promise. A future. Hope.

When she leaned back, she said, "Are you going to tell

me why we're freezing our butts off on a mountain this early?"

Jacob lifted his chin. "Somewhere you need to be?"

"We couldn't watch the sun come up from your apartment?"

"The view from there is good." He'd watched it every day since he got home from the hospital. "But this is better."

They set off again.

"This is where your grandpa brought you when you were little?"

Jacob nodded, a lump in his throat.

"Thank you for sharing it with me."

"We won't be long. Then you can go to work."

"As if I'd rather do that than spend the day with you." She glanced over.

"How are Kyle and Stella?"

She chuckled. "Complaining that they keep finding more things to *like* about Benson and then threatening to pack up and leave. It's pretty hilarious."

"They're hooked. They just don't want to admit it."

She glanced over. "I'd have said the same. But I'll freely admit it."

"I love you."

She squeezed his hand, her cheeks turning a gorgeous shade of pink. It was an expression he'd never seen before. Confidence and vulnerability. Strength and brokenness.

Life's journey was like the path up this mountain, with its twists and turns. Blind corners and tricky drop-offs. Patches of flowers that would bloom with the seasons.

This route saw winter. It saw the blazing sun and pouring rain. But in the end, they would reach the summit.

When the corner came, he picked up his pace. "Come on." The vista took his breath away.

Beside him, Addie gasped. "I've never seen this. It's beautiful."

"If you look to the left, you can see Benson. All the way over there." He pointed.

Between were mountain peaks—and patches of snow. Overhead, the dark sky above glowed to lighter blue, then a yellow haze. Below was a stripe of orange, then red met the horizon.

"It's stunning, Jacob."

"Jake is fine. I told you that."

"I like both."

He shifted to stand behind her, then carefully tugged her against him—*ouch*—as he wound his arms around her. "I'll have to find the tree where Grandpa carved his name."

"We should carve our names."

"I'm not sure I'm in favor of destroying nature like that, but I appreciate the sentiment." He shifted and pulled the tiny thing from his pocket.

So small in his big hand.

Jacob held it in front of her and spoke over her shoulder. Whispered in her ear. "Marry me, Addie."

She tensed.

Jacob held himself completely still, not sure what her reaction would be. It was on his heart to ask if she would be the subject of his next book. But maybe that was a story they'd write together—one that would last a lifetime.

Then she whispered back a single word.

"Yes." Addie's lips spread to a wide smile.

Jacob lifted his gaze to the sunrise. *You were right, Grandpa.*

There was always hope.

"Lisa Phillips is the master of edge-of-your-seat action and suspense!" - USA Today best-selling, RITA winning author, Susan May Warren

A new start.
An all too familiar threat.

Burned by the CIA, Lyric Thompson signed on with the Accountant's Office for the fresh start she needed. Running a resort of vacation cabins—the site of more than one murder—isn't going exactly to plan, but she wasn't trained to quit. When a developer puts the pressure on, she has to choose to fight back alone…or accept help from the one man she never let go of.

Isaac Amrakov has never been given the chance to plot his own course. When the Accountant's Office offers him a new life in Benson, he doesn't know just how much God plans to restore in his life. But the construction crew he's signed on with are up to something. The man he wants to be would wade in, but Isaac can't do the right thing and keep Lyric safe at the same time. Not without putting everything he wants in jeopardy.

These two trained operatives are in for the fight of their lives. But will they stand together, or let life tear them apart again?

***Hard Target* is a stand-alone story as part of the accountant's office series, Last Chance Downrange. An all-new setting. An all-new set of characters.**

**Find out more at:
https://lastchancecounty.com/downrange-series**

Christian Romantic Suspense

ALSO BY LISA PHILLIPS

This is only the tip of the Last Chance iceberg… find more stories based in Last Chance County at:

www.lastchancecounty.com

Find out about Lisa's other series and stand-alone books at her website:

authorlisaphillips.com

Other series:

Chevalier Protection Specialists

Last Chance County

Northwest Counter-Terrorism Taskforce

Double Down

WITSEC Town (Sanctuary)

Love Inspired Suspense titles

Coming Soon:

Last Chance Fire (Sunrise Publishing)

Brand of Justice (Stand Alone Thriller Series)

ABOUT THE AUTHOR

Find out more about Lisa Phillips, and other books she has written, by visiting her website: https://authorlisaphillips.com

Would you also share about the book on Social Media, leave a review on Lisa's page and share about your experience? Your review will help others find great clean fiction and decide what to read next!

Visit https://authorlisaphillips.com/subscribe where you can sign up for my NEWSLETTER and get free books!

Made in the USA
Monee, IL
09 April 2022

94447274R00184